DOWN

BOOK THREE IN THE DOYLE WITCH COZY MYSTERY
SERIES

KIRSTEN WEISS

Cover artist: wickedsmartdesigns.com

Alternate cover at back by Zack Weiss

Visit the author website: www.kirstenweiss.com

Misterio Press mass market paperback edition / November, 2016

http://Misteriopress.com

ISBN-13: 978-1-944767-19-8
ISBN-10: 1-944767-19-3

WHAT CAME BEFORE

Once upon a chill winter's night, the Bell and Thistle pub and its twenty-two occupants vanished. The next day all the baffled townsfolk found was a clearing filled with dead thistles. Some speculated the thistles had been planted in case the nearby pine forest considered staking a claim to the land. Others pointed to the saucer-shaped clouds floating above the Sierras and claimed aliens had taken pub and people.

The sheriff never even considered Doctor Toeller might be responsible. Doc Toeller was a valued community member, and how could she have made an entire building disappear? As to that, Sheriff McCourt certainly never would have believed Toeller was a fairy. Fairies were passé, the stuff of children's films, of nonsense and moonbeams.

So, the inappropriate authorities descended on the small, mountain town of Doyle with their SUVs and badges and guns. They investigated, examining maps, combing the woods, interviewing friends and relatives. Satellite imagery revealed nothing but trees, sonar equipment nothing but rocks and stone.

Doctor Toeller, whose magic was far older than man's science, smiled.

The media offered additional theories. Mass hallucination. Terrorists. A magic trick.

Finally, most of the humans returned to their willful blindness and declared the vanishing pub a hoax. And if the townsfolk heard a mysterious, tolling bell that sounded exactly like the one that had hung beside the pub door, it was probably tinnitus.

The Bonheim triplets, who knew better, understood it was magic all right, but it was no trick.

Doc Toeller was getting seriously annoyed with those three. It was a good thing that the middle girl would be dead before year end. The other two, however... She'd have to take steps to finish them. And then, she could turn her attentions to the Rose Rabbit.

Then things would get interesting.

CHAPTER 1

"Of course they're unrealistic." Officer Connor Hernandez curled the book in his meaty hand, and I tried not to wince at the damage to its cover. After years working in the bookstore, I should have had thicker skin. "It's an urban fantasy," he said, "a book about magic. Just ask Lenore."

I darted a quick glance at him. Okay, so I hadn't exactly kept it secret I was a shamanic witch, but I didn't advertise it either.

Fortunately, Connor's partner, Owen, didn't follow that thread. Fair-haired and good looking in a smooth-faced, rascally way, he shook his head. "Yeah, but come on. Fireballs?"

I pulled my long, blond hair over one shoulder and shelved a book. It was no use telling him magic didn't work that way. That magic was more subtle than fireballs and levitating motorcycles. Magic was more dangerous in ways people preferred not to imagine.

Behind the bookstore counter, my elderly boss, Mike Gallin, spoke in a low voice to a stranger in a well-cut suit. Afternoon sunlight streamed through the paned windows behind the register. It glinted off Mike's balding head.

The visitor wore too much suit for a May day in the California foothills, and I wondered what he was trying to hide. Then I wondered why I'd wondered that. Maybe it was the sharp, wary expression on Mike's wrinkled face.

Since last winter, we all wore that expression.

"This weather." Owen groaned and winked at me. "I wish the Sheriff would let us wear shorts on days like these."

I snapped my attention back to Connor. His muscular thighs strained against his slacks. On behalf of the women of Doyle, I thought shorts for the deputies were an excellent idea. Not that I would ever say that out loud.

"So what do you think?" Smiling at me, Connor stepped backward on a carpet the color of cigarette ash and bumped one of the bookshelves.

I opened my mouth, closed it. Seriously, I wasn't going to talk sheriff's sexy summer fashion with these two characters.

Connor's raven hair curled around his ears in black, dangerous spirals. In his police uniform, he looked like a hero from one of my sister's romance novels – tall and muscular and with the sort of tortured, olive-black eyes novelists think cops should have and cops would rather not earn. His right eyebrow quirked upward in a perennially amused expression, though I'd seen it switch to a scowl quickly enough. There was something about his masculine solidity that I admired. His taste in reading was eclectic: urban fantasy, mystery, and political history. He was currently working his way through a book on John Adams.

Owen didn't read unless he had to. That's not a criticism. I just felt kind of bad because of what he was missing.

"Think?" Owen examined the lurid cover of a graphic novel and haphazardly jammed it back onto the shelves. "I think it's nuts. Another story for Doyle's F'd up Files."

Confused, I smoothed the front of my cream-colored, sleeveless tunic and felt the lump of my notebook in its front pocket. Obviously, I'd missed a step in the conversation. We'd gone from shorts for deputies to… what was he talking about? Though From Doyle's F'd Up Files would make a good title for a prose poem. What would be in these surreal files? A mayor who thought a paperclip was a turnip? A rose rabbit? Urgh, I didn't even know what the damned rabbit was, and I couldn't get the alliteration out of my head. But the name kept coming up. Muttered by a dying woman. Encountered in a sister's vision. Weaving through my dreams. It had to be related to Doyle's magical problems somehow.

I returned the graphic novel Owen had taken to its proper place.

Noticing my action, Connor's eyes crinkled with weary amusement. He rested his elbow on the rolling ladder. "I was talking to Lenore about getting the author in for a talk. I hear he's local." He jammed the sleeves of his white, sheriff's deputy shirt to his elbows.

"It never hurts to ask," Owen said to Connor rather than me.

I nodded and glanced again at Mike and the stranger. Most authors leapt at the chance for exposure. But the bookstore – the entire town – had experienced a sharp decline in visitors since the Bell and Thistle event. We'd even taken to calling it that: The Event. Capital letters.

"Thanks, Lenore." Connor rapped me playfully on the shoulder with the book the way a big brother would tease a baby sister.

I bit back a sigh. I could drool over the deputy all I wanted, but it would never work. He couldn't see beyond the twenty-two missing people standing between us. And I worked at a bookstore because fictional relationships were easier than real ones. I'd been disappointed too many times before, by men who wanted more or just got bored or couldn't handle the real me. I could hardly blame them. Watching someone else read isn't exactly riveting. The only thing worse was someone who's attention constantly wandered to loitering ghosts.

A woman in a bonnet strode past the windows. Carrying a basket, she walked through a Mini Cooper.

"You going to the concert at the winery?" Connor asked his partner, but I could see his heart wasn't in it. Pretending Doyle was normal only took one so far.

"I have to work it," Owen said, ignoring me. It wasn't intentional. I'd perfected the art of fading into backgrounds, right down to my colorless tunic and slacks. "How'd you get off?"

"I asked," he said.

At the counter, Mike wore his fixed, the-customer-is-always right expression. Which meant the customer, whoever he was, wasn't right at all.

I bit my bottom lip.

"Lenore?" Connor asked.

"Hm?"

"Are you going to the concert?" he asked.

"I don't think so." I brushed some loose strands of blond hair behind my ear. I avoided crowds. Even at the most innocuous events there was an undercurrent of violence. It attracted things I'd rather not deal with.

"Why not?" Connor asked.

"I'm behind on my reading," I lied. "Jayce is probably going though." Concerts were more my sister Jayce's thing. Our other sister, Karin, of romance writing not-quite-fame, might attend in a pinch. But lately she'd been so caught up in her wedding preparations that I doubted she'd find time for this one.

"Books aren't life," Connor chided gently.

"They're my life." And I'd learned that fiction was often more true than what you read in the news.

Uneasy, I glanced again at the counter. Mike's expression had shifted to annoyance.

The stranger's arms crossed, his chin down, his legs apart. The body language said confrontation, but their voices remained low. The stranger turned. I caught a quick glimpse of a handsome face chiseled into a frown, dark brows slashed downward. Then he was striding to the door, his back to me again.

"Still, you should come." Connor's expression turned grim. "The town needs a break."

"I can't–"

"Lenore?" Mike waddled around the counter. He wore a short-sleeved, brown-checked shirt, khakis held in place by suspenders, and a comb over. He looked like an elderly egg, and I adored him.

I glanced to the open door. The stranger stormed outside.

My skin twitched.

"Would you start unpacking the new inventory?" Mike's mouth tipped upward. "That nephew of mine has found another reason not to be here, and the new shipment's in."

"Sure." I smiled briefly at Connor and Owen. "I'll ask about that author." And then I realized I didn't know which author he'd been talking about. But the two deputies were already joking and laughing and moving to the register with Mike.

My cheeks warmed with embarrassment, and I hurried toward the back room. The bookstore was deep and narrow, so deep that the storage room at the rear was always a bit of a surprise. I flipped on its overhead light, and the florescent bulb pinged and flickered. Its beery light steadied.

Glancing one last time over my shoulder – Connor was buying the book after all – I shut the door. The deputy would be the perfect man – he liked to read, was honorable and handsome. But he was a Doyle cop, and that was rough on a person's psyche. Our sheriff had lost thirty pounds in the last six months.

Doyle was caught in a web of powerful, fae magic. It had preserved the town, keeping the people who lived here dazzlingly beautiful. But there was a high price tag.

Twenty-two missing people.

I found the box cutter inside a battered metal desk. Slashing harder than I needed to, I attacked the boxes and sliced through the packing tape. I stacked the books on the desk by title, pausing to flip through a new urban fantasy. Connor might like this one.

Picking up a new romance by my sister, I smiled. Mike had set me up – he'd known Karin's book – a bundle of romance novels about shifters – would be in the box. Which meant he wouldn't mind me skimming its pages.

I read the first few pages, then a few more, finally losing myself in the story world. Karin's stories always had happy endings – such lovely fantasies.

Karin, Jayce and I were triplets, and we each worked our own flavor of magic. I worked shamanically with the spirit world and had seen plenty of weird spirit forms. Shifters though. Could they exist? I'd only recently come to believe in fairies. And if they were real...

Something thunked in the bookstore, and I raised my head.

Silence.

I listened, intent. "Mike?"

Nothing.

Scalp prickling, I walked to the door. My hand paused, raised above the knob.

Something shuffled behind me, and I whirled.

A massive turkey vulture perched atop Karin's stack of romance novels.

I gasped, stepping away and bumping against the closed door.

A vulture, an omen of death and rebirth.

The bird cocked its ugly, blood-red head.

"What are you doing here?" I croaked.

Slowly, the turkey vulture extended its brown and gray wings.

My breath quickened.

And then it vanished.

"Mike?" Dread pooling in my stomach, I wrenched open the door to the bookstore and hurried through it. Mike wasn't behind the register. I hurried down the center aisle. A tasseled loafer stuck out from behind one of the shelves.

My heart stopped. "Mike!"

I raced around the bookshelf.

Mike lay sprawled beside the ladder, his head at an unnatural angle. Blood pooled around his head. His blue eyes were open, staring.

"Mike," I whispered, my eyes burning, growing damp. No, not Mike. Anguish twisted inside my chest.

"I got your favorite coffee." Mike's nephew Peter strolled into the bookstore holding two paper coffee cups. He tossed his shaggy blond hair. "It's not as good as Ground's, but..." He stumbled to a halt, his blue eyes widening. "What did you do?"

CHAPTER 2

I stared at Mike, dead.

Slumped against a bookcase, he lay folded like a marionette on the gray carpet. One of his suspender straps had slid from his shoulder and hung loose about his short-sleeved, brown plaid shirt.

My chest squeezed so tight I forgot to breathe. Mike, dead.

I looked to Peter.

Mike's nephew held the coffees at an angle. In spite of their plastic lids, brown liquid dribbled onto the thin carpet. Peter's soft, baby mouth was slack. His Nirvana t-shirt bagged around the hips of his jeans.

"It's Mike," I croaked.

"What did you do?" he repeated.

The accusation jerked me from my bewilderment. "I just came from the storage room and found him like this." I fumbled in my pocket for my cell phone. "I'm calling nine-one-one now."

He blinked, shook himself. "Is he...?"

"He's gone," I said, my voice choked. His life force was gone. This wasn't Mike anymore. His spirit had fled, and only a shell remained. But that shell was so vulnerable, so fragile, that there was something almost childlike about it.

"If he's dead," he said, "nine-one-one won't help."

He was right, but I was already dialing. I explained the situation to the dispatcher, and she promised to get someone to the bookstore.

Doctor Toeller, frowning over a list, walked inside the bookstore. Her silver-gold cap of hair shone beneath the overhead lights.

My adrenaline spiked, breath quickening, heart jackhammering, flight or fight kicking in. But I could neither fight nor flee. I glanced away, schooling my expression. Not her. Not here. Not now.

"Have you got that book I ordered?" She looked up, and twin lines, the only furrows on her perfect skin, appeared between her brows.

My heart made another frantic scramble for freedom.

She hurried to Mike's limp form.

"What's happened?" she asked me.

I swallowed my bile along with the impulse to fling myself over Mike and keep her from touching him.

"She said she found him like this," Peter answered.

My throat tightened, and I looked at the gray carpet, glad for the first time that someone had spoken on my behalf. I didn't trust my voice.

Kneeling in her white linen slacks, she pressed two fingers to the side of his neck. "I'm too late," she said, her voice laced with regret.

I clenched my jaw. Toeller was good. Good at pretending ignorance. Good at pretending she cared. Good at pretending she was human.

Her magic brushed against my skin, and I shivered.

She turned to me, her eyes wide with sympathy. "Are you all right, Lenore?"

"It's Mike," I said faintly.

She patted my shoulder, and it was all I could do not so sheer away. "I'm sorry," she said. "You two were close, weren't you?"

Peter's expression flickered.

I nodded. She wasn't here to harm me, and she hadn't killed Mike. I frowned. Why had the idea of murder popped into my head? It hadn't been more than a minute or two between the time I'd heard Mike fall and I'd gone into the bookstore proper. He'd been alone. It was only a terrible accident.

"I told him to leave the ladder climbing to me." Peter scowled. "He still thought he was steady as a mountain goat."

Connor strode inside, his partner Owen in tow. Like Peter, Owen was a shaggy blond. Unlike Peter, Owen had a certain toughness to his manner, in spite of his boyish face. "We got a call," he said. Taking in the scene at a glance, he came to stand beside us. "Doc?"

Rising, she shook her head. "It's too late for the paramedics, I'm afraid. It looks like he fell off the ladder and cracked his head. A simple fall can be so deadly." The corners of her mouth turned downward, and she met my gaze. "Humans are so fragile."

I stiffened.

"Lenore, did you witness the fall?" Connor asked, his swarthy face serious.

"I work here too," Peter said, his expression sour.

"Did you witness his fall?" Owen asked him.

Peter flushed. "No. I was out getting coffee for Mike."

My nostrils flared. He'd been out getting coffee for himself to avoid work, as usual.

"Lenore?" Connor asked. "Did you see anything?"

"I heard him fall," I said. "I called to him through the door. When he didn't answer, I came out of the back room. That's when I saw him."

"Was he alone?" Connor asked.

I hesitated. "It seemed so." Mike had been alone when I'd found him, but something about this didn't feel natural.

"I knew we shouldn't have called nine-one-one," Peter said.

"It's the natural thing to do under the circumstances," Connor said.

"Would you come over here?" Owen asked Mike's nephew. "I'll need to take your statement."

The two men moved beside the cash register.

"What's going on?" a man asked from the front of the shop. Town councilman Steve Woodley, his tonsured scalp gleaming with sweat, stood in the open doorway.

Abandoning Peter, Owen hurried to the bookstore's front door. He said something to Woodley in a voice too low for me to hear.

The councilman shook his head. "Terrible. Terrible." He strolled away.

Owen shut the door and flipped the sign in the window to CLOSED.

Connor snapped photos of Mike's body with his phone and spoke quietly with Doctor Toeller.

I backed away. Over the last year, my sisters had found their share of corpses – all murdered. Maybe that's why my internal alarms were clanging. When a Bonheim finds a body, odds are the circumstances aren't natural.

Paramedics arrived, and the decibel level in the bookstore rose.

Ignoring everyone, I rested my hand on the top of a freestanding book case and relaxed my vision, letting my mind float in a light trance.

Something, flashed, rose-gold in the corner of my eye.

Instead of looking at it directly, I turned, keeping the movement in my peripheral vision.

Mike paced between two bookcases. He muttered and wrung his hands, a gesture I'd never seen him make in life. But I'd never seen a pink flash presaging a ghost before either.

In the movies, ghosts are semi-transparent figures. I see them as real people. Mike looked solid, but he hadn't fully manifested. That was why I could only see him when I was trying, in my half-trance state. But I shouldn't have been able to see him at all. It was too soon after his passing. Was this another mark of things in Doyle getting weirder? I rubbed my arms. Or was Mike desperate to tell me something?

Still not looking at him directly, I edged toward the spirit and steeled myself not to weep.

Mike's ghost babbled under his breath, his movements manic, jerky, fast. He pinballed off the bookshelves.

My heart twisted anew with grief.

Mike's spirit raced back and forth in front of me now. One corner of his brown plaid shirt had come untucked, flapping behind him like a schoolboy's. I swallowed the hard knot of grief in my throat.

If I'd believed that ghost was all of him, I couldn't have borne it, but this was just a remnant, a fragment of his soul. Still, it was all I could do not to run sobbing from the bookstore.

"Mike," I whispered, facing away from the others. "I'm here for you."

But he didn't listen to me anymore than anyone else did. Mike's spirit raced back and forth, oblivious, and I swear I felt a breeze stir.

"Mike. It's all right," I said, keeping my voice low.

He spun to face me and clapped his hands to the sides of his face. His jaw hinged downward, elongating. His words were a shriek, long and deafening and raising the hair on the back of my neck.

I keeled forward, pressing my hands to my ears. My skull was splitting, agonizing.

His scream went on and on.

"No," I whispered. No, no, no. "Mike."

And then he was gone, and I was left with ringing in my ears, a dry mouth, and a tangle of fear and despair in my chest.

"Lenore?" Connor laid his broad hand on the curve of my lower back. "What can I do?"

I straightened, gasping. He probably thought I'd been crying, and I wanted to cry, but not now. "This can't have been an accident," I said.

Something shifted behind his near-black eyes. He drew me further towards the back room. "Did you see something?"

I couldn't explain Mike's ghost to the handsome cop. "No," I said. "I think... I feel like there's more here."

"I know his death is a shock," he said. "It is to me too. I was just here..." He trailed off and shook himself. "It's understandable if you're not ready to accept this."

"Please." I touched my fingers to his arm and as quickly withdrew them. "Please, just... look."

"All right," he said. "We'll treat Mike's death as a question mark until we have evidence that says otherwise."

"Thank you."

The skin between my shoulder blades heated, and I glanced behind me.

Peter and the Doctor watched us.

If they'd overheard me, that was too damn bad.

Mike had told me to run.

CHAPTER 3

That day, we kept the sign in the window to CLOSED.

Peter said something about reopening later, "for Mike."

Fighting tears, I'd nodded, numb, and walked out the front door.

I walked, but I didn't see Main Street's western-style saloon. I didn't see the cool stone walls with iron shutters. I didn't see the colorful gardens behind white picket fences. I didn't see the tourists giddy from wine tasting. And Doyle was worth seeing. A relic of the Gold Rush, it was a beautifully preserved mining town in the California foothills. But all I could see was the memory of Mike's ghost.

I turned left, walking past weathered Victorians and dappled pine forest. A squirrel loped across the road, his tail an ashen wave.

I brushed tears from my cheeks. Mike had been like a kindly uncle. I didn't want to think of not having him around to talk books with. Every good reader spends time in wonderland, so Mike had never poked fun at me whenever I'd drifted off into my own netherworld. Mike had understood.

Mike, gone. My breath hitched.

I hadn't told him everything about my chronic mental drifting. He knew I had an interest in spirits and shamanism, but not even Mike would believe a fairy curse – or an unseelie curse, as Karin insisted on calling it. Despite that secret between Mike and I – a secret that affected him as well – we'd been close, our relationship easy, sharing our passion for books. We'd loved more than just the stories and the characters. We'd loved the scent of the paper, the feel of the pages beneath our fingers, the fonts and patterns of words on a page. These things had been lost in the digital age.

I swallowed the ache in my throat.

Finally, I reached our gabled stone and shingle house, and a weight dropped from my shoulders.

I trudged up the three porch steps.

A woebegone black cat huddled on the porch swing.

"It's okay to come inside," I said.

The cat, Picatrix, had attached herself to Jayce. But she refused to come into our house.

Picatrix looked away.

"Your choice." I ruffled the black cat's fur, hot on the summer day.

After checking to make sure Picatrix's food bowl was full (it was), I unlocked the door and let myself inside. We'd inherited the house from our aunt. Its scent hadn't changed since she'd passed – drying herbs and love and a hint of four thieves vinegar (our cleanser of choice).

I toed off my sandals and stood on the blue rag rug, feeling its softness against my soles. And then I walked upstairs to my bedroom and cried.

A lot.

But eventually, I had to stop.

In the window sat the calico Cat With No Name. His whiskered sneer told me to get over it.

"What do you know?" I asked. "You're a cat. Even if you are rare." Male calico births were roughly one in three thousand. I'd looked it up.

He swished his tail and yawned, unimpressed.

"You're also dead. That makes you zero for two."

Offended, the ghost cat hopped from the sill. Tail high, he strolled out the open bedroom door.

Someday, I'd figure out how to pass the cat on. But how do you tell a cat he's dead? Go to the light, there's catnip in the light... Picatrix wouldn't help. The two cats hated each other with a feline vengeance.

I lay on my bed and stared at the white ceiling. Mike's ghost had been wild with fear. I'd never seen him that way in life, but this wasn't the full Mike, just a wayward piece of his spirit. I believed ghosts were remnants of the soul. A person's soul could split into pieces when they were alive due to physical or emotional trauma, or after they were dead if their death had been unexpected or violent. The job of shamanic witches like me was to retrieve those missing pieces and return them so the person could move on in wholeness. Part of Mike's spirit had moved on, but a piece had split away, remained.

My breathing quickened. Had Mike been murdered? Or was his death the accident it appeared?

I rolled off the bed and walked downstairs, to my workroom at the rear of the house. Its single, square window faced the rear garden. Unlit candles lined the windowsill. Taking a matchbox from a cubby in the antique, rolltop desk, I lit them.

I rolled up the thick, white carpet.

Seated at the rolltop, my feet planted firmly on the ground, I centered myself. I kept the desk neat, because it's hard to get centered amidst chaos. So every cubby was tidy, the desk empty except for a thick, black, leather-bound journal, where I kept notes of my magical experiences. Small blue spray bottles – magical cleansing mists that Jayce had brewed – lined the desktop. They smelled of ginger and cedar and sandalwood, but I still preferred good old stinky burnt sage. The room still smelled faintly of sage from my last smudging.

I opened the magical journal – a modern grimoire – and flipped through its pages.

The dead cat crept through the open door and sprang to the top of the rolltop. He wove between the bottles, his calico tail coiling.

"Seriously?" I flipped through my grimoire. "You want attention now?"

I rarely had to summon spirits. They usually came to me. Or they had until I'd moved into my aunt's old house. She'd spelled a web of magical protection around the house and yard. Not having to worry about bumps in the night or shades at my bedside was a relief. But generally, I liked talking to ghosts. They had interesting stories, they listened, and in the end, they all went away.

I reviewed the spell, nodded, and shut the book.

The cat meowed.

"I don't have any ghost cat food, so you're just going to have to cool it."

Standing in the center of the room, I called in the four directions and the helping spirits. "The circle is cast," I intoned. Energy shivered through me.

The cat hunched, bristling.

From the desk, I took a bit of white chalk from a drawer and drew a circle on the floor. I wrote Mike's full name – Michael Bartholomew Gallin – around the inside circumference.

The cat peered from the edge of the desk, his whiskers twitching.

Grabbing my salt canister, I covered the chalk in salt. My aunt had expended a lot of magical energy keeping the wards around the house strong. If I was inviting a ghost inside, it was going to materialize directly inside my circle and stay there. Even if I was calling a ghost that would never harm me, a ghost I loved, the circle was inviolate.

I grabbed a brown and white patterned meditation cushion from one corner of the room and set it outside the circle. Sitting, I folded my legs, closed my eyes. "Michael Bartholomew Gallin, come."

Electricity whispered inside the circle. The atmosphere grew dense, as if the molecules were expanding, pressing against each other. The hair rose on my arms.

Sometimes magic really is as easy as calling someone's name.

I opened my eyes.

A slender woman in red corduroy bell bottoms and a floral-patterned tunic stood in the circle. A bead and feather hung from the tip of her narrow braid.

I swore. And sometimes, magic isn't easy at all. I'd gotten the wrong number. I glared at the dead cat. "Some familiar you are."

He meowed.

"Your name can't be Michael Bartholomew Gallin," I said to the woman. Judging from her clothes, she had died sometime in the sixties.

The woman frowned and adjusted her green-tinted glasses. "He said this was a portal."

"Who said this was a portal?" I asked sharply. Dammit. Yes, the salt circle was a portal of sorts, but it wasn't meant to be public access. How had I screwed it up?

Tentatively, she reached toward me, and her hand disappeared as it crossed the invisible barrier of my salt circle. She gasped and drew her hand to her chest. Her hand reappeared, and she massaged her fingers. "This doesn't seem right." She turned and vanished.

"Of course it wasn't right," I said to the cat. Her hand shouldn't have dematerialized and then rematerialized. The barrier should have acted like a concrete wall – impenetrable. Her hand should have pressed against it, not disappeared through it.

A handsome young man in an old-fashioned narrow, tweed coat and slacks appeared. He wore a brown derby and a comically large mustache. "What is this place?" he asked. "Who are you?"

At least I'd gotten the gender right this time. "I'm Lenore. Who are you?"

He shook his head. "Uh, uh. Telling a pretty lady my name was what got me into this mess in the first place." He took a step toward me.

"Don't–"

He vanished across the salt line.

What the hell? That had never happened to me before. The man reappeared, walking backwards. "Oh yeah, he told me to keep your eyes peeled. He's coming for you."

I untangled my legs and stood. "He? Who?"

But the man backed over the salt border and vanished.

A warm breeze caressed the back of my neck, and I stiffened.

White lady. The words were a masculine whisper.

I gasped and leapt to my feet, feeling someone's gaze upon me. But I was alone in the room with the ghost cat.

I hurried to the desk and reviewed my notes. I'd followed the spell exactly – to the last squiggle on the sigil. If something had gone wrong, it was because of me. Had my concentration broken? Maybe I hadn't been in the right emotional place for this sort of magic.

In the distance, a bell tolled.

I shuddered, coldness washing over me, turning my skin clammy with fear.

Are you willing? the voice asked.

Mouth dry, I whipped toward the circle.

A pink and gold mist swirled inside the salt.

"Oh, shi—"

My hands fell limp to my sides, panic gone. The light was gorgeous, swirls of pink and gold making patterns I could almost make out. There were mandalas in that mist, beautiful things in that mist. Things I wanted. Wanted so badly...

"Lenore!"

I blinked. I stood on the edge of the circle. My big toe nudged the line of salt. I leapt backwards.

The mist folded in on itself until it was the size of my hand, then my thumb, then my fingernail. The light winked out.

Stunned, I gaped at the empty circle.

"Lenore?"

I turned.

Jade eyes wide, my sister, Jayce, stood framed in the doorway. "What the hell was that?" Her long, nut-colored hair cascaded over her crimson tank top. Her jeans looked painted-on.

I braced one hand on the rolltop desk, my fingertips brushing through the cat.

He hissed and leapt to the floor.

"I'm not sure," I said, shaken. "I was trying to call a spirit." And I'd wanted whatever had been inside that circle with a longing that still left me hollow. I straightened off the desk. My palm left a damp print on the wood. I was sweating from the encounter. And the worst part was, I wanted more.

Her brow furrowed. "Mike?" Her expression shifted to sympathy. "I heard. It's all over the town. I'm so sorry. I know he meant a lot to you."

The front door bammed open, light footsteps hurrying toward us.

I grabbed a broom and began sweeping up the salt.

"Lenore?" Karin huffed to a stop beside Jayce. Her baby bump was hidden beneath a loose, blue top, but I suspected her matching blue slacks had an elastic waistband. Our sister was six months along and starting to show. She walked into the room and hugged me. "I heard about Mike's accident. How are you doing?"

"It wasn't an accident," I choked out.

My sisters glanced at each other.

"I thought he fell off a ladder," Jayce said.

"I found his body near a ladder," I said. "His spirit was already in the bookstore, and he was erratic, disturbed."

Karin took in the remains of the chalk circle and his name inside it, the lit candles on the windowsill. Her lips pursed. "Aren't spirits usually confused at first?"

"Yes," I said, "but it's also unusual for a ghost to manifest so quickly, right after the moment of death. Mike was afraid."

Karin cocked her head, her auburn hair loose. "But again, isn't that... normal? A sudden death can be a jolt."

"Not like this." I collapsed in the desk chair. "He told me to run."

"Run?" Karin asked. "Run from what?"

"His killer?" I asked. "The fairy? Doyle? Pick one."

Karin's brow creased. "But if he's confused—"

"If Lenore thinks there's more to his death," Jayce said, "then there's more."

I shot her a grateful look. Jayce had always been my defender, the one who understood me best.

Karin frowned. "I suppose you're right," she said, surprising me. "Lately, when one of us finds a body, there always is more, isn't there?"

"There's something else," I said. "The doctor was there."

"When Mike died?" Karin asked.

"No," I said. "After we found him."

"We?" Jayce asked.

"Peter and I." The memory tightened like a noose around my neck. "He'd been out for coffee and just returning. I was in the backroom. I think I heard him fall. I found Mike when I came out, and then Peter showed up. The doctor arrived a minute or two later, asking about a book she'd ordered. She confirmed he was dead."

"Oh, my God." Jayce pressed a hand to her mouth. "That must have been awful for you."

"So either of them could have killed Mike," Karin said.

Peter could have pretended to have just returned. The doctor could have as well. I'd have to talk to them both about what they'd seen. But I couldn't imagine approaching Toeller for anything. Not knowing what we did.

"But Toeller's never directly attacked anyone," Jayce said.

"As far as we know," Karin said. "Though after what happened to the Bell and Thistle, I'm not sure we can say that anymore."

"That's different," Jayce said. "That was magic."

I didn't reply. Our family had been entangled with Toeller for over a century, blasted by her fairy curse. Every one of our ancestresses had died at the birth of her first child, and every child was a woman. Their husbands died too, within months of the birth. And now Karin was pregnant, engaged and glowing and doomed. My fists clenched, fear scorching a path from my heart to my throat.

"Did you contact Mike?" Karin nodded to the chalk circle.

"No," I said. "Something went wrong. I kept getting other people, and they weren't behaving like normal ghosts. It was as if they knew me, or expected to find me, but didn't expect to be where they were?"

"Huh?" Jayce asked.

"I know, it makes no sense," I said, frustrated. "And then something else came into the circle. An energy."

"It was more than energy," Jayce said. "When I walked in, you were in a trance. You almost walked into the circle before it disappeared."

"What did this energy look like?" Karin asked.

"Sort of pink and gold flashes," I said.

"Is that what you saw?" she asked Jayce.

Jayce nodded.

Karin rubbed her hand against the swell of her stomach.

"What are you thinking?" Jayce asked.

"Well, was it pink?" she asked. "Or was it rose?"

We stared at each other.

My stomach lurched, and I tasted something sour.

"The Rose Rabbit," we said in unison.

"But it couldn't have been, could it?" Jayce asked. "I mean, he's… it's never made it into this world."

"And whatever it was, it still didn't," Karin said. "You said the energy stayed in the circle and vanished, right?"

I nodded. I didn't want to think about what might happen if that thing succeeded in becoming fully corporeal in this world. One fairy was a disaster. Two were unthinkable.

"If the Rabbit works for Toeller like we think…" Karin trailed off. "What did it want?"

It had wanted me.

CHAPTER 4

The next morning, I awoke from a dream of dangerous gardens and winding paths of stone. I was looking for someone but couldn't find him, and my search grew frantic, nightmarish.

Dressing quickly, I jotted the dream into my notebook. It was the beginnings of a poem, as so many of my recent dreams were. And it was probably about Mike. The memory of that loss hit me again, and I sat on my unmade bed for a moment, mastering my breath.

Picatrix, the black cat that had adopted Jayce, leapt onto the outside windowsill and peered inside.

The ghost cat leapt onto my bed and hissed, his back arching.

Picatrix whipped around and leapt from the sill.

"Honestly," I said, glad for the distraction, "you two."

Ignoring me, ghost cat (I really needed to choose a name for him) turned once on the white duvet and curled into a satisfied calico ball.

Still thinking of the dream, because it was easier than thinking about Mike, I walked to the bookstore, unlocked the front door. Peter hadn't responded to any of the messages I'd left on his phone, but it didn't seem right to keep the shop closed.

Besides, I had nowhere else to go.

Feet dragging, I walked to the spot where I'd found Mike. An iodine-colored stain had set into the thin, gray carpet.

I could almost hear the bookstore owner's voice in my ear, chastising me for letting the stain set. A perfectly good carpet – ruined.

I turned, thinking his spirit had returned, but his voice was just an ordinary psuedo-memory.

Hanging my head, I sighed. The carpet would need a professional cleaning and fast if we were to salvage it. It might already be too late.

Something thunked in the back room.

I straightened.

Heart banging against my ribs, I cocked my head, listening.

A soft scrape, metal on metal.

I crept behind the counter and grabbed the baseball bat Mike kept there. He'd never had to use it on anyone, not even to threaten them in tiny, low-crime Doyle. But Mike had been a careful man from a different era. The sort of man who'd be seriously pissed about that carpet.

Another soft scrape.

Clenching the bat in my hands, I tiptoed to the closed storeroom door. I drew a deep breath, flung open the door.

It bammed against the wall, and I leapt inside. The door ricocheted, hitting me in the shoulder hard enough for me to stagger sideways.

Gretel shrieked.

So did I.

Peter's wife clutched her chest, her angular face flushed with annoyance. "What the hell?" Her short brown hair stuck up in angry spikes. She was roughly my age – 29 – and she wore tight, jeans and a crop top, exposing her slim waist.

I lowered the bat. "Sorry. I heard someone in here–"

"And you didn't think it might be me?" Her tanned neck corded.

Since I'd only seen Gretel in the bookshop once before, and Peter had never set foot in the store before noon, I hadn't. But I should have, and my face warmed. I leaned the bat against the door molding. "I'm sorry. I... I tried calling Peter to find out what the plan was."

Her gaze shifted to the desk. "He was busy."

Mike's old-fashioned ledgers lay open on the desk. His precise, narrow handwriting filled the wide volumes of yellow paper. He'd never mastered the computer age. Whenever he'd wanted to type a letter or open a computer file, he'd referred to my step-by-step guides. No wasting time on the Internet for Mike. No texting over dinner with a friend, or checking social media posts while walking down the street, oblivious to the world moving around him. His generation had been perfectly delighted by ordinary reality and imagination.

"Hello?" Gretel snapped her fingers. "Earth to Lenore."

The rear alley door opened, and Peter walked in, his blond hair rumpled. "You won't believe who made an offer–" He stopped short, two paper coffee cups in his hands, and stared. "What are you doing here? We're closed." He wore baggy jeans and a black t-shirt with a comic book character I didn't recognize.

"She thought we wanted her here," Gretel said.

He looked at me.

"She said she called you," Gretel said.

"I tried," I said weakly. "I left messages. I didn't think Mike would have wanted to keep the store closed."

"Mike doesn't want anything," Gretel said. "He's dead."

"That's not..." I bit off the last word. It was true he was dead. But it was untrue that the dead didn't want things. Their desperate needs could be even hungrier than the living's. I glanced at the ledgers, sprawled open across the metal desk.

Gretel slammed the top book shut. "I was just trying to figure out where we are financially. I'm not sure if we can afford to keep the shop open while the estate is in probate."

Probate. I should have asked my sister Karin for advice. She'd know what had to happen now that Mike was dead. Like many writers, she couldn't quite live off her romance novels. So she earned a living as a part-time estate attorney. I forced a smile. "Mike taught me his accounting system. If you like—"

"It's not hard to understand," she said. "I've got it."

I wilted, the dismissal stinging.

Peter set the coffee on the desk. "Look, there's nothing you can do here. Go home. If you're worried about your pay—"

"My pay?" And then the realization struck. I was out of a job. Maybe whoever bought the bookstore would hire me back, but who knew how long that would take?

"Consider this a long vacation," he said. "Gretel and I will let you know if we need you."

"Gretel and you?" My brain stuck like drying gum, grasping at the words that made the most sense.

"We'll be taking over the bookstore," Gretel said.

I stared, thunderstruck. The idea Peter and his wife would run the bookshop hadn't even crossed my mind. He didn't care about the books and hadn't bothered to learn the business. Mike had practically told me he'd hired Peter out of pity. And Gretel and Mike had never got on.

"Since I'll be working here now," Gretel said, "we may not need you. But of course, we'll have to finish our review of the financials to get a better understanding of the business before making any decisions."

"Of course," I said faintly. I swallowed. They were Mike's only family. It made sense he'd leave them the store. "Well, let me know if—"

"We'll pay you what you're due," Gretel said. "As soon as we can."

I backed from the storage room. "Okay. Thanks. I'll lock the front door on the way out."

Gretel slammed the storage room door behind me.

I stood for a long moment, my head spinning. Losing my job wasn't as bad as losing Mike, but the two disasters coming so thick and fast left me stunned. My eyes teared, and I struggled for control.

Gretel laughed, her cackle drifting through the storeroom door.

Anger flared in my skull. I stalked to the front door and onto the sidewalk. I almost didn't lock the door, as promised, but then I shook myself. Gretel probably hadn't been laughing at me, and not locking up would just be irresponsible.

Deflating, I walked through town, past the wounded ghosts of miners and men in fifties hats and women in flappers' finery. None of the specters approached me, but it was with relief that I stepped across the threshold of my aunt's house. I didn't want to talk to anyone, not even the dead.

On the blue rag rug in the entry, I kicked off my shoes. "Jayce?"

No answer.

She was no doubt supervising the renovation at her coffee shop by now. The building's owner was paying Jayce to supervise the contractors. Jayce didn't know anything about architecture or contracting. But the owner was on the east coast, and Jayce knew what she wanted her new coffee shop to look like. I hoped she hadn't cast a spell on the poor man.

Anxious, I paced from room to room. I needed to start job searching, figuring out my next steps. All I could think about was Mike and what I'd lost.

Fortunately, spring in the Sierras is a great place for inducing a zen state of mind. So I stuffed a backpack with a bottle of water, my wallet, and a granola bar, and got into my car, drove east into town. Ghosts paced beside tourists on its sidewalks.

Turning onto Main Street, I slowed at the bookstore. I should have looked for Mike's spirit when I'd been there earlier. But I wasn't about to make a second visit now, not with Gretel and Peter there.

I cranked down the window. But I owed it to Mike to return, even if I had to face down his relatives, and–

Movement flashed in the corner of my eye.

A man sauntered into the road on the opposite side from me and toward my Volvo.

I slammed on the brakes, rocking forward.

"CROSSWALK!" he bellowed.

It was the man from the bookstore, and I stared, shocked. My car was in the crosswalk, and I'd been on auto pilot.

The stranger had ditched the suit jacket and wore creased gray slacks and a dress shirt, unbuttoned at the collar. Muscular and olive skinned, the man was a lot less handsome with his face distorted by rage.

He grasped my driver's side doorframe, his broad fingers coiling through the open window. "Are you blind? You're supposed to stop for pedestrians."

"I'm sorry," I stammered. He'd still been on the opposite side of the divided road when I'd started to drive through. But that was just an excuse. He'd had the right of way, and I'd messed up.

"Sorry! I could have been killed!"

That was an exaggeration, but I'd been in the wrong, and my shoulders curved inward with shame. "I'm sorry–"

"You idiot! Do you even know how to drive?"

A Jeep honked behind me.

"I should move the car," I said, glancing in the rearview mirror.

"You should get your license revoked."

"Look–"

"Looking is exactly what you didn't do."

"It was a mistake," I said, "and I'm sorry, and I'm glad you're not hurt."

"Glad I'm not hurt? What's that supposed to mean? That what you did was okay?"

"No, I'm just—"

"Is there a problem here?" Connor Hernandez strolled to the car window. He was in uniform. His partner, Owen, spoke into the radio clipped to his shirt and trailed behind him.

"The problem is this moron nearly ran me down," he said.

Connor turned to me. "What happened?"

I didn't like Connor knowing I'd messed up, but there was something about his nearness that unknotted the muscles in my neck. "It was my fault."

"She nearly ran me down," the man repeated.

"Lenore?" Connor asked.

"I was in the crosswalk," he shouted. "I could have been killed."

"One moment, sir," Connor said. "Lenore, what happened?"

"I told you what happened," the man said.

"Yes, sir, and now I'd like to hear from Ms. Bonheim."

The stranger blinked.

I swallowed. "He was on the opposite side of the road and had started through the crosswalk. I didn't see him."

"And your name is?" Connor asked the stranger.

He blew out his breath. "Maybe I overreacted. I was on the other side of the road."

"May I see your license, sir?" Connor asked.

"My license? I'm not the one with the driving problem."

"I already know who she is." Connor jerked his thumb at me. "License?"

Grimacing, the man pulled a wallet from his back pocket, handed him his license.

Owen waved the cars backing up behind me around us.

Connor studied the plastic card. "Well, Mr. Van Oss, I didn't witness the traffic violation, so I can't give her a ticket. It seems you're all right though. Where are you staying?"

A vein pulsed in the man's jaw. "The Doyle Inn."

"Nice place." He returned the license. "Enjoy the rest of your stay."

Grim-faced, Mr. Van Oss stalked to the raised sidewalk and vanished into a wine tasting room.

"You all right?" Connor asked.

"I feel terrible." I clenched the wheel. "It was my fault."

"Technically, yes. But he was on the other side of the street. It's a big road. He wasn't in any danger."

"Wait, how did you...? You did see what happened."

"Owen didn't." One corner of his mouth curled upward. "Want me to give you a ticket?"

"No."

"Come on," he said. "We were on our way to get a cup of coffee. Join us."

"I shouldn't."

"You're too rattled to drive. The way I see it, getting you off the street is a public service."

"I don't know," I hedged. All I wanted was to be alone in the woods, and I had a crush on Connor I didn't want to feed.

"It's just coffee."

And he'd just diffused an unpleasant situation. I smiled. "Sure. Coffee sounds good." I pulled to the side of the road and parked, then stepped onto the street. A monarch butterfly flit past, its orange and black wings fluttering erratically.

His partner, Owen, nodded to a pretty tourist across the street. "I see someone I want to talk to. Meet you there?"

Connor nodded.

I hitched my purse over my shoulder. "Where are you getting coffee these days?" Jayce's coffee shop had been their favorite, but it was under construction after a fire and wouldn't reopen for months.

"The cupcake shop. We stay clear of the baked goods, but the coffee's decent."

Pedestrians ambled past, walking dogs, gawking at the 19th century buildings. What was I doing having coffee with the man?

Unsettled, I strolled beside the deputy. I liked him too much, and for such a simple, pathetic reason. Connor listened, and my desire to be heard was a hungry fox, needful, traitorous, insatiable. Once, when Connor had asked me about shamanism, I'd rambled on about the spirit worlds for a good twenty minutes. Stunned by having an audience, I couldn't stop my flow of words. But he hadn't interrupted once, nodding and asking all the right questions at all the right moments.

Connor stopped in front of a green, metal table on the sidewalk. Wisteria vines loaded with plump blossoms twined up the nearby trellis. "Wait here," he said. "I'll get the coffee." He winked. "I know how you like it."

"Wait, I should—"

But he'd already gone inside the shop.

I gazed longingly through its windows. The only way I ever resisted their cupcakes was by not going inside. Now I was dangerously close to running into the bakery and ordering a red velvet piled with cream cheese frosting. Resist, resist, resist – both cupcakes and Connor.

I sat in a chair facing the street and hooked my purse over its back. Though it was only May, summer had arrived, and the morning was already making rivulets of sweat on my back.

A ghost walked past bundled up in furs, his beard a tangled mess, a pick ax over one shoulder. He grinned and tipped his hat to me, and walked on.

I pulled out my notebook and wrote down the details. The dead man's rough energy. The weather-hardened hands, brown and calloused. The hope and desire in his stride.

"Lenore?" a man asked, his voice rich and filled with concern.

I looked up.

Councilman Steve Woodley loomed over the table, the sunlight haloing his tonsured head. His silver hair was as sleek as his pressed blue slacks and a button-up shirt, open at the collar and exposing his muscular chest. His goatee was elegantly devilish.

"Councilman Woodley." I straightened in the metal chair.

He motioned negligently. "Call me Steve. I was so sorry to learn about Mike. How are you doing?"

"I miss him." My throat closed, and I couldn't say anymore.

"Of course you do. I miss him too. We've been friends for ages. He went to school with my youngest brother." The muscles in his face shifted to disapproval. "Before my brother left town."

I didn't respond.

"I suppose Peter and Gretel will be taking over the store?" he asked.

God, I hoped not. But there was no getting away from it. "Yes, I think so."

"I'm glad. This town needs a bookstore." He hesitated. "I've heard that you're not convinced Mike's death was an accident."

"I think it should be investigated like any other."

"Mike was old," he said. "These things happen."

Not to Mike. "I suppose," I said, fighting irritation. Steve's attitude was logical, but he didn't know.

"Well. Let me know if you need anything." He nodded and strode down the shaded walk.

A black SUV drove past. It looked like Nick Heathcoat's, and I closed the notebook, squeezing it in my hands. In two months he and Karin would marry. In three months, they'd be dead.

I jammed my notebook into my pocket. We had to stop the curse that had hung over our family for generations, killing every Bonheim woman at the birth of her first child, ensuring the child was a girl, and killing the husband soon before or after. And we had a chance to stop it. For the first time since the curse began, there were three Bonheims to fight it. That had to mean we had a chance.

Connor emerged from the bakery with two paper cups. "Still thinking about that crosswalk, I see." He set the cups on the table.

"No. I mean, yes," I said. "There's so much to think about. Have you learned anything new about Mike?"

His expression shifted, and he scraped the empty chair across the concrete and sat. "We won't have anything back from the county coroner for at least a week or two."

"But the coroner is looking into it? So you agree his death was suspicious?"

He shifted in his chair. "An autopsy is routine when no one is there to witness a sudden death."

Disappointed, I lowered my head. "So you don't think it was suspicious."

"People fall, Lenore."

"Mike wasn't unsteady on that ladder."

"He was getting up there in years," Connor said.

My hands tightened on the mug. "Not all elderly people are doddering!"

"Anyone can slip up."

Biting my lip, I turned the coffee cup in my hand.

"Is there something you're not telling me?" he asked.

"No." Nothing admissible in a court of law.

He leaned closer and placed his broad hand over mine.

In spite of my grief, my breathing quickened.

"Lenore, you can talk to me. I know Mike meant a lot to you. If there's anything you need, let me know." Removing his hand from mine, he settled back in his chair. "After all, we're friends right?"

I swallowed. Right. Friends. "All I need is to get his death cleared up, and I know you're working on it." But was he?

CHAPTER 5

Smarting from my driving mistake (I'm a dweller), I drove across Main Street's troll-free stone bridge and onto the looping highway east.

A field of thistles flashed past. A woman picked her way through it, her head bowed.

My grip tightened on the wheel. Someone was at the site of the missing Bell and Thistle. But all of Doyle had come here once the police tape had come down. We'd stood and stared in silence, looking for some sign or explanation.

Later, we'd come looking for that damned bell, the one that had hung outside the Bell and Thistle's front door. Its phantom toll haunted the town, stopping us in our tracks, bringing sheens of panic to our faces. No one could predict when the bell would ring or fathom what it meant.

We'd searched for the source of the sound, hoping someone had found the bell and hung it as a prank or remembrance or warning.

In vain.

The town council banned all bells, wind chimes, and alarms over one hundred and ten decibels.

And still the ghost bell tolled.

Grimacing, I focused on the highway. I had human ghosts to worry about.

The road narrowed, and I slowed, crowded by the tightening loops of macadam and tall pines. I never knew whether to be relieved or disappointed that I'd never seen my father's ghost on this highway where he'd died.

My sisters and I had already outlived him.

Below a ski resort, small lakes glittered like sapphires against milky granite boulders. Patches of snow dotted the jagged mountain peaks, the far-off trees appearing near-black.

The woods in Doyle had become no-go zones for my sisters and I. Karin and Nick had gone in once and the paths had changed, getting them lost. Jayce had gone inside and been attacked by a murder of crows. The Doyle woods were fairy territory.

But higher up, in the true Sierras, we were safe, and I drove there now. I wasn't going to give up my connection to the woods and mountains. And I wasn't going to give up my solitude either. Both were too important for a shamanic witch.

I parked in a dirt lot beneath a trio of pines and locked my Volvo. After I'd hiked in a hundred meters, I ditched the dusty trail and clambered over boulders and moss-covered logs and up a steep hill.

At the top of the hill, a twisted pine grew out of a granite slab. Leg muscles groaning, I sat against the tree and enjoyed my ghost and fairy-free view of the lakes.

I opened my backpack and drank from my water bottle and thought of a future without Mike. Tears leaked from my eyes and mingled with my sweat. I dashed away both and dug my notebook and pen from my pack.

The branches whispered in the breeze. I closed my eyes and listened. There were no words in this wind to haunt me, and a sense of peace descended, loosening my limbs.

I wished Connor were here. He didn't need to talk and analyze every experience. The deputy was the sort who could just be. I imagined leaning against his broad chest, the feel of his well-muscled arms enfolding me. His—

My eyes flashed open, my sense of peace gone. What was I doing?

Hurriedly, I finished my poetic notes, tucking the notebook into my pack. I stood, dusting off the seat of my shorts, and climbed higher.

The trees thinned on the steep slopes and made way for wildflowers – yellow mule ears and red paintbrush and purple lupine.

A stitch pinched my side, but I drove myself onward, wanting the exhaustion.

Finally, panting, I stopped beneath a pine and dropped onto a flat rock. I gulped water and closed my eyes, tilting my head back against the bark.

The Sierras had their own magic, and I felt it now, an electricity that raised the fine hair on my arms. When I opened my eyes, I wasn't surprised to see the white wolf seated, panting, beside me.

I looked over the lakes. They glittered, dazzling, and I shielded my eyes from the reflected sunlight. "I understand now what the vulture was trying to tell me. What brings you here?" I turned my head.

The wolf was gone.

"That's not helpful." Unless the messenger was the message. Was someone waiting in Doyle for me with news? Or perhaps I'd already received the message and needed to figure it out?

I pulled out my notebook and pen and let the words flow – scraps of images and feelings that I'd later shape into a poem. The more I observed and thought about what I was observing, the more the world seemed to unfold. The ripples of light off the lakes. The silent wheeling of a bird of prey overhead. The scent of the pines. In spite of my sorrow, my heart swelled.

When I ran out of words, I repacked my backpack. Nearly ninety minutes had passed. I picked my way down the hill. Down was always more treacherous than up, and off-trail I moved carefully, each step a meditation. Finally, I reached the trail and strode to my Volvo.

Something white glinted in the soft earth of the trail.

I bent and pulled a cattle jawbone from the dirt. It was smooth, angular, and narrow as a blade, with a single molar. I found its twin a foot away. It too had a molar in exactly the same place as the first. Shaking my head, I wondered at that, and at what had killed the animal, and why it had been left to rot for so long. But that's the problem with spending so much time in Middle World – the ground we walk on and which I perceive so differently. Things get muddled. It gets hard to tell the difference between real and metaphor.

I listened to the forest for answers, but all I heard was the wind soughing in the pines. Why hadn't a tourist plucked these bones from the earth to mount on the wall? Why had they been left for me?

I jammed the jawbones into my pack and continued down the trail.

Driving back, I treated the road as a meditation as well, paying deep attention. Maybe that guy, Van Oss, had been too far away to be in any real danger, but it frightened me that I hadn't seen him. I'd been lost in thought, and driving in a trance state is the quickest road to disaster. The not-so-near miss had been a wakeup call.

I turned onto the road to town. In front of a yellow house, strings of grapevines rustled in the breeze, their grapes small and hard and green. Winding past a stone barn that had been converted to a wine tasting room, I turned onto Main Street

Tourists were out in force this sunny afternoon. I slowed, my gaze flicking from the cars to the people crowding the sidewalks.

Heedless, a blond boy, no more than six, raced into the street in front of my car. I braked hard, stopping a few feet from his startled face.

He goggled his eyes, widening his mouth and touching his tongue to his chin in a gruesome grimace.

In spite of myself, I burst into laughter, shocked by his youthful audacity.

His mother ran into the street. Scolding him, she grabbed him roughly by the arm and scooped him up. They hurried to the shaded sidewalk and into a boutique.

I blew out my breath and relaxed my grip on the wheel. So the morning's clash with Mr. Van Oss had been a warning message. I'd thank the man if I didn't suspect he'd take it badly.

I drove on and drifted to a halt behind a sand-colored Range Rover. It didn't budge from its spot in the middle of the road.

Ahead, horns bleated.

Five minutes passed. Releasing a loud breath, I leaned out the window, but I couldn't see past the Range Rover.

Finally, I pulled off the road and parked between two young maple trees. Doyle was too small for me to be stuck in traffic.

Grumbling to myself, I strode past frontier-style buildings housing boutiques and restaurants and tasting rooms.

"…atmosphere is thinner here," a florid tourist told her husband. She adjusted her floppy hat. "You must be careful."

Her husband held a leash, a terrier straining at its end. The man licked an ice cream cone and looked skeptical.

Past a blue Prius, the source of the traffic hold-up came into view. Alba Pollard, wearing a sandwich board, was blocking traffic. Angry black scrawls raced across her board. She shouted, rambling and waving her arms.

Tourists stopped to watch the show then realized the woman was insane and scurried down the sidewalks, their faces averted.

Fifty-something and scrawny, Alba made a u-turn in front of the Prius. Her sandwich board clunked against its bumper.

The driver honked, cursing out his open window.

I slowed my steps. No one listened to Alba, the town schizophrenic, so we had that in common. "Hi, Alba. How are you doing today?" Working with spirits, I'd found the only way to calm them down was to keep calm myself.

It didn't work with Alba.

Her blue eyes blazed with rage. "You! You!" Her long gray hair was lank and wrenched into a pony tail. Her skin was suntanned, leathery. Her loose, black tank top and jeans were two sizes too big for her. The fabric slithered around her narrow frame, threatening to expose too much Alba.

"What's wrong?" I asked.

"The corporations are using psychic attacks to keep people sick. You know all about it."

"Y— yes, you told me about it before. Remember?"

She pointed at me, and the sandwich board over her shoulders shifted. "Witchcraft!"

I stepped away. "What?"

"That phone is witchcraft!"

I glanced at the cell phone clutched in my hand. Quickly, I slid it into the pocket of my shorts.

"You're corrupted like the rest of them." She jabbed me in the chest with her bony finger. "You're not real! Nothing here is real."

Scalp prickling, I rubbed my breastbone. "Alba—"

She grabbed my arm and yanked me close. Alba stank of sweat and garlic, and I was close enough to see every wrinkle, every discolored patch of skin. "You need to run," she said. Her scent turned acrid – the odor of fear. "She's coming for you and your sisters. She needs a sacrifice to stay in this world. The Bell and Thistle wasn't enough."

My breathing quickened, turned shallow. "What—?"

"Alba, what on earth is going on?" Doctor Toeller strode toward us. Her short, silver-gold hair glinted in the sun, but she looked ice cool in her blue silk shirt and wide-legged white linen slacks.

I stiffened, forced a smile. Then I realized how inappropriate a grin was and settled for a worried look. Worried was easy. The doctor scared the hell out of me.

Alba's grip tightened on my arm. "Run," she said, her voice hoarse. "She'll get you. She and Britney Spears!" Her voice rose to a howl.

It was Mike's warning, his shriek, all over again. My stomach turned, and I pressed my hand to my mouth to suppress my rising nausea.

The doctor put her hands on her hips. "Not Britney Spears again. Alba, you're blocking traffic. Now go home."

Alba glared at her battered tennis shoes. "Britney's part of the corporations," she muttered. "They're making us sick with their psychic powers."

"And you'll make yourself sick out here in the heat," the doctor said. "Now go home before the sheriff comes. You won't like it if she takes you to jail."

Releasing my arm, Alba shrank behind me. "Don't let the sheriff take me away."

"She won't if you go home." The doctor nodded up the street.

Alba turned and ran off, the sandwich board flapping against her thighs.

I stared after her, my lips parted. Like the rest of the town, I'd never looked too closely at Alba. Until today.

The doctor turned to me. "Are you all right?"

I swallowed, mouth dry.

A car honked, and I jumped.

The doctor waved to the blue Prius. "We should get off the street."

"Ye-es." I hurried to the sidewalk and stood in the shade of the balcony above Antoine's Bar.

"Poor Alba," the doctor said. "In another age, she would have been committed. But the laws today..." She shrugged. "Refusing to commit the mentally ill doesn't seem particularly compassionate, does it?"

Sweat trickled down my temple. Normal. Everything was normal. Be normal. "Are you her doctor?" I asked.

"No. Alba refuses to see a doctor." The doctor shook her head. "I'm afraid neither of us can do anything for poor Alba. But how are you?"

"I miss Mike." My voice cracked.

"Of course you do." She grasped my hand, and I flinched. "How long have you been working for him?"

"Since I returned from college. He was a good person."

"I couldn't help but overhear what you said to Officer Hernandez. Do you think his death was foul play?"

One way or another, Doc Toeller had a hand in all Doyle's recent, sudden deaths. If Mike had died, she'd pushed the murderer his way, just like she'd done for all the others. A sudden fury boiled inside me. "You would know better than me."

Her blue eyes narrowed, turning arctic, and something... other, feral and dangerous, slipped out. "What do you mean?"

That otherness had the effect of an ice bucket challenge, turning my anger to chill fear. I'd been stupid, and I had to fix this, fast. "You were the first doctor on the scene to examine him," I floundered. "What's your opinion?"

Her expression smoothed. "I'm not a coroner, but his injuries appeared consistent with a fall."

"Then I suppose that's what it was."

A line of cars cruised past.

"But why did you say otherwise?" she asked. "Did you hear or see anything?"

"It sounds like you're not convinced it was an accident."

"And you're avoiding my question. What's wrong, Lenore? You seem agitated."

"Isn't everyone?" I babbled. "The Bell and Thistle. Mike's death. Last year's murders. We're all on edge."

A hot wind rose, drying a gritty sweat to my skin. It tangled my hair and rattled the elm beside the sidewalk.

A melancholy bell tolled.

I glanced down the street. Neighbors looked fearfully over their shoulders and away, refusing to meet each other's eyes.

She frowned. "Everyone knew someone in the Bell and Thistle. I don't suppose we'll ever get closure on that mystery."

My pulse accelerated. Closure. The bitch. "Oh?"

"I'm no psychologist, but I do know a bit about loss. This town is grieving and in denial."

"Loss? You talk as if they're dead. They've only been taken."

"Taken?" She cocked her head. "Don't tell me you believe the UFO theorists?"

"Taken." I looked her in the eye, and in spite of my fear, I said, "And we'll get them back."

She went quiet, her face as still as the grave.

I'd gone too far, and suddenly I couldn't speak either. I froze, rooted to the spot, my knees trembling.

I felt it then. Her magic was overwhelming, electric, everywhere. The earth and sky flowed through the woman before me.

I'd only been playing at magic, dancing between the worlds, chatting with ghosts and animal spirits. I hadn't understood magic at all. This was power. And I was small.

The world went translucent, time and space folding together, blurring. I saw men in battered hats on horseback. I saw Doyle's low, wooden buildings vanish, replaced by a thick wood.

I wanted to fall to my knees, tell her I loved her, I'd do anything for her, my queen. She was a queen. It was so obvious now. A golden, unbearable light danced around her head – her crown.

I swayed, bending, but something snapped me upright, locked my legs into place.

Something about a queen in America seemed off. I cocked my head, thinking about that.

The twenty-first century rushed toward me, and it was just me and the doctor on a normal Doyle sidewalk again.

So we weren't playing games anymore. Me, quiet Lenore, had been the one to break the silence and reveal my sisters' knowledge. The doctor and I knew each other now.

I gritted my teeth. "Why didn't you use your unseelie influence to get Alba to move? Did you have to scare her with threats of arrest?"

Her eyes glowed blue fire. Her face distorted.

The sidewalk cracked before me. The crack widened, deepened, ran up the wall of the wooden building, splintering it in two. It raced, a jagged line, across the road. The cement crumbled at my feet, pebbles bouncing into the darkness.

I should run, I thought vaguely. But my legs wouldn't move. The street darkened. Overlapping images swirled around me, dizzying. Women in fifties dresses and gloves and hats. A deer, grazing beneath a pine. A miner whipping a donkey, driving him onward.

Out of nowhere, a rope appeared, coiling around my waist and torso. It tightened, and I gasped for breath. Something tugged me backward, away from the gap. A green maiden walked toward us, her eyes the color of ivy. Reaching into the chasm, the maiden grabbed a fold of earth and whipped it across the gash.

And then I was on the sidewalk in Doyle.

A car drove by, too fast, its wake stirring my hair.

Jayce, in an emerald tank top and brown shorts stood in front of me and glared at the Doctor. Karin stood beside me, her hand braced on my shoulder. She was pink from exertion, her blue t-shirt stretching taut against the swell of her stomach.

Doc Toeller nodded and smiled. "Enjoy your day, ladies." She sauntered down the street.

"What the hell was that?" Jayce's voice trembled.

I slumped against the wood-plank wall of Antoine's Bar. "She knows we know."

Karin's grip tightened on my shoulder. Abruptly, she released me. "If she didn't before, she knows after that display." She rubbed her stomach. "Did we actually beat her?"

"No." I swallowed. "That was a draw. She was testing us." She'd been testing me, probing to figure out what I knew. And when I'd pushed back, she'd unleashed a taste of her magic. I was depressingly sure a taste was all it had been.

"We need to talk." Jayce angled her head toward the door to Antoine's.

And I did need a drink. Desperately.

I followed my sisters inside. A long, curved bar with brass fittings lined one wall. Brass lamps hung from the wooden ceiling, bare except for the water stains. We found a table in the back of the long, narrow room.

Karin lowered herself to a bench and scooted close to the wall. Before long, she wouldn't be able to fit. I slid in beside her.

"Mineral water?" Jayce asked her.

Karin nodded.

"Cider," I said.

Jayce went to the bar.

"Are you sure you're okay?" Karin asked.

"I'm fine."

She gasped, her eyes widening, and clapped her hand to her stomach.

"Karin!" No, no, no. She had to be okay. We died in childbirth, and she was only six months along, and—

She blinked rapidly. "She moved. She kicked!" Karin grabbed my hand and placed it on the gentle swell of her baby.

I didn't feel anything beyond the gentle rise and fall of her breath, and then something small thudded into my palm.

Her eyes grew watery. "She kicked." She shook her head. "It's the first time I've really felt her. I was starting to think... You felt it, didn't you?"

There was another shift beneath my palm. "I felt her," I said, grinning, and took my hand away.

"What's going on?" Jayce slid in across from me and passed a glass to Karin. She handed me a brown bottle, moisture glistening on its sides.

"The baby kicked," Karin said.

"No way! Lemme feel!"

I changed places with her, and Jayce pressed her hand to Karin's stomach, an expression of sheer joy on both their faces. My heart squeezed, and I had to look away.

Jayce laughed. "I felt her! She's amazing!"

Karin ducked her head and sniffed. "Now. What exactly happened?"

I told them.

They glanced at each other.

"What did you see?" I asked.

"I didn't see the history of Doyle on parade," Karin said. "All I saw was you standing in front of Toeller. You were pale and sweating. There was an energetic cord between you, so black it seemed to absorb the light around it. And I could feel..." She shuddered. "You're right, we didn't beat her. She walked away."

Jayce took a swig from her beer mug. "I didn't see a cord, but I felt her magic. Yours too. And it was cold." She shivered and rubbed her bare arms.

I looked around the bar. No one was near enough to overhear, but I leaned across the table anyway and lowered my voice. "There's something else," I said.

"Alba Pollard."

Karin's face creased with sympathy. "What about her? You said she left the street under her own steam."

"She's not like the rest of us," I said.

Jayce raised a brow. "No kidding."

"Her skin," I said. "It's aged differently. She doesn't have the Doyle glamour."

Karin bit her lip. "Are you sure?"

"Trust me, I got an up close and personal look today," I said. "Her skin is normal for a woman her age who doesn't take much care of it."

"But why wouldn't we have noticed earlier?" Jayce asked.

"Because no one looks at Alba directly," I said.

"And we should know better," Karin said bitterly.

"That's not the point," I said. "Alba grew up here. If anyone should have the glamour, it should be her. But she doesn't. And another thing... Doc Toeller scared her. I mean really scared her. It wasn't just the threat of calling the sheriff."

Karin rubbed the lip of her water glass. "There are theories that the mentally ill can see the truth behind unseelie glamours."

"Or maybe the unseelie is the one who drove Alba crazy," Jayce said.

"Alba told me the unseelie needed a sacrifice to stay in this world," I said, "that the Bell and Thistle wasn't enough." What more would she take from us? When would it be enough? My bottle slipped between my fingers, and I caught it before it hit the table.

Karin nodded. "It's said fairies take human sacrifices every seven years. Some of the legends say the humans are sent to hell, but it's more likely they go to the unseelie world. That would explain why some managed to make their way home last year."

"They didn't last long though when they got back," Jayce said.

"No," Karin said. "But they did return."

"So what's changed?" I asked. "If Toeller was taking one person a year every seven years, why take twenty-two people at once and an entire pub? Why make it look like the pub never existed? Seven years haven't passed since the last hiker disappeared." I put the last word in air quotes.

Karin cocked her head, and a lock of auburn hair slid off her shoulder and onto her breast. "The Bell and Thistle must be different somehow. It was always important to the unseelie, wasn't it?"

"Right," I said. During Prohibition, Doyle had been split and a new town, Arcadia, built nearby. The Bell and Thistle should have fallen within Arcadia's town boundaries. Instead, the property had become a special island of Doyle. That had to mean something. "And the old wellhouse. Toeller fought to keep it from being developed."

"She succeeded," Jayce said.

I nodded. The Historical Society, which the doctor spearheaded, was trying to get the old wellhouse declared a historic monument. I hated to agree with them, but the old stone folly did deserve preservation.

"Maybe she doesn't like change," Karin said.

"No," I said. "The wellhouse has a meaning too." Once while exploring it, Jayce had seen a crumbling castle and tangled garden in a vision. Jayce wasn't prone to visions. Unfortunately, we still had no idea what any of it meant. The more we learned, the more ignorant we became.

I didn't like that I was getting used to that feeling.

CHAPTER 6

I stood at the kitchen island and sliced mushrooms. My hair brushed against the drying herbs, hanging from the iron pot rack. Outside the open window, the light dimmed, the sky turning dusky blue. It was too hot to bake, but I warmed the old-fashioned gas oven anyway, kneaded dough, cooked tomatoes and garlic on the stove top for pizza sauce.

I punched the dough. I'd walked past the bookstore again today. Its doors had been locked. Mike would never have closed the bookstore on a Friday.

I hadn't called Peter to find out what was going on or if I could help. His message had been clear: don't call us, we'll call you... When hell ices over.

I should have spent the rest of the day job-hunting, but I hadn't the heart for it. So I'd lost myself in my books and my poetry and the soft silence of the garden. But my nerves were as hot and electric as the summer day. The words wouldn't flow. The spirits wouldn't come.

Now it was Friday evening in the kitchen, and the pizza dough wouldn't rise. I couldn't figure out what I'd done wrong. I'd been careful not to make the water too hot. It was certainly warm enough in the kitchen for the dough to rise naturally. The yeast wasn't past its sell-by date. And yet the dough sat there, gray and lifeless.

Someone hammered on the door, and I started.

I wiped my hands in my apron and removed the saucepan from the heat, slopping tomato sauce across the stove. It sizzled on the burners, the smell acrid, and dripped into crevices the depths of which I'd never probe.

The pounding grew louder, more demanding.

Annoyed, I strode to the front door and wrenched it open.

Gretel Gallin stormed past me, her shoulder banging into mine. She wheeled around, her sandaled foot catching in the rag rug. Her short brown hair stood in angry spikes. Her denim cut-offs and faded orange t-shirt were tight enough to make Jayce proud. "You conniving bitch!"

I gaped, stunned. "What?"

The ghost cat trotted down the steps. Whiskers twitching, he crouched beside the door and readied to make his getaway.

Gretel poked me in the chest. "I warned Peter you were up to something!"

Too shocked to fight back, I rubbed my breastbone. Why did people keep poking me there? "Your husband? What are you talking about?"

"Don't play innocent! I never trusted you. Never!"

Because I'm quiet, people think I'm a pushover. But sometimes, I push back. My voice hardened. "Tell me what you're upset about or leave."

"Leave?" Her brown eyes blazed. "This isn't even your house!"

The cat growled, a warning only I could hear.

"It is—" I shook my head. One third of it belonged to me, but I wasn't going to argue with Gretel about that now. "Please leave."

"I'm not leaving until I get what's mine."

"What's yours? I don't know what you're talking about."

"Gretel!" Her husband leapt up the porch steps and hurried inside. He scowled at me, his soft, babyish mouth thinning. "Let's go." He grasped her narrow arm, and she twisted away.

The dead cat hissed.

"I'm not leaving until I get what I came for," she snarled.

"Gretel, this isn't helping." He raked his hand through his shaggy blond hair.

I gaped, nearly as shocked at his wrinkled chinos and button up shirt as by Gretel's outburst. It was the first time I'd seen him in something other than a t-shirt and jeans. Had I missed Mike's funeral?

"Helping what?" I asked. "What's this about?"

"Let's go." He tugged his wife's arm.

"This isn't over," she said to me. I guess when you're really pissed off, only clichés will do. "You won't get away with this. I'll make sure of it!" Leaving a few choice curse words in her wake, she let her husband draw her from my house.

I trailed after them. "Peter..." I said helplessly. "What can I do?"

I stopped in the doorway as they walked down the porch steps.

He glanced over his shoulder. "You've done enough."

I closed the door and locked it.

The ghost cat sneezed.

"Thanks," I said, flattered the cat had stayed to defend me rather than bolting outside. He didn't seem to know he was incorporeal and could leave whenever he wanted, doors be damned.

Pensive, I walked to the kitchen and resumed slicing and dicing mushrooms. But indignation and worry sent my nerves jittering. What the hell had that been about?

Finally, I grabbed a lavender and sage bundle from my workroom and set a match to its end. The lavender had come from Karin's garden, where we'd built a labyrinth out of the bushes. The sage was from our aunt's garden – now ours. When the tips of the bundle were burning, I blew the flames out and carried the sage bundle through the house. Peter and Gretel's energy hadn't been left behind, but my emotional attachment to her fury was still here. The ritual helped me detach. A little.

The cat followed me through the house. I guess burning sage doesn't work on animals, at least not the dead ones.

When I finished, I ran the end of the smoldering bundle beneath the tap in the kitchen sink, extinguishing it. Beneath the cat's watchful gaze, I hung it from the pot rack to dry out and returned to my pizza.

The dough still hadn't risen, but I rolled it out anyway. The pizza was just for me, so I didn't care if it wasn't quite right. But I still cared about Gretel's cryptic rant. She'd seemed to think I knew what she'd been talking about. What had I done now?

I drizzled cheese and mushrooms over the crust and slid it into the oven, set the timer. "What about Mambo for a name?" I asked the cat, now atop the refrigerator. He'd hissed at Gretel. He'd earned a real name.

He yawned.

"Jupiter?"

No reaction.

"Okay, how about Hex?"

The cat met my gaze.

"I'll take that for a 'yes.' Hex it is."

I washed my hands and searched for my cell phone. Finally, I found it wedged between the fat, white sofa cushions in the living room, its walls painted a pale blue. My aunt's sapphire-colored witch ball turned slowly in the window.

A message awaited me from an unknown number – never good news. Frowning, I dialed voice mail.

"Hello, Ms. Bonheim," a rough, male voice said. He coughed, phlegmy, and I imagined an older man. "My name is Harold Pivens. I was a friend of Mike's, and I'm the executor of his estate. Would you please call me when you can?" He added his phone number and condolences and urged me again to call as soon as possible.

I checked my watch. It was six o'clock – a bit late for a work call, but curiosity had me in its teeth. I dialed Mr. Pivens.

He answered on the fifth ring, just as I was about to hang up. "This is Harold Pivens. How may I help you?"

"Hi, this is Lenore Bonheim. I got your message. I hope it's not too late for me to call?"

"No, no, not at all. I'm glad you did. And my condolences again on your loss. I know you and Mike were quite close. He spoke of you often."

"He did?"

Hex strolled into the room, his tail high.

The man chuckled. "But I don't suppose you know about me. Mike liked to compartmentalize his life. I'm his attorney."

"But you're not from Doyle," I said. I would have known him if he was.

"Correct. I'm in Angels Camp. I know this may seem rather sudden. Poor

Mike isn't even in the ground yet. But there is some urgency. Mike's bookstore is a going concern, and the longer it's closed, the more damage to its value."

"I'm sorry. Are you a business partner of his?" I asked, muddled.

"No, as I said, I'm the estate's executor. There's no way to say this but to say it. He left his book business to you. Every bit of it."

My legs folded beneath me, and I collapsed onto the white sofa. "What?"

"You helped manage the bookstore, and he knew how passionately you felt about literature. He felt his legacy was best left in your hands."

"The bookstore," I repeated, not quite believing.

Hex leapt onto the sofa and settled beside me, his calico fur icy pinpricks against my bare thigh.

"Not only the bookstore," the lawyer said. "You may not be aware, but Mike also dealt in rare books. That part of the business he ran from his house."

I hadn't known, and my mind whirled like a demented merry-go-round. Rare books? Why hadn't Mike mentioned anything about rare book dealing to me?

Interpreting my silence correctly, he chuckled. "As I said, Mike liked to compartmentalize. At any rate, the important thing is to keep the bookstore running. I'm not sure how you want to handle the rare book side of things, but all his inventory belongs to you."

"I see." But I didn't see – not at all.

"We should meet. There are funds available so you can continue to run the bookstore. Fortunately, it's moderately profitable. The rare books are where his real income came from though."

I swallowed, my mouth dry. "I had no idea."

"He said you wouldn't. Oh, there is one thing. I'm afraid his niece and nephew may be a bit unpleasant. They believed everything was going to them. If they give you any trouble, please let me know at once."

"They came by my house tonight," I said dully.

"To your house? Did they threaten you in any way?"

Hex rose and kneaded his two front paws into my thigh. It felt like a tiny ice cube massage – not an entirely bad thing in this heat.

I thought back over the conversation. "I don't think so. But they were upset."

"I'd recommend firing young Peter. I'm afraid keeping him about won't go well."

"Firing him?" Peter worked for me now?

"He is on the payroll."

"I don't think I could do that. It doesn't seem fair. And he is Mike's nephew."

He sighed. "I was afraid you'd say that. Well, the decision is yours. But if he causes you any trouble, let me know. I'll help in any way I can. My specialty is estate law, but I do know a thing or two about employment law. Do you have the keys to the bookstore?"

"Yes."

"Does Peter?"

"Yes."

He sighed again. "You might want to ask him to return them."

"But..."

"But what?" he asked.

My chin dipped toward my chest. "Peter did get something, didn't he? I can't believe Mike would have left him out of the will." I'd feel terrible if he had. Peter might be shiftless, and his wife might be evil (or at least unpleasant), but he was Mike's family.

"Don't worry, the remainder of the estate went to Peter. Mike's house will sell for a pretty penny."

"Good," I said, but guilt gnawed at my bones. I couldn't blame Peter and Gretel for being upset about the will.

"The bookstore will be closed this weekend, of course. We'll have to go to the bank on Monday to get you onto the accounts, and then you can reopen for business. In the meantime, are you free on Sunday? I'd like to go over the papers for the other side of his business. They're all at his house. Can you meet me there?"

"Sure. What time would you like?"

"I'm a morning person. Nine o'clock?"

I was not a morning person – the bookstore opened at eleven. But I agreed. We said our farewells, and I hung up.

My arms fell, limp, to the couch cushions, and my right arm dropped through the cat.

Eyes burning like only a dead cat's can, Hex leapt to the floor and turned to glare at me.

I barely noticed. Mike had left me the bookstore.

My eyes warmed, and I rubbed them. I didn't want to cry anymore. I was tired of it. But this... I'd always thought of Mike as more than an employer. Now I knew he'd felt the same. I guess I'd always known it, but I'd never expected being remembered like this. Mike and I weren't blood. Peter was.

The oven timer dinged. I zombie-walked to the kitchen and slid the pizza from the oven. Mind churning, I drizzled chopped basil over it and set the pizza to cool on the work island.

Slipping into my sandals, I walked out the back door and into the yard. Stars appeared in the darkening sky. The moon wouldn't be far behind.

Solar-powered lights dotted the garden paths. I walked past knots of herbs and bunches of flowers – purple foothill penstemons, pink showy milkweed, yellow bush poppies. I trailed my fingers across the cool surface of a bird bath and walked on. Oaks lined the property boundaries. I walked to one now and lay my hand against its rough bark, feeling the pulse of its sap, feeling its roots reaching into the earth. I let the tree ground me.

I had a job again. More than a job. I had an actual business. Two businesses, if I could figure out what to do with the rare books. I rubbed my throat, which had gone painfully dry. But could I? I knew enough about the rare book world to know it was cutthroat. I couldn't count on an honest deal for Mike's inventory. I'd have to do some serious research before I made any decisions. The most likely one would be to sell the inventory and be done with it.

Reluctantly, I stepped from the protective embrace of the oak and walked toward the house. Lights in the windows shone, inviting.

Things would work out.

From behind me came a terrible groan. A crack.

Startled, I whirled.

The oak tilted toward me, and there was a rending sound, its roots tearing from the earth.

I stared, uncomprehending.

And then I ran.

A crash. Something caught the back of my leg. Pain flashed through my calf. I kept moving, branches snapping.

Heart thundering, I didn't turn around again until I'd reached the door. I grasped the knob, leaning against the door and panting. The oak lay on its side, plants and the bird bath crushed beneath its swaying branches. Leaves showered the ground.

I stared. I had just communed with that oak, and I hadn't felt any signs of illness or weakness. Its roots had been healthy, digging deep into the earth.

There was no reason that oak should have fallen.

I slid down the door and sat on the wood porch. There was only one reason that oak had fallen.

Magic.

CHAPTER 7

Legs shaky, I returned to the kitchen and poured a glass of water from the tap. We'd believed this house had been a safe zone, protected from the unseelie's dark magic. But I saw how dumb that idea was now. Doctor Toeller had been inside this house, ministering to my aunt in her final illness. Or killing her.

In spite of the stifling kitchen, my sweat felt cold against my skin. We'd trusted the doctor with our lives. What fools we'd been.

My elbows pressed into my sides, as if I could make myself smaller, disappear from her radar. And that was even stupider.

Tight bundles of fear knotted my muscles, and I rolled the cool glass across my clavicle. The doctor had lived for centuries. She'd moved among us, manipulated our town, made people vanish without a trace. Blessed some with good luck and others with bad. Inflicted – I suspected – strange compulsions that were too easy to chalk up to psychological disorders. The modern world, in its attempt to label and categorize every oddity, had made us blind and vulnerable. But even if we'd all known the truth, what defense was there against an evil this strong?

The front door banged open.

I jumped, dropping the glass.

It shattered on the tile floor. A shard nicked the top of my foot, drawing blood. It was a tiny cut, but the pain was sharp, and I flinched.

"It's me!" Jayce called.

"Back here," I said, and my voice wasn't wobbly. I plucked the biggest fragments of glass from the floor and deposited them in the trash bin beneath the sink. A crimson bead trickled along my foot, formed rivulets between the bones. I grabbed a paper towel and blotted the blood.

My sister strode into the kitchen. Her hips swayed, the charms on her long, silver necklace bouncing against her flat stomach. A piece of sawdust clung to the low-cut front of her amethyst tank top. Beneath her gray shorts, her legs were impossibly tan. Her feet were bare, any footwear no doubt kicked off in the entryway and lying about for me to trip over. She braced her hands on the butcher block island and sniffed. "That smells fantastic. Mushrooms and olives?"

"Don't move. I broke a glass." I went to the tall cupboard and got a broom and dustpan.

She straightened. "What's wrong?"

My throat closed. We were no longer safe in Ellen's house, but maybe that safety had always been an illusion. I swept up the glass, and drops of moisture dampened the straw broom.

She jammed her hands on her hips. "Something's wrong. The house smells like sage and pizza, and you broke a glass."

"I drove through a crosswalk the other day. I didn't even notice someone had entered it from the other side." I'd tell her about the tree once I figured out what it meant. And my crap driving bothered me.

"Was anyone hurt?"

"No, but I should have seen him. I was thinking and not paying attention."

"That's the life of a shaman," she said.

"It shouldn't be." My jaw tensed. "I'm supposed to see more, not less."

"But our brains are built to filter out the noise, so we can pay attention to what's important. Yours doesn't."

"A pedestrian isn't noise. Maybe I shouldn't be driving." Seeing too much was the danger of Middle World. Unable to meet her gaze, I stared at the drying herbs hanging over the island.

"How close was this?"

"Not that close, but still... He was really mad."

"He who?"

"Some guy named Van Oss. He was in the bookstore earlier."

"And he's still in Doyle?" Jayce frowned. People didn't linger in Doyle – it was a transit point to the Sierras, no more.

I pinched my bottom lip. Why had Van Oss stayed? And what had he been talking to Mike about?

"That's not enough to make you cry," she said. "You have been crying, haven't you?"

"Mike left me his business." The admission was easier than telling her about the oak, the failure of our aunt's magic. It had been bound to fade at some point. Nothing lasts forever. But it was a knife twist reminder of our loss.

Her mouth fell open. "What? But that's wonderful! Isn't it?"

"It is. It was... I never dreamed I was in his will." Or that dark magic could attack us in our safe haven. I swallowed. "The lawyer called. He wants me to get the bookstore started up again as soon as possible."

"That makes sense. You have to pay rent on the space." She grabbed a pizza cutter from a drawer and a plate from the cupboard, and cut herself a slice.

"A mortgage," I corrected. Good God, did I own a building now too? Or had Peter inherited it, and now I'd have to pay him rent? I shook my head. I couldn't delay any longer. "There's something else."

"What?" She bit into the pizza and closed her eyes. "This is good."

"A tree fell in the backyard."

She grabbed a paper towel and wiped her hands. "Is that all? You had me worried. I guess we'll have to get some tree trimmers out here to take it away, but—"

"It wasn't natural. Not normal, I mean." Because there was nothing more natural than magic.

She stilled, the paper towel crumpled in her hands. "Which one?" she asked, her voice hardening.

"One of the oaks."

She hurried from the kitchen.

I followed her out the back door and to the porch.

Giving herself a little shake, she trotted down the steps and into the garden. Jayce paced around the fallen tree. The solar lights still glowed through its branches, though most had been knocked sideways by the impact.

She paused in front of its exposed roots. Crumbles of dirt sifted from their wooden tangle and into the pit gouged from the earth.

Jayce raised her hand, palm toward the roots, and closed her eyes.

A breeze stirred her mahogany hair, and I felt the swell of her magic, a current that made me think of earth and sky. I smelled a warm forest, mosses and wild grasses and water on stone.

Opening her eyes, she dropped her hand to her side. "You're right. This wasn't normal. We should call Karin and get her over here. She may be able to sense something we can't. The three of us can cast a cleansing and protective spell."

"No," I said quickly. "The tree was meant to fall on me. It's not safe here anymore, and Karin's more vulnerable than we are."

She gnawed her bottom lip. "Why would the fairy knock over one of Ellen's trees?"

I relaxed. She wasn't arguing about bringing Karin into this. "I was beneath it at the time."

"But you weren't hurt. Was this a warning? Something to shake us?"

It had sure shaken me. "It is strange that something with that much power hasn't acted directly against us," I said. "I wonder if Toeller can." Something had stopped her display of power on the street earlier, and it hadn't been us.

"Do you think...? Well, the curse is specific, isn't it? Maybe she's bound by it as well. We have to die in childbirth, not crushed by falling trees."

"There are rules." Rules were Karin's specialty.

As if she could read my mind – and I think subconsciously she could – Jayce said, "We need Karin."

"Not here. Not now."

She studied the tree and grimaced.

Something small shifted beneath the oak's branches.

We took quick steps back.

An animal, anonymous in the darkness, scampered away.

"All right." Jayce blew out her breath, her gaze tracking the animal by the rustling in the bushes. "We'll tell her tomorrow. But we do need to tell her. The two of us will have to do for now. Where's Ellen's book?"

"The attic." I hadn't had the heart to dismantle our aunt's magical workspace.

My sister gave me a long look, and nodded. We walked into the house together. She went upstairs to find my aunt's "recipe" book.

In my workroom, I gathered my sage bundle and mason jar filled with Jayce's black salt mixture. She was our mistress mixologist, and had created an anti-fairy blend of dead sea salt, ash from a sacred fire, and iron filings. Fairies hated iron. I only hoped we had enough.

Jayce walked inside my room, her head bent to the open, leather-bound book in her hands. "I've got the incantation." Her hip banged against the rolltop desk, and she winced. "Ready?"

I lit the smudge bundle, watching the flames grow at its tip, and blew it out. "Ready."

We walked upstairs and up the ladder to the attic, through the maze of cardboard boxes and family antiques.

In the center of the unfinished wood floor, Jayce took my hand and began to chant. Energy grew between us, a living thing that pulsed and made my scalp tingle.

We walked in a circle around the attic, then down the ladder to the second floor and repeated the process. On the first floor, we spiraled outward and then outside, pacing the garden. The stream of sage and lavender smoke trailed behind us. A fingernail moon crested the mountains, bathing the garden in silver. The leaves of the fallen oak gleamed. A branch swayed, as if moved by an invisible hand. A bat flapped overhead, its dark track blotting out the stars.

At the property boundary, by the uprooted oak, I uncapped the mason jar. I poured a thin line of the black salt mixture along the edge of the garden, around the side yard, across the driveway, and back.

When we reached the fallen tree, Jayce closed the book and took my hand. We stood in silence. White light streamed from the sky through the crown of Jayce's head and out every pore. She glowed, though I knew she couldn't see it. I was seeing with my Middle World vision, and I was glowing too, an enlivening, hot-cold electricity.

At the same instant, our muscles relaxed, shoulders lowering. Her light winked out.

"Well?" Jayce asked.

"I felt it, but against something that powerful, it still may not work." If Karin had been here, her magic would have added to ours. But I didn't know if it would make a difference against something that could make a pub and twenty-two people disappear.

Jayce smirked. "Toeller won't like those iron filings."

"Which will stay in place exactly until someone drives a car across the driveway," I said.

"Don't be so negative."

"We need more iron."

Jayce laughed, a rich, unstoppable burble.

"What?" I asked.

"You. All of this," she said between snorts.

And then I was laughing too. But it was laughter tinged with fear.

A male figure, stooped and round, paced outside the boundaries of the yard, and I stilled.

"What's wrong?" Jayce said.

"Mike." His spirit had come at last. And we'd just set up a nuclear version of a protective barrier, keeping him out.

He stopped and stood facing me, waiting.

"Wait here," I said.

I picked my way down the moonlit path. Mike looked as solid as any living person. But moonlight shone through his khaki trousers and his short-sleeved, brown plaid shirt.

"Mike." I smiled sadly at his suspenders and stopped at the magical boundary. "I'm here. I'll help you any way I can."

He gazed at me, his expression sorrowful, and my throat squeezed shut.

"Mike." My voice broke.

He threw back his head. His jaw hinged open, and he screamed that terrible scream of despair, horror, outrage. The sound was a rusted blade, cutting through me, driving me to my knees.

I pressed my palms to my ears. "Mike!"

And then he was gone, and Jayce was kneeling at my side.

"What happened? What is it?" she asked. "Are you all right?"

"Yes." But I'd never be all right again. Any doubts I'd had had been banished. I'd seen ghosts like this before. I knew what it meant. "Mike was murdered." I knew it, marrow deep. His spirit hadn't needed to speak the words. The injustice had been coiled in his dreadful shriek.

CHAPTER 8

The CLOSED sign in the bookstore window wrung my insides for too many reasons. I drove past slowly, the warm breeze through my window fluttering my loose, white cotton tank. With an effort, I wrenched my gaze to the road, its sidewalks thronged with pedestrians in shorts and t-shirts.

Mike had never missed a sunny Saturday in the bookstore. It was one of the best times for book sales. People traveling up to the lakes stopped into our small mining town to sample wines. Once they realized an evening in the mountains without cell service might not be so entertaining, they found the bookstore.

My hands grew clammy. I'd dealt with distressed spirits before, but none that I'd loved. Mike's spirit in pain was unbearable.

Mike needed justice.

I needed justice.

I clenched my hands on the wheel and drove through the town and onto the main highway. This time I wouldn't look for my father's ghost. But hope and dread spiraled inside me every time a pine branch bent in the wind, or a mushroom forager appeared along the roadside. I couldn't not look, and I despised myself for it.

The sheriff's station was a three-story building of aqua-tinted windows and rounded corners. In its parking lot, I stepped from the Volvo, unstuck my white, not-quite-linen slacks from my thighs and grabbed my purse off the seat.

The macadam was deep black and smelled of a recent re-tarring. I imagined my heels sinking into the asphalt and through the earth. The impression was so vivid, I glanced behind me to check for footprints I'd left in the pavement. There were none.

I had no standing to be here, but I hurried up the low concrete steps and inside. As far as the sheriff was concerned, I was only Mike's friend and employee. But the memory of his tortured spirit drove me onward.

Sheriff McCourt stood in the high atrium beside a potted palm and a cluster of chairs. Her short, curly blond hair was as rumpled as her white blouse. Her khaki slacks hung loosely on her, and her cheeks were hollow.

She spoke to a man and woman in business suits and sensible shoes, and I immediately recognized them as FBI agents. Agents had flooded Doyle after the disappearance of the Bell and Thistle. None of them looked or talked like

Mulder or Scully. The man was weather-beaten and woebegone, with graying hair and lines around his hazel eyes. The female agent was tall – nearly six feet – and slim with dark skin and cropped, black hair. I guessed she was of Indian or Pakistani descent.

I straightened. She was the woman I'd seen at the site of the missing Bell and Thistle.

The sheriff shook their hands and tucked her broad-brimmed hat beneath one arm. They nodded at each other, and the agents walked toward the glass front doors. The woman glanced at me, her brown eyes appraising.

Sheriff McCourt spotted me and looked away. Then she met my gaze, and her mouth crinkled downward. In a resigned sort of way, she angled her head, as if to say, what are you waiting for?

I forced myself to hurry to her. "Sheriff McCourt, hello." I didn't like having to talk to her. I didn't know her well, and her encounters with my sisters had never been good. But there were things I needed to know.

"Lenore. What brings you to my station?"

I swallowed. "I wanted to ask if there was any indication that Mike's death might have not been natural."

"What?" Her expression pinched. "Speak up. I can barely hear you."

I repeated myself, more loudly.

The automatic doors slid open for the agents. The woman stopped in the doorway and rummaged in her brown leather purse. Heat from outside flowed into the atrium.

One of the sheriff's brows shot upward. "Not natural?"

I glanced at the agent, certain she was eavesdropping. "Could there have been foul play involved?"

"You think there was foul play?" the sheriff asked.

The male agent said something to his partner. She shook her head and followed him outdoors, stepping aside for a young blond man in jeans and a worn t-shirt. A manila envelope was tucked beneath one tanned arm.

"I do," I said.

"What evidence do you have?"

If only I couldn't claim a tormented ghost as proof. "Mike wasn't wobbly on his feet. He ran up and down that ladder every day."

"Even young people fall and break their necks."

"Is that how he died? A broken neck?"

Her mouth compressed. "We don't have the coroner's report yet."

"When do you think you will?"

The young man strode to us. "Sheriff McCourt?"

"Yes?" she asked, wary.

"You've been served." He handed her the thick envelope and strode away.

"Thanks," she said without irony and looked to me. "What were we saying?"

"Do you need to…check that?" Cheeks warming on her behalf, I motioned to the envelope.

"Divorce papers," she said, and her expression shifted – a quick tightening and release. "You were asking about the autopsy."

"Um, yes." McCourt's husband had recently been released from jail. Word was, he'd moved to the nearby town of Angels Camp. I couldn't even imagine what that must be like for her. "When do you think you'll get the results?"

"A week or two, most likely."

"But what if he was murdered? Won't that be too late?"

"Is there any reason to think he was murdered? Do you know someone who'd want him dead?"

I drew away slightly. "No." Peter and his wife were hungry for the inheritance, but it didn't feel right to throw them under the bus. "Something just seemed... wrong, about the scene."

A trio of uniformed deputies walked past us. One laughed, his voice echoing off the white tile floor.

"Wrong," she echoed, her voice flat and dry as the high desert.

"I know that isn't much, but–"

Her brows drew downward. "When someone dies suddenly, it can be difficult for us to process. We go into denial."

"I don't deny he's dead, just the way he supposedly died."

"Until we get a coroner's report, there's nothing to warrant further investigation."

"But... he's dead!"

"And I've got twenty-two people missing who may still be alive," she snapped. "You get any feelings about them, let me know. Otherwise, I need to go find them." A vein throbbed in her temple.

"What if...?"

She glared.

"What if they're connected?" I asked in a small voice.

The sheriff's eyes narrowed, and she closed the distance between us. "Connected?"

"It's a small town. A disappearance, a suspicious death–"

"For the last time, there's nothing suspicious about an old man falling off a ladder. Now stop trying to make this into something it isn't, and get out of here before I detain you."

"But–"

"Lenore?" A uniformed Connor strode toward us, his handsome face drawn. He had the beginnings of a five-o-clock shadow. "What are you doing here?"

"Wasting my time," the sheriff said. She turned on her heel and stalked toward an elevator. It swished open at her approach, and the two deputies emerging leapt aside to make way. She didn't acknowledge them.

"What's going on?" His olive-black eyes tracked the sheriff's departure, his expression unfathomable.

"I came to ask about the status of the investigation into Mike's death." I drew a deep breath to calm myself, and inhaled Connor's aftershave – woodsy and spicy, warm and sensual. My heart fluttered like a caged sparrow. This was silly. Connor was one of my kind, a book lover. I'd always found it easy to speak to him, so there was no reason for palpitations now.

He scrubbed a broad hand across his face. "You shouldn't have done that."

My belly knotted. "Why not?"

"Look, I just got off duty, and I need coffee. Come with me to the cafeteria?"

"Sure," I said.

I followed him through the atrium and into a small cafeteria. Floor-to-ceiling windows overlooked the nearby woods. The pines pressed close, as if trying to crowd the station out.

We approached the register.

"What'll it be?" he asked, his smile returned. "I'm buying."

"Coffee," I said. "Black." The skin sagged beneath his deep-set eyes, lines carved into the corners and around his mouth. He must have worked a night shift, and I fought a sudden urge to reach out, squeeze his rough hand. I didn't know much about the deputy aside from his reading material. But what a man reads can speak volumes, pun intended.

He ordered for us both, and soon we were seated at a round, formica table by the window.

I dropped my paper napkin on a suspicious-looking brown stain and sipped the coffee. It scalded my tongue, and I drew a quick breath of annoyance.

"It's not Ground," he said, smiling wryly, "but it's got enough caffeine to wake an elephant. When's your sister's coffee shop reopening, by the way?" He watched me intently.

A burst of insecurity washed through me, and I adjusted the collar of my white, cotton tank. "In three months, if all goes well."

"So." He turned his paper coffee cup on the table. "Mike. How are things going?"

"He left his book business to me, which is amazing. But now Peter and his wife are furious. His wife accused me of... I'm not sure what she accused me of. She seemed to think I'd tricked Mike into naming me in the will."

"That's bull. Mike wasn't senile. And you took as much interest in that store and those books as he did. He wanted his business to go to someone who cared about it, who'd carry it on."

"He told you that?"

He smiled, lopsided. "He didn't have to. I'm surprised you learned about his will so fast."

"His executor wants to keep the business going while we sort out his estate. I guess he felt it would be easiest to just tell me everything right away.

Apparently, Mike did some rare book trading on the side from his home." And the more I thought about that, the weirder it seemed. I rubbed my forearms. Even if rare books and trade paperbacks were two wildly different markets, why not display some of the rare books at the store? Why not share his finds with me?

"Do you know anything about rare books?"

"No. But I'm supposed to meet the lawyer tomorrow at Mike's house to go over the inventory." I drummed my fingers on the table. "And you have successfully changed the subject. What have you heard about the investigation?"

"I can't discuss an ongoing investigation."

"So there is an investigation at least? Because it doesn't sound like the sheriff cares."

"Sheriff McCourt has a lot on her mind since the Bell and Thistle." He gazed out the window. The pine branches shifted in the breeze.

He brightened. "Hey, Owen and I might have figured out that bell business. You know that old abandoned farm south of town?"

I nodded.

"There was some scrap metal banging together. I think that's what we've been hearing."

"That's great," I said, unenthusiastic. The bell we'd all been hearing wasn't scrap metal, and he knew it.

"What's wrong?" he asked.

"Mike was murdered."

His head jerked toward me, and his coffee-colored eyes widened, startled. "McCourt told you that?"

"No, I'm telling you."

"What do you know?"

"Would you believe it came to me in a dream?" I asked, bitter.

"I might," he said, surprising me. "The subconscious can be a powerful tool."

"Please don't try to rationalize this." Rationality only went so far when your family was under the thumb of an unseelie curse.

"I'm not discounting what you're saying, but you can't take dreams to a jury."

"Do you think I don't know that?" My hands bunched in frustration. "I need proof."

"The police need proof."

I crossed my legs, uncrossed them. "Proof which they're not bothering to find, because McCourt thinks there's nothing there. That Mike was a doddering old man who fell off a ladder."

"When the coroner's report comes in—"

"It will be weeks before that happens, and if any evidence exists, by that time it will have disappeared," I said. His calm, cool, rational demeanor was really irritating. But it wasn't his fault I lived my life in the irrational between of ghosts and animal spirits and dark fairies.

"You don't know that. So far, there's no evidence of any wrongdoing."

I rose. "Then if you won't find anything, I will."

"What's that supposed to mean?" he asked, curt.

I grabbed my cooling coffee. "It means I'm going to be taking over Mike's business, and going through his papers, and talking to his friends. I may as well keep my eyes open for evidence while I'm at it."

"No, Lenore. You need to stay out of this and let the police do their job."

Through the windows, beneath the pines, Mike's ghost stood, his shoulders slumped. A breeze tossed the branches, but his short sleeves didn't flutter. His thinning, gray hair remained unruffled. I felt his desperation, a jagged, metallic vibration in the air that tore at my heart.

The ghost shook its head, an expression of sorrow etched in the lines of his face, and I had to look away.

"If I find anything," I said, "I'll turn it over to you."

"No. Look at all the trouble your sisters got into last year. I thought you were smarter than them."

My neck stiffened. "Right. Thanks for the coffee." I strode from the cafeteria.

"Lenore!" he called after me.

Ignoring him, I walked on. The station's glass doors slid silently open. The mid-Sierra summer sun slammed into me, and I slowed, shielding my eyes with one hand. Waves of heat writhed above the macadam.

Connor didn't follow, and I felt an odd disappointment. But what had I expected? I'd pretty much insulted his profession, or at least his department. Not my finest hour, but Mike's need was greater than sheriff's deputy egos.

I wrenched open the door of my Volvo and sticky heat flowed from the car. Someone had killed Mike. Someone clever and quick. But I had resources and abilities the police didn't. It was time I used them.

CHAPTER 9

I parked in front of Mike's gray and white Victorian. He'd often threatened to repaint it in true, garish Victorian colors. Fortunately for his neighbors, he'd never carried out his threats, because the ivy was too thick. The greenery clutched the house, as if it would drag it down the steep, straight road that tumbled into Doyle.

It had stormed last night, thunder booming against the granite mountains and rattling windows. Thin wraiths of steam rose from the puddles dotting the street, the morning sun warming the town. The Sunday tourist flood would arrive in the afternoon – people returning to the Bay Area from their weekend in the mountains. They'd stop in Doyle for a quick bite or to stretch their legs. And the bookstore was closed, missing all those potential sales.

I stepped from the car and walked to the picket fence, placed my hand on the gate.

A woman shouted. "Get away from there!"

My hand jerked away, and something sharp scraped my palm. I hissed from the pain and glanced at my hand, but there was no mark.

Dragging her sandwich board behind her, Alba Pollard stalked up the sidewalk. The tendons in her scrawny neck bulged. Her eyes blazed with rage. The sandwich board bumped over a crack in the sidewalk, and the two pieces of plywood clattered. The air seemed to vibrate red and black around her quivering form. "I said, get away from there! Corporate stooge! That isn't your house."

Since it really wasn't my house, I couldn't argue. "I'm meeting someone," I said, edging away.

"All you thieves sniffing around here now that he's dead. I know what you want! Drugs!" The collar of her ragged gray tee slipped sideways, exposing her bony shoulder.

"No, I honestly don't." Drugs? WTF?

"You've been touched by darkness." She drew closer. Her breath stank of rotting food, and I fought to keep a smile on my face. "You're like the rest of them. A puppet."

"Ms. Bonheim?" A tall, elderly man in a tan, three-piece suit walked down the porch steps. The front door stood open.

Relieved, I whipped inside the garden, shutting the low gate behind me. "Yes. And you must be Mr. Pivens."

"Thief! Puppet!" Alba paced the sidewalk, the sandwich board scraping the concrete.

He frowned at her. "Why don't we go inside?"

I followed him into the high-ceilinged foyer. Sunlight streamed through the stained glass window above the door and painted the oriental rug in geometric yellows and greens and blues.

He shut the door, dampening Alba's shrieks. "Mike was a patient man when it came to Alba. More patient than I would have been. But I'm afraid her presence next door will lower the value of this property." His hands were white and papery, and something about them made me shudder.

"It's a beautiful house."

A grand staircase, its wooden steps polished, wound up to the second floor. White, crown molding framed high gray walls.

Alba's shouts drifted through the paneled walls.

"The library is this way," he said.

I knew the way, had been there many times before, but I nodded and let him lead me to a library straight out of a British historical drama. The walls – where you could see them behind the bookcases – had been painted a deep burgundy. A rolling ladder stood against one wall. Three arched windows, blocked by ivy, faced Alba's house. Opposite was a fireplace.

"Is this part of his rare book collection?" I asked.

"We'll have to check his inventory, but I believe everything here is from Mike's personal collection. That would now belong to his nephew, Mr. Gallin." He walked to a shelf and pulled a book forward. There was a snick, and the bookcase opened inward. A light flickered on automatically.

I gaped at the secret door.

He grinned, enjoying my reaction. "Mike never showed you this?"

"No, he didn't." And how Mike must have enjoyed his secret.

"Mike was a generous man, but he did enjoy his privacy." He gestured to the open door. "Come and see."

Hesitant, I walked through the bookcase. The small, octagonal room was lined with glass-fronted bookshelves. I scanned the spines. A hardback with its cover intact – black with a white skeleton – American Ghost Stories, 1928. A slim volume with a pebble-gray cloth cover – Secret Symbols of the Rosicrucians. A blue volume the size of a hymnal– The Magician, by William Somerset Maughan.

"Notice a theme?" Mr. Pivens asked.

"These are all occult books," I said, stunned. What had Mike been up to? "I had no idea he was interested in the paranormal."

Mr. Pivens sniffed. "I don't know about interested. He said it was a profitable sideline."

I rubbed my forehead. That didn't track with what I knew about rare bookdealers. They were usually scruffy, down-at-the-heels types. But my knowledge of that world was limited. I pointed to the Somerset Maugham. "Is this a first edition?"

"Possibly. You'll have to check his records." Mr. Pivens nodded toward a Wooton Desk over six feet tall. Its three hinged sections hung open – a center piece with a fold-down writing desk, and a deep door on each side. Cubbies lined the doors, filled with ledgers and journals and loose papers.

I grasped one side and pulled. It hinged inward smoothly, and I whistled. The entire desk could be folded up like a tall box.

"The desk is yours as well as the contents, of course. But I'm afraid going through his records will be a bit of a challenge," he said. "Mike had his own organizational system, and he kept everything." He shut the bookcase behind us, and the room was suddenly too small, stifling.

Biting the inside of my cheek, I picked up a book lying on the open desk. The Works of Geber. I opened the cover. It took me a moment to process the date in roman numerals: 1678. I whistled and put the book down quickly. I'd need to wear gloves to handle any volumes that old.

I pulled a wide ledger from the back of his desk. Mike's neat script filled the lined, sand-colored pages. I blinked. The Works of Geber was worth eighteen thousand dollars.

Slowly, I scanned the shelves. There were hundreds of books. Not all would be worth that much money, but... "Oh, my God."

"Indeed," he said.

"I don't know anything about rare books!"

"I doubt that matters much. Even if you simply sell the rare book inventory and abandon that side of the business, you will be left with quite a tidy sum."

I choked. Tidy sum?

"I understand you write poetry?" he asked.

My face heated. "Mike told you." It wasn't something I advertised.

"He was quite proud of you. I do hope you keep writing. Perhaps this extra funding will allow you to continue, even self-publish. I hear self-publishing has become respectable."

"I don't think I can stop writing even if I wanted to." The poems came, flowing out of me. If I didn't write them down, the words and images kept me awake at night.

"I suggest you take that ledger with you, and any other records you can find which will provide you an accurate inventory."

My forehead scrunched. "Take it with me?"

"For now, the books will have to remain here. You and I are the only two people who know about this room, so they'll be safe." He walked to a glass case. Taking a key from his vest, he unlocked it and pulled out a hardback with a blue and gold cover.

I winced at his bare fingers on the leather.

"The Sword of Song, by Aleister Crowley. First edition, one of only three copies printed on vellum for Crowley's personal use. It's worth over fifty-thousand dollars."

I swayed, the ledger clasped to my chest. How was I supposed to manage such a bequest? Why had Mike left something so precious to me? "You seem to know something of rare editions," I choked out.

"Only this one." He slid it back onto the bookshelf and locked the case. "Mike wouldn't stop crowing over this acquisition. It really will be safer here."

"I'm fine with keeping the books at Mike's." I couldn't imagine anything so valuable in my home.

"Fortunately, Mike had a trust, so we can avoid probate. That will make settling his estate much smoother." He turned to peruse the books.

Taking that as a hint, I rummaged Mike's desk. "Aren't you worried I'll take something I shouldn't?" I asked.

"Everything in this room belongs to his rare books business, and that now all belongs to you. There's nothing here you can take that you shouldn't."

Except for the books themselves. I sat down hard on the rolling chair and it skidded a few inches from the desk. I rolled closer and studied the ledger more intently. Each entry described a book – its title, a description, the seller and price paid, the estimated resale value, the date Mike had sold it and for how much. My finger paused over a name – Heath Van Oss.

I chewed the inside of my cheek. Hadn't the man in the crosswalk been called Van Oss? That would explain why he'd been in Mike's bookstore. Two years ago, he'd sold Mike a book of American folktales for three hundred dollars. Mike had left a question mark by the estimated value, and he hadn't resold it yet.

I flipped the pages, wishing Mike had entered the computer era. He'd put lines through books that were no longer a part of the inventory, so they were fairly easy to pick out. But there were a lot of pages. Still, this ledger couldn't contain all the books in the room. There had to be other records. I longed to be alone, to dig through his notebooks and papers for the evidence the police weren't bothering to gather. But I couldn't do that with the lawyer looming over me, so I stuck with the ledger.

I froze, staring blankly at a yellowish page. A poem had been scrawled across it.

The Queen Vanishes
Dread drives my pulse, a ragged rhythm.
Her absence blights the trees, their trunks paper cutouts, their twisted leaves dying slugs. Her absence cracks the fountain, its brackish waters a seeping wound that drip, drip, drips to the paving stones. Her absence dims the sun, a cheerless, painted disk. I cannot say how long she has been gone. Long, I worry, for the world to feel her disappearance and fold in on itself, a wilted lover.

I slip through the seam to the Otherworld of nightmares and hard lines and hunger. Man and magic rustles the tall, red trees, the scent acrid, searing.

My Queen crouches beside the spring. Her hands fist. The babble of water drowns her muttering, ripples off her lank hair, raises the flesh on my scalp. She turns, her expression a diamond grotesque on a burning castle wall.

Silent, I extend my hand. Silent, she takes it, follows me through the glass spring. I do not see the heart she's left behind, fractured into three. But dread drives my pulse, a ragged rhythm.

My ears rang, my head aching. It was a poem I'd written.

"How lovely," he said. "Though I never got the hang of poems that don't rhyme. What is it called? A prose poem?"

"Yes," I whispered and shut the book. "It's one of mine."

"Mike must have kept it as a tribute to you."

Knowing he hadn't, I stood quickly, gripping the ledger. "This seems to be his most recent book of accounts."

"Yes, I believe it is, but there may be others. There are so many books, you see."

"I think I'd like to start with this one."

"Yes, I imagine you have a lot of research to do. Well, then. Monday at the bank? We can get the bookstore account put into your name?"

"Won't they need a death certificate?" I asked.

He waved aside my concern. "You let me worry about that." He opened the bookcase and paused beside it, waiting for me.

I walked into the library, and he shut the door behind us. "Well, then. You have your homework, and I will see you–"

Peter and Gretel walked into the library and stopped short.

Peter's baby face flushed. "Where did you two come from?" Though we were over a hundred miles from the ocean, he wore his usual board shorts and a gray t-shirt stained with what I guessed was ketchup. His wife's army-green shorts and khaki tank displayed every curve and angle.

Guilt struck me dumb. I held the ledger to my chest like a shield.

The lawyer folded his arms. "I could ask you the same thing. We hadn't scheduled a visit."

"It's my house, isn't it?" Peter asked.

"Mike was quite specific," the lawyer said. "The house was to be sold, and you were to be given the proceeds."

"But the stuff in it belongs to us," Gretel said. "You're not going to sell that."

"Not all the contents are yours," Mr. Pivens said. "Some belong to his business, and others have been bequeathed to friends."

Her face contorted. "How do we know you're not giving away what's rightfully ours?"

"You have a copy of the trust and of his list of bequests." He reached into his breast pocket and drew out a sheaf of folded papers. "And here is a copy for you, Miss Bonheim."

"He wasn't in his right mind." Gretel pointed a long finger at me. "She influenced the old man."

"In my opinion," Mr. Pivens said, "he was of sound mind. This house is valuable. Your husband will receive a handsome settlement."

"We should have gotten the bookstore," Gretel snarled. "You haven't heard the last of this." She turned and stormed out.

Peter hurried after her.

"I wouldn't worry, Miss Bonheim," the lawyer said. "Mike was no more addled than I am, and I can assure you, everything is clear and in order."

Numb, I stared at him. Because everything was not clear nor in order.

It had been a week since I'd composed the poem we'd found in Mike's ledger, but I hadn't written it for Mike. No one had seen the poem, kept folded and secret inside my notebook at home. And the poem in the ledger was in my handwriting.

CHAPTER 10

The lawyer was as good as his word. On Monday, he talked the bank manager into putting my name on the bookstore's accounts in spite of the lack of a death certificate.

"The advantage of community banks, Ms. Bonheim," the lawyer said as we strolled onto the bright sidewalk. He shot his cuffs and blinked in the sun. "They'll do the right thing, even if it's not quite by the book. A pity we no longer have any like that where I live, but Doyle is a world unto itself, isn't it?"

Startled, I glanced at him. "You noticed?"

A pickup drove past on the street. The morning was already warm, and I unpeeled my white blouse from my back. I'd worn a cream-colored, linen skirt today in honor of the elegant Mr. Pivens. The blouse was already rumpled.

"Doyle doesn't have any fast food restaurants or chain stores," he said. "Every business is charming and unique." He motioned toward the false fronts of the old west buildings – boutiques and tasting rooms and restaurants. "I don't know how your town council manages it, but I'm envious. I know one can't stop progress, but Doyle has made a valiant effort."

In the distance, a bell tolled, empty and echoing, and the skin prickled on the back of my neck. Along the street, people missed a step, glanced over their shoulders, ducked their heads.

He smiled. "Church bells. Lovely."

It was Monday morning, and that was no church bell.

Mrs. Reynolds walked past pushing a stroller, and we stepped aside. Her shoulders hunched, her expression haunted. Her husband had vanished with the Bell and Thistle.

"Now," he said, "you will let me know if you need anything. I'd like to do a complete inventory of the rare book business at his house before I officially turn that over to you. I want to make sure there is no confusion between his personal and business collection. There must be no misunderstandings among the heirs."

I nodded.

"The bookstore is simpler. It's separate from his home. But with Mike's personal library so close to his work space... I doubt things were mingled, but you never know."

"It's fine," I said. "I understand."

"You have my card. And one more thing." He handed me a key ring. "This key is to the store. I know you already have one set, but now you have Mike's set as well." He frowned. "Have you got young Peter's set back?"

"Not yet." I'd been avoiding the chore.

"Don't put it off." He nodded to me and strolled down the road.

I watched his straight back, until he disappeared around a corner. Then I turned and walked to the bookstore. My bookstore. Ye Olde Bookstore, because Mike had never been able to think of a better name. I wouldn't change it now.

Unlocking the door, I stepped inside. The bookstore was stuffy, and I toed down the door's kickstand and left it open. We were normally closed on Mondays, but if someone wanted to buy a book, I was ready to sell.

I slid open the window behind the counter, creating a cross-breeze, and turned on the electric fan. Mike had been too cheap for air conditioning. I thought I'd figured him out – frugal and honest, funny and kind. But that had only been the surface Mike, hiding an interest in rare occult books. What else had I missed?

The thin soles of my caramel-colored shoes were soft on the carpet. I unlocked the cash register and turned the key. The register hummed to life.

I traced one finger over the keyhole in the locked drawer beneath the counter. Mike had given me my own set of keys, but never a key to this drawer. He'd told me it was only for junk, and I hadn't pursued the issue. But junk didn't need a lock. I sifted through the small key ring the lawyer had given me, smiling with relief when I found a tiny key.

I held my breath. It fitted neatly into the lock. "What are you hiding?" I whispered.

"Ms. Bonheim?" a man asked.

My muscles spasmed, and the key fell to the gray carpet.

The man from the crosswalk stood on the other side of the counter. Why hadn't I heard him come inside? The front door had been open only a minute or two. Had he been following me?

Stomach knotting, I stooped and grabbed the key, pocketing it. "Mr. Van Oss, isn't it?"

"I wanted to apologize for the other day," he said, towering over the counter. He looked as sleek as a seal with his slicked-back hair and pressed white shirt. The top buttons were undone, hinting at a muscular chest, and I felt myself flush. "Anyone can make a mistake," he said, "and I may have overreacted."

"No," I said. "I should have been paying more attention. I'm sorry I gave you a scare."

"I wasn't scared," he said sharply, then smiled. "And you can call me Heath." He stuck out his hand, and I shook it. His grip ground my bones, and I struggled not to wince. "I'm a rare bookdealer."

Which explained why he'd sold a book to Mike. But he was awfully well dressed for a bookdealer. Karin's fiancée favored Armani, so I knew what designer menswear looked like. Van Oss was wearing expensive threads.

A coyote trotted into the bookstore, and I drew a quick breath, forced my gaze to the man. The animal was a spirit with a message. Coyotes were tricksters, teaching us the balance of wisdom and folly. What was it trying to tell me?

"I'm Lenore." I retrieved my hand. Dropping it to my side, I clenched and unclenched it to restore the circulation.

He edged around the counter and casually braced his arm on the top of the register. "The fair Lenore from The Raven?" His gaze raked me from my flats to the top of my blond hair.

The coyote's head swiveled, as if scanning for the proper section of the bookshop to browse.

"No," I said. "I don't think so, since that Lenore died young." My sisters and I might be doomed, but my parents wouldn't slap that sort of label on me. They'd never got the chance to explain their choice of names though.

"But we're all going to die," he said. "Life only has one exit."

"So I've heard. You said you're a rare bookdealer? Is that why you were meeting with Mike?"

"I'd asked him to appraise a book for me. I doubt it's of much value. I probably shouldn't have bothered him."

My eyes narrowed. "I didn't realize he did book appraisals."

"Not officially," he said, "but all rare bookdealers are appraisers to some degree. We have to be in order to know what to buy and sell the books for." He smiled, leaning closer.

If I had whiskers, they'd be twitching. "What was the title of the book?" I asked, raising my voice.

"You know Mike was a specialist in occult books?"

"Is that what you asked him to appraise?"

"A book of American folktales. Vanity published. The author thought he was going to be America's version of the Grimm brothers. It's likely only worth a thousand or two, but I need it back."

The coyote sniffed at the cuffs of the man's trousers.

I gave the man a fake smile. There had been a book of folktales from Van Oss, but according to Mike's ledger, he'd paid three hundred dollars for it. Was it a different book, or was Van Oss up to no good? "I suppose folktales would fall into the occult category," I said. "Who was the author?"

"Are you taking over his business?"

"Yes."

"Buying it out?"

"I inherited it," I said, growing annoyed.

His smile was slow, sly. "I didn't know Mike had a daughter."

"We were friends." I folded my arms.

"And you shared a love of... books."

I raised my chin. "Mike's executor is going to be conducting a complete inventory of his rare books–"

"Pivens, is it?"

"You know him?"

"I know of him."

"Then I'm sure if you show him a receipt for the book you lent Mike, he'll be happy to assist you." Maybe the man had lent Mike a different book of folk tales, but I wasn't going to admit anything to this jerk without seeing a receipt.

"Of course. In the meantime, if you happen to come across it, you'll let me know?"

"Sure." I'd agree to anything if the creep left.

He gave me another long look, then turned and departed, the coyote at his heels.

I'd sage the store to rid it of his atmosphere, if Mike would let me. My throat tightened, and I remembered that the store was mine now, Mike was gone, and I could sage as much as I wanted.

I inserted the key into the mysterious drawer and opened it. A tattered copy of a booksellers' magazine lay inside. I set the magazine aside. Beneath it there was a small metal cashbox. I pulled it out and set that on the counter too.

The box was locked, but I rifled the key ring and found a key that fit, opened the lid. The inside of the cashbox had been sectioned off -- small trays for change and a long tray for bills. What looked like a Roman coin lay in one of the change trays. An iron railroad spike lay in the section for bills. I lifted off the top section. The bottom was empty.

My shoulders slumped. Just junk. I'd really thought the box might hold something important.

I reached deep into the back of the drawer and touched paper – three wrinkled envelopes. A yellowed envelope with a faded Christmas card from Mike's mother, long dead. An envelope with a land deed in nearby Angels Camp – the lawyer might like to see that. And an envelope postmarked only eight days ago from an auction house with a name even I recognized. I pulled out the letter.

It was handwritten.

Mike–

The provenance looks good. If you have what it seems like you have, we'll be happy to set the minimum bid at one million.

Sandra

I stared, stunned. One million? Mike had a book worth a million dollars? That couldn't be the folktale collection that Van Oss had asked about – he'd said it was only worth a few thousand. But would Van Oss hang around Doyle for days waiting for a valuation on a thousand-dollar book? He'd spent less on his suit.

My forehead wrinkled. No. Either this wasn't the mysterious book of American folktales, or Van Oss was lying about its value. And those two possibilities weren't mutually exclusive.

A million dollars. If anyone else knew about the book, it was a motive for murder.

I pulled the drawer out further, in case there was something I'd missed, and found a wrinkled piece of binder paper. I unfolded it and sucked in my breath.

"Nathaniel hied away to the fae spring
To gather herbs and flowers for his bride.
Belle, mischief mad, behold anon the man.
Oh Moon, she raved, smit dreadfulle to her heart,
She wove her magic spelle and bound him close.
Away to me, she called, forget your love,
Forget your mortal pledge, a haunting cry.
Three days he tarried in the unseelie bower.
His home and hearth forgotten in her couch.
Then fire more fierce than fae's blew through his soul,
And waking, stumbled to his mountain home.
Return! She cried. I bind you with my charms,
I call the Morrigan, tie fast his fate,
If he resists, its Uffern's gate he'll knock on."

My hands shook. It was the origin story of our family curse.

Mike had known the curse story. How was it possible? Had our aunt told him? She must have given it to him, but why would she?

I looked more closely at the page, and my head swam. This wasn't happening. Not happening, not happening, not—

Someone knocked on the door frame, and I crumpled the paper in my hands.

A woman in a blue business suit and white blouse stood in the entry. "The sign says CLOSED, but the door's open. It's confusing."

"I'm trying to air the place out, but if you'd like to buy a book, you're welcome." She looked familiar, and then I remembered where I'd seen her before – at the sheriff's station. Inside the bookstore, she didn't look quite so obviously like an FBI agent. Her black hair was up in a bun, and I could see the bulge beneath her blue blazer where a gun no doubt hid.

She strode to the counter, and I had to crane my neck again.

"I understand you had some trouble here," she said. Her voice had a faint, Indian accent.

"The owner died a few days ago."

She glanced at the cash box and papers on the counter. "Not a natural death."

Nonplussed, I stared at the agent. What did she care about Mike's death? "He fell off the ladder." I gestured to the rolling ladder against one of the bookshelves.

"You're one of the Bonheim sisters."

"Yes, I'm Lenore."

"I'm Agent Manaj." She held out her hand, and I shook it. This time, I didn't get a bone crushing squeeze.

"What's the FBI doing in Doyle?" I asked.

She arched an ebony eyebrow. "You have to ask? Or is Doyle so used to people vanishing that the loss of twenty-two people and a pub is no big deal?"

Pain stiffened my neck. "I knew people in that pub."

"Not as well as your sister knew them. Her name's Jayce, isn't it?"

What the hell was that supposed to mean? "What do you know about Jayce?"

"She was a suspect in several murder investigations, and she found a missing person – Ely Milbourne. We'd been looking for him for decades."

The general consensus was that he'd been in hiding in the woods all that time, on the run from the law. But Jayce had found Ely all right – or his body at least. And it hadn't aged a day since he'd last been seen in 1995. I wondered how the authorities had managed to explain that detail. "So it was Ely's body."

"Oh, yes. Your other sister ran into some trouble too – Karin?"

The paper crackled in my hand. "I wouldn't say that. She was trying to help Jayce." I said a silent apology to Jayce.

"You go into the woods much?" she asked.

"Everyone does. That's why we live in the mountains."

"Ever seen anything odd?"

"No," I lied. "Why? Do you think the missing twenty-two are in the woods?"

"Mr. Milbourne was. And another missing person, Dante Cunningham. Your sister, Karin, found her last summer. Dante didn't survive the encounter though."

"Dante Cunningham?" I felt the blood drain from my face. Dante had gone missing in 1911. Karin had found her last year, ancient but alive and stumbling in the woods. We'd understood later she'd been taken by the same force that had taken the twenty-two. It was the same force that took a hiker every seven years. What we didn't understand was how she and Ely had escaped.

How had the agent recognized Dante for who she was – a missing person from over a century past? Or had they made that connection? "I think I remember hearing that name," I said. "Was she related to the local Cunninghams?"

"It seems so. An elderly aunt."

"Was she visiting?"

"No, she was born here. She disappeared in 1911."

"That can't be the same woman then," I said carefully. "She'd have to have been well over a hundred years old."

"People are living longer these days," she said, bland.

"There's not a lot of modern medicine in the forest. Do you think she left Doyle on her own and then somehow made her way home years later?"

"It's a mystery." Her dark gaze bored into me. "But as I'm sure you know, there are a lot of mysteries in Doyle. You were the first to report the missing persons at the Bell and Thistle."

Jaw tight, I stretched my mouth into a smile. "My sisters and I did."

"Yes," she said. "Your sisters. There are rumors going around town that the three of you are witches."

Going cold, I leaned against the window sill behind me. "This is California. The New Age never left."

"Old age now. Of course, most witches are harmless. Only a few are delusional and dangerous. So are you? Witches?"

"We didn't make the Bell and Thistle disappear, if that's what you're asking."

"I asked if you were witches."

"We're not Wiccan," I hedged.

"That wasn't the question. Wicca is a religion. Witchcraft is a practice."

"I practice shamanism. You'll have to ask my other sisters about their hobbies."

"I will." She turned on her heel and strode out.

Hurrying after her, I shut and locked the front door. I didn't want any more surprise visitors. There was nothing wrong with practicing witchcraft in California these days. You couldn't swing a cat without hitting someone who worshipped the goddess or read Tarot cards. But why the devil had she been asking about it? I knew a supernatural force had taken the twenty-two, but the FBI certainly couldn't believe it. Could they?

Something slipped to the floor, and I bent to retrieve the paper I'd dropped. The curse story.

I blew out my breath.

It was written in my handwriting.

CHAPTER 11

"I'm sorry." The woman's voice crackled over the phone. "But that information is confidential."

I shifted, leaning my hip against the bookstore counter. The auction house was trickier to deal with than Mike's bank.

A ghost in a World War II G.I. uniform walked past the paned window. Half his face had been sheared away, exposing bloodied muscle and bone and grinning teeth.

Swallowing bile and sympathy, I turned my head. When the soldier was ready to cross over, he'd find me. They always found me, their damaged bodies and souls exposed to the raw. The contented dead didn't stick around.

My grip tightened on the old-fashioned rotary phone. "The executor and I are in the process of inventorying Mike's business. I found your letter about the minimum bid, and–"

"And I can't help you without a death certificate."

"Seriously?"

She sighed. "I am sorry to learn of Mike's passing, if it's true."

"If?"

"But you have no idea how cutthroat his business can be. I can't simply give that information out over the phone without verifying that what you're saying is true."

"A death certificate," I said.

"And proof that you have the authority to discuss his estate."

"All right. I'll get both for you."

"Very good." She hung up.

"Goodbye to you too," I muttered and dialed Mr. Pivens.

"Hello?" the elderly lawyer asked.

"Mr. Pivens, this is Lenore."

"Ms. Bonheim? I just left you. Is there a problem already?"

"I'm not sure. I found a letter from an auction house." I read it to him.

He whistled. "Good Lord. A million dollar starting bid? And there's no mention of the book's title?"

"No. I called the auction house, but they won't give me any information without a death certificate. They also want proof I have the legal right to discuss his estate."

"Do they think they're a bank?" he asked, indignant. "I've never heard of anything so ridiculous."

"When will we be able to get a death certificate?"

"Not for a month."

"A month?" I parroted.

"This is the government, my dear, and they do things in their own time. However, I do not like the idea of a book of that value lying around Mike's house. Thank you for calling me. I'll return there now and see if I can locate it."

"Would you like my help?"

He chuckled. "I was counting on it, Ms. Bonheim."

"I didn't find any mention of a book valued over a million in the ledger I have."

"You said the letter from the auction house was recent?" he asked.

"Yes, it was postmarked last Monday."

"And would have taken two days to arrive."

"He received it the day before his death," I said.

"And he might not have had time to record it."

I scanned the letter, open on the counter. "Maybe." But the letter looked like a response to his request to set a minimum million-dollar bid. Mike had known what he had, or he'd suspected.

"Where are you?" he asked. "Can you meet me at the house, or shall I come to collect you?"

"I'll meet you there."

"An hour then."

"Perfect. Good bye."

He said farewell and hung up.

A chill breeze rustled the letter on the counter. The paper lifted into the air and fluttered to the floor.

I stooped to pick it up, and a gray shadow moved in my peripheral vision. I straightened. "Mike?"

But I was alone in the bookstore. I studied the letter again. It had been locked away, and as far as I knew, only Mike (and now I) had the key to that drawer. But could someone else – Peter or Gretel – have seen it? I shifted, uneasy. A million dollars didn't go as far as it used to, but people killed over less. And a million was just the opening bid.

Peter and Gretel were suspects. I walked toward the storeroom. If they'd killed Mike, I'd make them pay.

I yanked open the door, and everything stopped – my brain, my bravado, my breath. "What the hell?"

The drawers had been pulled from the desk. Open manila folders and papers lay scattered about the cement floor. Books, their spines bent and damaged, spilled from overturned boxes. The desktop computer monitor lay on its side on the floor, and its screen was cracked. One metal bookshelf canted at an angle, propped against a wall. All the boxes its shelves had held lay in a rough pyramid beneath it.

Anger flushed through my veins, warming my skin from the inside out. Peter and Gretel. They'd had a key to the bookstore...

I went cold. They still had a key. They could get inside whenever they wanted. I weighed the options – demand they return the key or change the locks – and chose the path of least resistance. "Change the locks it is."

Cursing, I collected the papers off the concrete floor, glancing at them and organizing them into stacks on the desk. Slowly, I cleared a path to the alleyway door. I turned the handle. It was unlocked, and I cursed. Not content with trashing the storeroom, Peter and Gretel would have let someone else stroll into the bookstore after them.

I cracked my knuckles. Those two had better not come to me for help after they died.

Needing to calm down, I stepped outside and leaned against the cool bricks. I breathed deeply and studied the clouds. Karin had recently learned how to read them and had tried to teach me. But I simply enjoyed watching their slow, inexorable drift.

My anger seeped through the pavement and became fertilizer for the earth. The earth was good at taking crap and turning it into something useful, and my mini tantrum was small beer by comparison.

When I no longer wanted to throttle Gretel, I straightened off the wall, brushed off the back of my skirt, and reached for the door.

I paused, my hand over the knob. Peering at the metal, I bent closer. Fresh, shiny nicks marked the edge of the keyhole. I jerked my hand away and clutched it uselessly against my chest.

Working in a bookstore, I'd read my share of mystery novels. Trashed storeroom plus scratches and dents on the lock screamed lock picking. My gaze darted around the alley, but it was just me and the garbage cans.

Shaken, I returned inside and locked the door, walked to the register. I studied its lock. It seemed okay. But the lock on Mike's mystery drawer was scratched. There were faint gouges at the top of the drawer as well, as if someone had tried to pry it open.

I called Connor. And yes, I could have just called the sheriff's department, but...

"Hey, Lenore." His voice was as rich and warm as hot chocolate. "What's up?"

"I think someone broke into the bookstore."

"I'll be right there."

I winced. "Actually, can you come by later? I have to meet Mike's lawyer, and it doesn't look like anything was taken."

"You want me to come by when it's convenient," he said in a flat tone. "For a burglary."

"I just... Someone vandalized the storeroom. I thought it was Peter or Gretel. They have a key. But there are scratch marks on the alley door and in one of the drawers at the front counter." I wavered about telling him about the million-dollar book, but I decided to wait. I really did need to meet Mr. Pivens.

"What about the register?"

"That seems okay."

"All right. Don't touch anything."

I grimaced. "I already have."

His exhalation was heavy with disappointment. "The bookstore's closed today, right?"

"Right."

"Then do what you need to do. I'll stop by in the afternoon. Three o'clock?"

"Thanks," I said.

"You know most cops wouldn't let you schedule an appointment."

A warm glow flowed through me. "You're not most cops."

"Damn straight, I'm not." Chuckling, he hung up.

I locked up and walked home to collect the ledger. Doyle's streets were quiet, the tourists fled, the iron shutters on the boutiques and tasting rooms closed.

A spirit staggered out of Antoine's. He stank of gin and tumbled into the street. A ghost 1960s Buick struck him, sending him flying twenty feet down the road. Then a very real SUV whizzed through them both, and the vision disintegrated.

My life. And people wondered why I kept quiet.

I collected the ledger from my house and drove to Mike's Victorian.

Alba was thankfully absent, and Mr. Pivens rocked on the front porch's swing. He rose when he saw me park on the side of the road. "Good morning again." He checked his watch and frowned. "Or should I say good afternoon? Have you had lunch?"

"No, but I'm not hungry." I shut the car door, leaving the window cracked open, and walked into the garden. "Are you? We don't have to do this now."

"I grabbed a bite earlier, but I should have planned better," he fretted. "We can order something, if you like. There must be some restaurants in Doyle which deliver."

"Really, I'm not hungry," I said, climbing the porch steps.

He opened the front door for me. "Very well, but if you change your mind or feel faint, please let me know."

Feel faint? I bit back a chuckle. Mr. Pivens was old school.

The old house smelled of Mike – pipe tobacco and wood polish – and unwanted emotion surged through me. Silent, I followed the lawyer into the library and through the bookcase into the secret room. It was cooler in the octagonal space. Up high, an air conditioner hummed. I looked up and spotted vents high on the walls.

The lawyer noticed my glance. "This is the only room with air conditioning. I assumed it was because there are no windows, but perhaps Mike wished to keep the books temperature controlled."

"Makes sense." But I'd never dealt with old books, so I really had little idea. Another bullet of insecurity tunneled through me. There was so much I didn't know. I handed him the ledger. "How do you want to do this?"

"Why don't I comb through his desk again?" He nodded to the three-piece Wooton desk. "You can check the ledger against the books on the shelves."

"Sounds good to me." Cradling the open ledger in one arm, I traced my finger beneath the entry for the book at the top of the yellow page, the Aleister Crowley. Fortunately, the books were alphabetized by author, so the work went quickly. I paced in front of the glass shelves, resisting the temptation to open them and thumb through the books. Mr. Pivens shuffled papers at the desk.

After two hours, I'd reached the bottom of the last entry. "All the books except one are accounted for," I said.

He gazed at me over his reading glasses. "Which one?"

"A book of American folktales Mike bought for three-hundred dollars."

"Not our million-dollar book then," he said. "Did you find anything that might fit the bill?"

"There are three books in the ledger that don't have estimated prices listed. A third edition set of The Golden Bough, a first edition of something Latin by Richard Argentine, and an illustrated William Blake."

He smiled and leaned back in the cane chair. "Ah, Blake, the great mystic poet and artist. Did you know he had very little formal education? The son of a stocking seller, he was looked down upon by the establishment all his life. It really irritated him."

"I like the idea of Blake – he was a real mystic poet, a poet who had visions and wrote about them. But I never was able to get into his poetry."

"It's an acquired taste," he said. "But what is this Latin text?"

"De Praestigiis et Incantationibus Daemonum et Necromanticorum." I read the words slowly, certain I was mangling the pronunciation, and a shiver crawled up my spine.

"Of witchcraft and spells of the demons and necromancers," he intoned. "How intriguingly creepy."

"You speak Latin?"

"We had to learn it in my day," he said dryly, "the benefits of a classical legal education. I assume it's old?"

"From 1568."

He swiveled the chair to better peer over his spectacles at me. "Good Lord. It's hard to imagine a book surviving that long."

"It was printed on vellum. That lasts longer than our modern paper."

"It would have to. Where is it?"

I guided him to the shelf.

He gazed through the glass at the stained and warped cover. "I found some gloves in the desk, but I won't touch it. Not something that old. I wouldn't dare. Could that be our mystery book?"

"I don't know," I said. "Age doesn't necessarily correlate with value. Rare books are like anything else. Their value is determined by supply and demand."

He tilted his head, and for a moment he looked like an elegant vulture. "For someone who claims to know little about rare books, you seem to know a great deal."

I flushed. "I've picked things up here and there, but I'm no expert. And there is another mystery I forgot to mention."

"Oh?"

"A man came to the bookstore this morning, Mr. Heath Van Oss. He said he was a rare bookdealer, he'd given Mike a book to value, and he wanted it back. When I asked for details, he said he'd speak with you."

"If he has a receipt, and we find the book, then of course we'll return it. But he hasn't contacted me yet."

"And if he doesn't have a receipt?" I asked.

"Then he's a liar or a fool. Mike would never have accepted valuable property without delivering some sort of receipt. Did he tell you he didn't have one?"

"No, not exactly. I just got the feeling he wasn't being entirely honest. According to the ledger, Mike bought a book of folk tales from Van Oss for three-hundred dollars."

"The book that's missing." His reflection wavered in the clear glass.

"Yes."

"And now Mr. Van Oss wants it back for free." He chuckled, a dry sound. "I may not know much about rare books, but I heard an earful from Mike. Not entirely honest is practically the definition of rare bookdealers. But I suppose there could be a second book of folktales, particularly if this fellow, Van Oss, specialized in them. And as professionals, we all have occasion to consult others in areas that aren't within our expertise. You're certain there isn't a second book in the ledger?"

"Not that I saw, but Mike's descriptions were sometimes a little too brief." He'd left me with so many mysteries.

"Well, we'll have to wait and see what this fellow has to say for himself."

"There's something else."

His white brows rose. "More? My dear girl, you have had an eventful morning."

"Someone vandalized the bookshop's storeroom."

"What?" His expression turned thunderous.

"At first I thought it was Peter or Gretel. But then I noticed scratches around the lock on the rear door and on one of the locked drawers beneath the cash register."

"Was anything taken?"

"Nothing from the register. A policeman will meet me later this afternoon to look at the place."

"This afternoon?" He bristled. "Making you wait that long is outrageous! I shall have words with your sheriff."

"No," I said quickly, "he offered to come sooner. I asked him to wait. Since nothing was stolen, I didn't want to delay our meeting."

"These books aren't going anywhere, but I understand your rationale. Mike's strange death, and now a break-in. It beggars belief."

"So you think it's strange too?" The tension I didn't know I was carrying, released.

"Perhaps I'm simply in denial at the loss of another friend. But I saw Mike scamper up and down ladders more times than I can count. And now with so much money at stake and all these odd occurrences, I can't help but wonder if there isn't more to Mike's death than it appears."

I wasn't alone. I wasn't crazy. Mr. Pivens thought something was off too, and I grasped his hand.

Lightly, he squeezed, his skin cool to the touch.

"We shall speak to the sheriff about this together," he said. "Today."

"Thank you," I said, grateful. Maybe the sheriff would listen to a lawyer if she wouldn't listen to me.

"What time was this policeman due to arrive?"

"Three o'clock."

"Then we should go now to speak with him together. I did find a notebook which may help us." He returned to the desk and plucked a small, black, leather-bound journal from it. "It seems Mike made his initial notes in this when he acquired a book. Later, he transcribed and fleshed them out or corrected them in his ledger. There may be something in here which didn't make it into the ledger." He handed it to me. "I'll allow you to make the comparison. My eyes aren't what they used to be."

"I'll let you know what I find."

"I know you will. And now?" He pressed the latch in the wall, and the bookcase glided silently open.

We walked into the library, and he shut the bookcase behind us.

"We have just enough time to—" He straightened, his eyes blazing. "What the devil?"

I turned.

A man in a black ski mask and gloves stood beside one of the tall bookcases. He grasped a book in one hand.

I sucked in a quick breath, too startled to move.

"This is a citizen's arrest," Mr. Pivens thundered, he strode toward the man. "Don't move!"

The man in black rushed forward.

"Look out!" I shouted, frozen in place. But I was too late.

The burglar drove his shoulder into the lawyer's midsection.

With a gasp, the elderly man flew backward and sprawled on the parquet floor.

The man in black raced from the room, his footsteps heavy. A door slammed.

Swearing, Mr. Pivens rolled to his side, his hand stretched outward. And then his eyes rolled up in his head, and he collapsed.

CHAPTER 12

Stomach churning, I dropped the notebook and knelt beside the lawyer. His face had gone gray, his breath coming in shallow gasps. A triangle of sunlight found its way through the ivy-covered windows and crossed his chest, knifing to a point over his heart.

"I've called nine-one-one," I said and took his hand. "They'll be here soon." Eyes closed, he squeezed my hand.

I glanced toward the entryway to the foyer. I was alone. Safe. The burglar was long gone. Returning my attention to the lawyer, I relaxed my gaze. A short, inky snake wriggled into the lawyer's chest.

"Come to me, my helping spirits," I murmured. "Spirits who are here in this man's greatest and highest good, come."

A presence filled the space behind me, a tingle of magic at my back, but I didn't turn. With my astral hand, I grasped the snake. It writhed, cold as ice, in my grip. And then it bit me.

Its venom coursed up my arm. I pulled, clinging to the serpent, trying to wrench it from the lawyer's chest. Sweat beaded my brow.

A shuffling sound, a footstep.

I looked over my shoulder.

A man stood in the foyer. Battered and bruised, scars crossed his face. His golden hair gleamed in the light from the foyer's stained glass window. A beam of sunlight caught in red glass turned his white t-shirt pink. His jeans were too large and his t-shirt too small, straining against his muscles. He watched me, an intent expression on his face.

I should have been startled, scared, angry. But his presence seemed... right.

Then the venom reached my heart, and a sharp pain split my chest, jerking me from my drifting. I gasped. "Don't just stand there," I said. "Help me."

The man vanished.

Dammit! Another stupid spirit. Gritting my teeth, I wrenched back my arm. The snake popped free. Flying into the air, it dissolved in a beam of sunlight.

I dropped to all fours, panting. Shadows from the ivy rippled across the hardwood floor, stretched over the bookshelves.

A siren wailed in the distance.

I sat on my heels and held the lawyer's hand. He seemed to breathe more easily now, his chest rising and falling beneath his suit.

The man with the scars – I'd recognized him, but from where?

Heavy footsteps clunked and clattered up the porch steps.

"In here," I shouted and scrambled to my feet.

Two paramedics, a man and a woman, hurried into the library.

I moved aside and they dropped to their knees, checking the lawyer's pulse, emptying tackle boxes full of medical equipment.

"Lenore?" Connor strode into the room and grasped my shoulders.

A gasp of relief broke from my lips.

His olive-black eyes sparked with emotion. "What's happened?"

"There was someone in the house," I said. "He wore a mask—"

"An intruder? That wasn't in the dispatcher's call."

"Mr. Pivens had a heart attack, I think, and whoever broke in ran off. I was more worried about the lawyer than the burglar." I glanced at the paramedics. They'd strapped an oxygen mask to Mr. Pivens's face.

"All right," Connor said. "Wait here." He strode into the foyer.

Uselessly, I watched the paramedics. The male paramedic ran past me and out the front door.

I blinked rapidly. "Is he—?"

"He's going for the stretcher," the woman said. Her broad, sympathetic face was spattered with freckles. She tossed her short, curly brown hair. "We're taking your friend to the hospital."

"How is he?"

"I don't like making predictions," she said, "but he seems to have stabilized for now. But we need to get him to the hospital. Are you a relation?"

"No, I'm a client. His name is Harold Pivens. He's from Angels Camp. I don't know if he has any relatives there." I didn't know much about him at all outside of his friendship with Mike, and I raked my hand through my hair.

"It was a good thing you were here and able to get him help so fast," she said.

Her partner lurched into the room. He set the stretcher on its side next to Mr. Pivens and flipped it flat.

"One, two..." They nodded and lifted the lawyer onto the stretcher, then unfolded its legs with him upon it. They wheeled him from the room.

I stood, dazed. Half a dozen books lay tumbled from their shelf. I walked to them and knelt, picking up one bound in red leather with gilt lettering. Zamboni, by Edward Bulwer Litton. An early edition of the occult gothic novel, but not the first. I took another off the floor. The Californians, by Gertrude Atherton. This was a gothic, and not at all occult that I could remember.

"What are you doing?" Connor asked behind me.

I started, nearly dropping the books. "These were on the floor." I rose. "They were on the shelf earlier."

"You mean the intruder pulled them from the shelves?" His chin lowered, his brow furrowing. "And now you're getting your fingerprints all over them?"

"Sorry." I should have known better, and I handed the book to him. "But the intruder was wearing gloves."

Connor stepped away, his broad hands raised. "Put it where you found it." I did.

"Now tell me what happened," he said.

"We were in the secret room—"

His eyes bulged. "What? There's a secret room? Where?"

"Connor, there's something I have to tell you. I found a letter from an auction house. Mike has a book worth at least a million dollars. The auction house wouldn't tell me which book—"

"You called them?"

"Mr. Pivens and I are trying to inventory the estate."

"Why didn't you tell me?"

"I'm telling you now."

"Show me," he said, grim.

I found the hidden latch, and the bookcase swiveled open.

Connor whistled. "Holy Hardy Boys."

In spite of everything, I gasped a laugh.

His hand on the butt of his gun, he prowled inside, his movements fluid and powerful and alert. I knew there was nothing to fear inside that strange room, and the feline gracefulness of his steps fascinated me.

Connor scanned the glass-covered cases and went to stand beside the open desk. "So which of these books is it?"

"We're not sure," I said. "We've narrowed it down to three possibilities."

"All right. Even if the burglar wasn't after the million-dollar book, you need to get all three of them somewhere safe. Do you have a safe deposit box?"

"Yes." The room seemed smaller with Connor in it, and I looked away, too aware of his appeal.

"Get the books. I'll take you to the bank."

He watched while I slipped on the white cotton gloves from Mike's desk. I removed the three books from the cases. When I picked up the sixteenth century tome on witchcraft, its warped cover crackled, and I winced. "Could you grab the ledger?"

He tucked it under his arm, and we left the room. Connor made me show him how to find the hidden latch and wouldn't leave until he'd practiced opening and closing the door several times. While he played with the mechanism, I retrieved the black, leather-bound notebook I'd dropped.

"What's that?" Connor asked.

"One of Mike's notebooks," I said. "He used it for notes when he first acquired a book, then he'd transcribe it into the ledger you're holding."

"You think the ledger's incomplete?"

"I'm not sure. A man came into the bookstore. You met him, Mr. Van Oss. He said he'd given a book of American folktales to Mike to value. There's no borrowed book listed in the ledger."

"But it wouldn't be if Mike didn't own the book, would it?"

The shadow of the ivy twined around his neck, as if strangling him, and I shivered. "No, but there is a listing for a book on American folktales that Mike bought from Van Oss. We can't find it on the shelves." Was it here, in the library?

"Does this guy have a receipt?"

"If he does, he's waiting to give it to the lawyer, not to me."

The pattern of the ivy shifted across his face. "But you inherited Mike's business. It was in trust. It's yours. You're the one to talk to."

"I don't care who Van Oss talks to. If the book belongs to him, I'll return it."

Connor followed me in his squad car to the bank. Escorting me inside, he waited outside the private room while the teller brought me the narrow, metal box.

I unlocked and opened it. Inside were legal documents and ten gold coins we'd inherited from our aunt. I pushed the coins to the back and gently set the books inside. Regretfully, I closed the box on them. How I would have loved to examine the books. But my examination wouldn't tell me their worth. I'd need to do research, possibly consult experts. Van Oss wouldn't be one of those experts.

I rang for the teller.

Smiling, she took the case off my hands and escorted me into the bank's green-carpeted waiting area. Beside a high table, Connor chatted with Councilman Woodley.

Connor glanced at me. "Everything all right?"

I peeled off the cotton gloves. "Yep. Hello, Council– I mean Steve."

"Lenore." He smoothed his silver goatee. "Deputy Hernandez was just telling me the news about the break-in at Mike's. Shocking."

"It's been one surprise after another," I muttered.

The councilman cocked his head. "There've been others?"

"Mike dealt in rare, occult books." I might have an information source in Woodley. The councilman had said he'd known Mike for years. "I'd no idea he had an interest in the occult, did you?"

The councilman chuckled. "His interest was the books, not the supernatural. He never took that sort of thing seriously."

My throat tightened. Was that why Mike had kept his side business secret from me? Because he didn't believe, and knew his disbelief in the face of my shamanism would sting? "I'd no idea he dealt in rare books at all."

"Neither did I," Woodley said. "I thought he'd given that up years ago. But why are you taking an interest in the business?"

"Mike left it to me," I said bleakly. "All of the business – his bookstore and the rare books. I don't know what I'm going to do."

"Run the bookstore, of course," Woodley said. "You were meant to be there. Sell the rare books to the highest bidder. There are auctioneers for that sort of thing, aren't there?"

I studied him, my brow wrinkling. Could he have known about Mike's million-dollar find?

Connor cleared his throat. "Speaking of your bookstore, we should check it out."

The councilman's white brows rose. "Trouble?"

"Some vandals," I said. "Nothing serious."

He shook his head. "Vandalism here, in Doyle? It's hard to believe how times have changed. If you need any help, let me know. I wouldn't mind taking a look at Mike's old books. I don't know much about the occult, but I do enjoy the smell of old paper."

We said our goodbyes. Casually, Connor laid his broad hand on the curve of my back as he escorted me from the bank, and my breath quickened.

He drove me to the bookstore, parking in the alley in the rear. Snapping on latex gloves, Connor examined the scratch marks around the lock. He straightened. "These look like the marks I found around Mike's back door today."

"You think that's how the man got into his house?"

"Maybe. I'm going to dust for prints." He moved away from me and said something into the radio clipped to his collar. He spoke too low for me to hear, and the response was too garbled for me to understand. Connor nodded. "Owen's going to print Mike's place, just in case the guy took his gloves off at some point."

"You didn't tell him about the secret room, did you?" I asked, anxious.

He angled his head. "No, but is there a reason I shouldn't?"

"I guess not," I said. "I just don't like revealing all Mike's secrets. It doesn't seem right."

"The intruder wasn't in that room, so there's no need to print it."

"So you won't tell him?"

"He's my partner. He'll kill me if I don't tell him. Lenore, it's a secret room!" His eyes crinkled with boyish delight.

"Then you need to swear him to secrecy."

"In blood beneath a full moon." He flashed a smile and as quickly sobered. "You said there was vandalism?"

I nodded and handed him the key. He unlocked the door and walked inside, stopping short at the fallen bookcase. Tumbled boxes, a river of books pouring from their cardboard. The desk, with its drawers gaping. The computer monitor, its screen cracked on the concrete floor.

He blew out his breath. "In my professional opinion, I'd say you've been vandalized. Did you touch anything?"

"I picked up some of the papers."

"Lenore," he said, rolling his eyes. "Stop touching things at crime scenes."

"I'm sorry! I thought it was Peter or Gretel."

"You thought they'd trashed the place?" he asked. "Why?"

"Because they still have their key, and they weren't happy I'd inherited Mike's business."

He arched a brow. "So you decided the best thing to do was let it slide."

"Peter is Mike's nephew. I didn't want to make things worse. And then I saw the scuffs around the lock and thought maybe it wasn't them and someone else had broken in."

"All right. I'll need to get your prints so I can separate them out."

Then he'd need Peter and Gretel's as well. They'd love that. "There were scuff marks on one of the locked drawers beneath the register too."

"Which you, of course, touched."

"I didn't notice the damage until later."

"So that's a yes?"

My face warmed. "It's a yes."

"Okay. I'm going to take prints. You go stand somewhere else and don't touch anything."

I edged around the fallen bookcase. Picking my way past boxes, I grabbed the doorknob to the bookstore.

"Lenore!" He glared from me to the doorknob.

I winced. "Sorry." But it was too late now, so I pulled open the door and walked into the shop.

The heat was smothering, a thick, musty coil. I resisted the temptation to open a window and turned on the fan. In the mystery section, I found a book I'd been meaning to read. I sat on the thin carpet, my back against the end of a wooden shelf, and read.

The writer was good, hooking me from page one, and soon I was lost in the story. The author knew how to observe things, and her metaphors were marvelous. I wondered if she wrote poetry. Then I stopped wondering and let the story take me.

Connor cleared his throat. "Lenore?"

I looked up.

He unpeeled his latex gloves.

"You can't be done already," I said.

"We've been here forty minutes."

"Oh," I said, surprised to find I was a quarter of the way through the book. "I assumed when you said 'touch nothing' you didn't mean the books."

"Don't worry about it. You're good." He sat beside me, stretching out his long legs on the carpet and nudged me with his shoulder. "How's the book?"

"So good, I didn't realize forty minutes had passed," I said, sheepish. "Did you find anything?"

"Lots of prints, but I can't tell you yet who they belong to. Now it's your turn." He held out a device that looked like a smartphone attached to a giant, black battery case. There was a white box in the center of the blue screen. "Give me your hand."

"You're kidding me."

"We're high-tech in Doyle."

I snorted. "Right." But I let him take my hand.

His strong fingers wrapped around mine, and I hoped he didn't notice the flutter of my pulse. He pressed my thumb to the screen. There was a beep, and he took my index finger, then the other fingers, pressing each to the screen and getting prints.

"What about in there?" I asked, my mouth dry, and I nodded to the back room.

"I had to do it the old fashioned way – fingerprint powder and a brush." He released my hand.

"You're multi-talented."

He laughed. "Right. I'm a real Renaissance man."

"So what next?"

"Next I see if we get a hit off any of the prints I took, and you do whatever you would normally do."

"I'd normally go to the hospital to see how Mr. Pivens is doing."

"That's a good idea," he said.

"And then I'd clean up the storage room."

"You're going to need help with that."

"Are you offering?"

"Maybe. My shift ends at five. You buy me dinner afterwards, I might see myself clear to helping you out."

Was he…? Was this…? "That sounds fair," I said, my voice thin.

"Then it's a date." He sprang to his feet and helped me up. "I'll meet you here at six."

"Okay." Dazed, I followed him to the storeroom, watched him clamber over the boxes and cases to the rear door. This wasn't a real date, was it? Because I couldn't do a real date. Unfortunately, I didn't know how to tell him that without sounding like a complete jerk.

He waved over his shoulder, without looking back, and left. The door clanged shut behind him.

Damn. I had a date.

CHAPTER 13

Sunlight glinted through the tops of the pines, casting prison bars across the highway. In spite of the heat, I had the windows rolled down and the air conditioner off. I wanted fresh air, the sweet scent of the mountains.

The hospital had told me Mr. Pivens was resting comfortably, and I could visit. But my stomach burned with anxiety. Doctor Toeller spent a lot of time at the hospital, and I worried about what she might do to Mr. Pivens. The lawyer's heart attack had seemed natural, but nothing was as it seemed in Doyle. And I really hated hospitals.

I parked in the wide lot. Bracing myself, I forced myself to enter the hospital's multi-story, blue-glass sarcophagus. Its cold miasma washed over me as soon as I walked through its sliding doors.

The new hospital had been built over the old, so it was chock-full of ghosts. They wandered the hallways wearing hospital gowns and desperate, confused expressions. Blue light from the windows tinted their skin, as if they'd been asphyxiated. Some of the spirits were missing limbs, others were more mangled. Doyle had its share of car accidents on the winding mountain highway, my father's included.

I kept my gaze forward, trying not to make eye contact. But I had to stop at the visitor's desk to learn where Mr. Pivens was.

A pleasant, round-faced woman smiled up at me. I knew she wasn't from Doyle, because her face was worn, her skin ashy. A volunteer from a nearby town, I guessed. Our hospital served the entire county.

"Can I help you?" she asked.

"Yes, I'm here to visit Harold Pivens. I called earlier, and the hospital said I could visit, but they were in the process of moving him to a room and didn't know the number yet."

"Let me check." She scanned her computer monitor. "Mr. Pivens?"

I shifted my weight. "Yes, Harold Pivens."

A woman, her hospital gown stained red at the abdomen, came to stand beside me. She'd probably been in her early twenties when she'd died. Her auburn hair reminded me of Karin's.

"Pivens, Pivens..." the volunteer muttered.

"Where's my baby?" the ghost asked me, her voice barely above a whisper.

My hands fisted on the desk. "He was admitted today."

"I woke up, and he was gone. Everyone was gone." Her voice rose to a shriek. "Where is everyone? Why won't anyone talk to me?"

I glanced sideways at her. "What's your name?" I asked in a low voice.

She started. "I'm Pamela Andrews," the ghost said eagerly. "My baby's name is Mark. That's what we agreed to name it."

"Martha Shelton," the volunteer said, not looking up from the computer. "And yours?"

"I'm Lenore," I said.

"Is my baby here? Where is he?" the ghost demanded.

"It's been a while since I've been at the hospital," I said to the volunteer. "Not since my cousin, Pam Andrews died."

"Oh, I'm so sorry to hear that," Martha said.

"I'm not dead," the ghost said. "Why did you tell her I was dead? I'm right here!"

"Complications in childbirth," I said to the volunteer.

Martha met my gaze, her broad face furrowed in sympathy. "I remember her. I was here when it happened. Such a tragedy. Her husband was devastated. Losing his wife and baby all at once."

"What? My baby? What is she talking about?" The ghost reached to clutch at me, but her hands passed through my arm. Her touch left an icy trail that made me gasp.

My vision blurred. The last things I wanted to think about were dead mothers or dead children. Not with my own sister pregnant and doomed.

"My baby's not dead!" The ghost slammed her fist on the counter, and the computer rattled.

Martha frowned, tapping the monitor. "The screen just... Oh, there it is again. Harold Pivens. Room three-oh-eight."

"Thank you." I hurried to the elevator.

The ghost hurried after me. "Tell me what happened. Where is my son?"

"I'm so sorry, but your son has passed on." I dug my cell phone from my purse and clapped it to my ear – my best defense against looking crazy. "You'll find him on the other side."

"What other side? There is no other side."

"Do you see a light?" I paused in front of the elevator and smiled at a middle aged woman. An elderly woman in a knee-length, violet skirt leaned heavily on her arm.

"A light? There's no light. There's no other side. I don't believe in that garbage."

"You'll have to look to find it," I said. "All you have to do is believe to see."

"But what if I look and there's nothing there?"

The elevator doors opened.

"Then you're not looking hard enough." Atheist ghosts were the hardest to cross over. They didn't believe in anything. That made it harder for them to accept they were ghosts, and even harder (for some reason) to believe there was a better place for them.

"You're lying to me. Why are you lying to me?"

I waited for the two women to make their way into the elevator, then followed.

"When you're ready, I'll help." I said to the ghost and pushed the button for the third floor.

"You're lying!"

The elevator doors rumbled closed.

"Do they allow cell phones in here?" the elderly woman asked pointedly.

"It depends on what section of the hospital you're in," I said. "They've got signs where phones are banned. I spent a lot of time here last year." Enough time to read every single sign. Twice.

The doors slid open on the third floor.

I smiled at the women and stepped into the green-carpeted hallway. Opposite, picture windows looked out over a sunlit patio.

I turned right and walked to the double doors that led to the nurses' station. After getting turned around twice, I finally found my way to Mr. Pivens's room.

A gray curtain on a curving track was drawn across the door. I rapped on the doorframe.

"Come in," a weak, masculine voice croaked.

Apprehensive, I drew aside the heavy curtain and stepped inside. The top of the bed was angled up at a thirty-degree angle. Sand-colored blankets puddled around the lawyer's waist.

He smiled, his skin whey-like. "Ms. Bonheim. How nice of you to stop by for a visit."

I ran a jerky hand over my hair. "How are you?"

"Only a mild heart attack. I'll be back on my feet in no time. Did the police catch the blackguard?"

"I don't think so. They found marks on the back door. They think the lock may have been picked."

"Marks on the lock?" he asked. "Didn't you say you found scratches on the lock to your storeroom?"

"Yes. The police took prints of my storeroom today."

"Someone's after that book." He raised his head. "Miss Bonheim, you must be careful."

"It's all right. I've moved the three books to my safe deposit box."

"I'm less worried about the books' safety than your own," he said dryly. "You could have been hurt."

My ribs squeezed. "You were hurt."

"This?" He motioned with his hand, and it fell, limp, to the blanket. "I can hardly blame the burglar for my weak heart."

The curtain swept aside, and Doctor Toeller strolled in, reading a chart.

I took a quick step backwards, fear speeding my heart. Stay careful. Stay cool. Stay calm.

The doctor's skin was luminous, her hair shining like spun silver and gold. Her lab coat was an unearthly shade of white. She was so obviously not of this world – how had we been fooled for so long? Careful.

"Mr. Pivens, I've looked at..." She glanced up, noticed me, and smiled. There was something feral in the curve of her lips. "Lenore. What are you doing here?"

"I just stopped by to see how Mr. Pivens was doing," I said, my words tumbling over each other. "I didn't know you were his doctor." She knew I knew. I didn't have to worry about hiding it. So why was my blood hammering in my skull?

"Mike said wonderful things about this good lady," the lawyer said. "If it weren't for Doctor Toeller, we wouldn't have this new, state-of-the-art hospital. Mike may have been a bit of a Luddite, but I'm determined to keep up with the times. The human brain is like a shark. It must keep moving forward or die. So what is the word, good Doctor?"

She glanced at me and hesitated.

"You can speak in front of her," he said. "Though Ms. Bonheim, perhaps you do not wish to hear? The broken down workings of an elderly body can be distressing."

I clasped his hand. Mine was moist. "I'm willing if you are."

"I have good news," Toeller said. "Your arteries are clear. There's no sign of heart disease."

"Then why the devil did I have a heart attack?" the lawyer asked.

"It's called a coronary artery spasm," she said. "It temporarily cuts off blood flow to the artery, and can be caused by drug abuse–"

"The only intoxicant I indulge in is alcohol."

"Cigarette smoking–"

"Not my pipe! I only smoke it once a month. Sometimes twice."

"Extreme cold or emotional stress," she finished.

He jerked upright on the bed, the blood rushing to his face. "Are you telling me that scoundrel nearly frightened me to death?"

"Mr. Pivens, you should be resting." The doctor laid a hand on his chest and gently pressed him into the mattress.

"I have never been so humiliated in my life."

"Maybe I should go," I said and regretted the suggestion at once. I couldn't leave him alone with... her.

"No, Ms. Bonheim," he said. "I may be embarrassed, but I know my duty. Stay, and we'll solve this puzzle together."

The doctor raised a brow. "Puzzle?"

I bit my lip and willed him to say nothing. I didn't know how or if any of this was connected to her, but I didn't want to take the risk it was.

"A treasure hunt, my good Doctor," he said airily. "Now how much longer must I remain your prisoner?"

"At least another day or two. We'd like to keep you for observation, and you are recovering from a heart attack, even if it was mild. This is serious, Mr. Pivens."

"Very well," he said. "I shall stay calm and eat my oatmeal."

She smiled. "You do that." She nodded to me. "Lenore."

I forced a smile in return. "Doctor."

She left, the curtains rustling behind her, and my limbs loosened.

He pointed a shaky hand at the laminate wardrobe. "My clothing. The key to Mike's house is in the pocket of my trousers. Would you retrieve it?"

Bemused, I opened the cheap, faux-wooden door and found his trousers, clamped into a hanger. I rummaged inside the pockets and drew out a small key ring. "These?" I turned and showed him.

"Yes. I want you to keep them."

"But the house doesn't belong to me."

"Please, just keep them. I don't like the idea of them falling into the wrong hands, and you have every right to be in that house. Your property is inside it – quite valuable property, I might add. But if you must go inside, I suggest you don't go alone."

"Okay." It wasn't quite a lie. He'd only suggested I not go inside.

The lawyer and I chewed over the mystery of the books. He was reluctant to believe someone might have killed Mike. But the burglar had been after something bookish Mike had possessed.

Mr. Pivens's middle-aged daughter strode into the hospital room. "Dad! What happened?"

I left, worried and no wiser. But the doctor had no reason to harm Mr. Pivens. If Mike had been killed because of a valuable book, then she wasn't involved. And I couldn't imagine any book, at any price, she cared about. Doyle was her storybook plaything, and we were her characters.

When I emerged in the hospital parking lot, the temperature had dropped but the light was still bright. I got into my Volvo and wound down the hill towards the main highway.

Something large and brown shifted between the pines. I braked hard, startled. "Bear!" I shouted to no one.

A black-and-white patchwork cow ambled onto the road.

Embarrassed, I unclenched my jaw. A bear? Really? At least Connor hadn't been around to witness my panic.

The cow lumbered up the hill and vanished into the thick trees.

I continued on, thinking hard as I threaded the Volvo around hairpin curves and over steep slopes. The bookstore storeroom and Mike's house had scratches around their locks. That implied someone without a key. Peter and Gretel had a key, but they could have scratched the knobs to make it appear like a regular break-in.

And then there was the rare bookdealer, Heath Van Oss. I scrunched my shoulders, my hands opening and closing on the wheel. The hotel he was staying at cost over two hundred bucks a night. If he really thought his book of folklore was only worth a few thousand, he was eating into his profits. Was the book an excuse? Or was he after the million-dollar mystery as well?

Could Toeller have been involved? My pulse sped at the thought. If she was involved, then her pattern had changed, and our assumptions were dangerously off. She'd been on the scene right after Mike had died. But I couldn't see a reason for her to want Mike dead. She wouldn't care about the book or the money, and Mike was no threat.

Or was he? I grimaced. He'd kept his interest in the occult well hidden. Why? Why keep his second business from me? He'd known I was interested in shamanism and would be fascinated by his occult collection.

Mike wouldn't have hidden his business from me out of embarrassment. Not in California in this day and age. Besides, he could always pass off his interest as academic. But had it been? Had Mike been a practitioner? I hadn't seen any signs in his house, but I'd only seen the library and lower rooms. What if there were other hidden spaces, upstairs, for rituals, or–

A man in loose jeans appeared in the middle of the highway as if conjured out of thin air.

Swearing, I slammed on my brakes, rocking forward. The brakes squealed, the back of my car slewing sideways. An odd noise emerged from my throat.

Casually, he turned his head.

I gasped at the map of scars crossing his face. It was the man I'd seen in Mike's library. The man who hadn't helped me when I'd been struggling to save Mr. Pivens because he wasn't a man.

I squinted. He didn't look quite dead either. This man was something else, and my gaze clouded with confusion, the sense of connection to him growing stronger. It was like seeing someone you thought was an old lover, and who then turned his head and revealed he was someone else entirely.

Our gazes locked, and I was falling. An apple orchard and a blizzard of white petals. Rusted prison bars. Bones on an ancient battlefield.

Are you willing?

A car honked behind me, and I jumped in my seat, the belt scraping against my neck.

The man was gone.

Shaken, I pulled off the road. What the hell. What the hell?

"Lenore?"

I gasped and jerked away from the voice.

Connor bent toward the open window. "What's wrong? I thought we were going to meet at your bookstore."

"We are." Dazed, I peered past him.

I was off the highway. Way off the highway and parked beside a tangle of woods and the old, Moorish wellhouse. Had I been driving on auto-pilot again? My insides writhed. I wasn't supposed to drift and drive, and shame heated my cheeks.

My mouth went dry. I couldn't have gotten here on autopilot. I'd traveled miles in moments.

"Are you okay?" Connor asked, his voice warm with concern.

I cleared my throat. "Fine. I just came from seeing Mr. Pivens." Something had happened. Something magic. Something big. And I'd sensed nothing. Had I teleported? Or had someone teleported me? And an entire Volvo? What kind of big magic would that take?

"How is he?" Connor braced his hand on the roof of my car. "I'm planning on going over tomorrow to take his statement. I didn't want to bother him today."

This sort of thing had never happened to me before... But it had happened to Jayce last year. She'd been having a vision inside my house and ended up in her coffee shop, scared witless. Not that she'd ever admitted to fear.

"Lenore?" he asked.

I blinked, returning to earth. "What? Oh. He's okay, I think. I'm sure he'll enjoy the visit."

He frowned. "What are you doing out here?"

If only someone could enlighten me. "I was... curious about the wellhouse. The Historical Society has taken it over, haven't they? They planned to fix it up," I babbled.

His brow creased. "I don't think it's theirs yet. Why are you interested?"

Um... "Readings," I said.

"Readings?"

"I thought it would make a nice spot for poetry readings and... stuff," I fumbled.

"It would be easier to sell books afterward at the store, wouldn't it?"

Damn. He wasn't just listening to me. Connor was really thinking about what I was saying. And I was talking complete garbage. "Yeah. You're right. It's a bad idea."

"No." His smile curved. "It's a creative idea. I like it. If they're going to fix this place up, they're going to need to do something with it. Readings sound good."

"Thanks."

"Look, I'm sorry, but I won't be able to make it tonight. I have to pull a double shift."

"Oh," I said, ignoring the twist of disappointment in my gut. "It's fine. What are you doing here?"

"We got a complaint some kids were fooling around out here. You know how dangerous that wellhouse is. It's falling apart. Of course, by the time I got here, all I found were some empty beer cans."

"Oh."

He leaned closer, and I caught a whiff of his cologne, spicy and seductive. "Lenore, are you sure you're okay?"

"Sure," I chirped.

Liar, the scarred man whispered in my ear.

CHAPTER 14

In the mountains, the sky is darker, and the stars are closer, more numerous. You can trace the path of the Milky Way, the bowl of Earth's atmosphere. But as I lay in an adirondack chair on my aunt's back porch, I didn't see the stars. I saw the vast spaces in between and felt my insignificance. My limbs grew heavy. Why hadn't Mike told me about his secret life?

I'd thought of him like a second father. I drew a shuddering breath. But I hadn't known him, and he hadn't trusted me.

He had left me the business, though. He'd wanted me to see it all at last.

I didn't understand.

A bat spiraled above, blotting out the stars behind its papery wings. I imagined its path was a poem, seemingly random but with an inner meaning. For the bat at least.

I checked my phone. It was almost eleven, and Jayce wasn't home yet. This was normal for Jayce on a weekend, but not a Monday night. Something scuttled beneath the branches of the fallen oak, and I jerked upright on the chair, my heart pounding.

A small animal scampered past the overturned birdbath. I sat back in the chair. I hadn't called to get the tree removed yet, and the fallen oak was an ideal hiding place for woodland creatures.

Sighing, I walked inside and locked the door behind me. I wouldn't call Jayce. She'd probably met up with her boyfriend, Brayden, and was spending the night.

Restless, I prowled the house, then went upstairs to my room on the second floor. I paused outside my door, then continued down the hallway.

A knotted rope hung from the trapdoor to the attic.

I stared, indecisive. How many times had I rummaged in that attic, searching for some clue to defeating our unseelie enemy? It was futile, I knew. Our aunt had searched that attic for answers longer than I.

But I grasped the rope, rough against my palm, and tugged. The door in the ceiling opened, and a ladder rattled part of the way down. Grasping it, I pulled it to the floor and climbed into the attic.

The air was hot, unmoving. I fumbled for the switches and flipped both on, illuminating neat rows of boxes, a rough wooden floor, a sloping roof. The ceiling fan groaned, barely stirring the air.

Dead Hex emerged from the trapdoor and meowed, plaintive.

"I can't pet you. And I can't feed you. You really need to go to the light."

He strolled to our aunt's antique secretary desk and sat in front of its glass-fronted bookcase.

"Trust me," I said. "There's nothing in there that will help." I'd practically memorized every damn line of the magical spell books inside. Aunt Ellen had refused to call them grimoires. They were her recipe books. No fancy airs for our Aunt Ellen.

I opened an attic window and leaned out, inhaling the scent of the sage in the garden below, enjoying the cooler air on my skin.

Pulling myself from the window, I walked down a corridor of cardboard boxes and stopped in front of a section I hadn't yet exhumed.

The calico cat followed, his tail lashing.

My family's history lay buried inside this attic. I hoped maybe, maybe, there was something here that Ellen had missed, something that could show us a way out from the under this curse. There had to be a way to break it, and Karin's pregnancy put us on a deadline.

My throat tightened. I pulled a box to the floor and tore open the neatly folded box lid. A cloud of dust puffed into the air, and I coughed.

Old clothes.

Hex pawed at the box.

"Are you giving me a sign here, or do you just want to be in on the action?"

I pulled out a navy swing dress with embroidered roses and a net collar.

Hex rolled onto his back and batted ineffectually at the hem.

Black, high-waist women's slacks. I held them to my hips. Scratch that, they were pedal pushers. Karin would love these, when she could fit into this size again. A wave of sadness swamped me.

If she could fit into it again.

Downstairs, a door slammed.

I closed the box and left it where I'd found it so I could continue my excavation later. "Jayce?" I shut the window, turned off the light and fan, and climbed down to the second floor.

"Here!" she shouted from downstairs.

I found her in the kitchen, scrabbling in the refrigerator.

She emerged with a bottle of beer. "Ugh, you wouldn't believe my day." She shoved the door shut with her heel. Slim necklaces looped over her loose, red tank. "The contractor got the wrong tiles. Well, some of them were right, but half of them were wrong, and you can't have two different types of bathroom tile on the floor. So guess who had to return the tiles and get the correct ones? Me." She popped off the bottle cap and took a slug of beer. "Waste. Of. Time. When I got back, they'd pulled everything out of the front planter boxes and chopped the jade plants into pieces. I loved those plants!"

"Why'd they do that?"

She shrugged. "They thought I wanted them to. How they came to this conclusion is a mystery." She took another gulp of beer. "I think I can salvage the clippings. Was your day better than mine?"

Frustrated, I rubbed the back of my neck. "Someone broke into Mike's house when the lawyer and I were there. Mr. Pivens had a heart attack, and the burglar got away."

She thunked the beer onto the butcherblock island and gaped. "What? Are you okay?"

"I'm fine."

Something shifted outside the kitchen window, and I turned. Flat, silvery eyes glowed against the glass.

My heart seized, and I took a leapt backwards, banging into the butcher block work island. A knife clattered to the floor.

Jayce swore. "Picatrix!" She shot into the hallway.

The front door clicked open, and I scowled at Dead Hex, now perched on the counter by the sink. The calico wore a smug look. "Really?" I whispered. "Is that how you're playing this?"

"Picatrix?" my sister called.

The door slammed shut.

Shaking her head, she returned empty-handed a few minutes later. "I don't get that cat. She had no problem taking over my old apartment, but she refuses to come inside the house."

Hex leapt gracefully from the counter. Tail high, he sauntered from the kitchen.

"And the racoons keep eating all the food I leave for her on the porch," Jayce continued.

"I've been meaning to talk to you about that—"

"I've heard burglars target houses of the recently deceased," she said hastily. "Maybe the burglary was random?"

Since I didn't want to talk about our ghost cat any more than Jayce wanted to talk about the rampaging racoons she'd attracted, I let her change the subject. "I don't think it's that. Some of Mike's private collection is more valuable than I knew." I told her about the letter from the auction house.

Her jade eyes widened. "A million dollars?"

"That was the minimum bid."

"Over a million dollars?"

"That's not all. A bookdealer claims he gave Mike a book on American folktales to assess, but I can't find it anywhere."

Her eyes narrowed. "Claims?"

"I found a record of a book of American folklore the dealer sold to Mike. And he didn't show me a receipt, and Mike was pretty good about keeping records."

"You think he's lying?"

"He's lying about something," I said. "He told me the book wasn't worth much, but he's been hanging around Doyle, staying in the local hotel, at least since Mike died."

"You think he broke into Mike's house."

"He would have fit the build of the burglar. But so would Peter."

She leaned her hip against the counter. "And I wouldn't put it past Peter, though a break-in seems more Gretel's style. They're both weasels." She opened the refrigerator and grabbed another beer, handed it to me. "Your need is greater."

Lowering my head, I unscrewed the top and took a sip. It was a local brew, a blond, and tasted faintly of peach but more of bitterness. I wrinkled my nose. Life would be cheaper if I liked beer. "I just don't understand why Mike didn't tell me."

"About the folktale book?"

"About any of it. He knew I was interested in shamanism."

She raised a brow. "Only interested? You are a shaman."

Okay, maybe I hadn't told him everything about my life either. "Still, he should have known I wouldn't judge him for having an interest in rare, occult books. I'd have loved to get my hands on them."

"And now you will. He left the business to you. He wanted you to know about it."

"Right, after he was dead." I gulped the beer to hide my hurt.

"All right, let's channel Karin and be logical. If you didn't know about his rare book business, what are the odds someone else did?"

"His clients had to know."

"But would Peter and Gretel?" she asked.

"Maybe. And a book worth over a million dollars makes a great motive for murder. What if Van Oss's folklore book is just an excuse? What if he's after this valuable book, and that's why he's in town? That's why he broke into Mike's house?"

"If he was the one who broke in."

"Peter had a key to the house," I said. "He wouldn't need to break in. He had a key to the bookstore too. There was no reason for him to break in there—"

"Whoa." Her expression tightened. "Someone broke into the bookstore? You didn't tell me that."

"I discovered it this morning. The storeroom was trashed, and it looked like someone had tried to get into the locked drawer beneath the register."

"But not the register itself?" she asked.

"No. So they definitely weren't after cash, they were after the book or information. Peter and Gretel could have faked a break-in in both places to throw suspicion away from them."

"Maybe."

We stood in silence, pondering that.

In the distance, that uncanny bell tolled, long and mournful. A cold wave of fear raised the flesh on our arms.

Jayce blanched and gulped the rest of her beer. Across Doyle, people would be shutting windows, children pulling covers over their heads. We'd all be looking anywhere but at each other, remembering the missing twenty-two.

"We're running out of time," I said in a low voice.

"I know that. I know that!" Jayce paced. "Nick and Brayden have been threatening to fill in the fairy spring."

"Can they do that?" I asked, horrified and intrigued.

"I don't know how they can, but Nick's frantic. He knows Karin doesn't have much time left. She's been able to talk him out of it, so far. Karin said if the spring's filled in, they may never be able to get the disappeared back."

And one of the disappeared was Nick's sister, Emily. "Do you think she's right?" I asked.

"I don't know."

"I'm not sure filling in the spring would work," I said slowly. "The spring may be Doc Toeller's way of passing between the worlds, but she's in ours now. And I don't think she'd react well if the spring was attacked."

She brandished her empty beer bottle. "We have to do something!"

"Filling in the spring could make things worse."

"But we don't know that."

"We don't know enough of anything," I said. And that was our problem. I glanced at the ceiling, thinking of the attic above. My mother hadn't borne triplets by accident. If the three of us together couldn't defeat this curse, then no one had a chance.

CHAPTER 15

Van Oss haunted Doyle.

I saw him when I glanced out the window of the bookstore. I saw him when I browsed for food at our local grocery store. I saw him on the street, lounging in a sidewalk café. And I didn't know what to do.

I wasn't a detective. Worse, my shamanic skills were failing. I don't know where I was going wrong. Every night I tried to call Mike, and every night other spirits came. One wouldn't leave until I'd called her daughter and told her a story about a barbeque at the Grand Canyon. Another insisted I tell his wife about a photo that had fallen behind a sofa. There was no question of ignoring them. The barriers around my aunt's house had lost their potency. The ghosts came and went as they wished. All I could do was their bidding.

And I still hadn't been able to find the mysterious book of American folklore Van Oss claimed he'd given Mike, or the one Van Oss had sold him. The man came into the bookstore at least once a day, asking after it, and denied ever having sold Mike a book. But my feeling grew that there was more to his persistence than a folklore book.

Van Oss was lying.

I'd researched the three "maybe million-dollar" books, but the going was slow. I didn't know what I was doing and had grown too paranoid to reach out to another expert. Certainly not to Van Oss. He'd offered his services in inventorying Mike's collection to "speed the process."

I'd declined.

Mike's mysterious notebook revealed nothing new except another one of my poems, in my own hand. Spooked, I'd turned to researching the folklore book listed in Mike's ledger from Van Oss – The Folk and Fairy Tales of America. The rare booksellers I'd phoned told me the book wasn't worth more than a few thousand dollars, at best. It didn't make sense for Van Oss to linger so persistently for a book of that value.

Peter and Gretel seemed to be stalking me. I'd offered Peter a job. Thankfully, he'd declined, his face twisted with resentment. Gretel seemed to have taken up a post on a chair outside the bakery across the street. She made no secret of watching me, glaring furiously whenever I walked out the bookstore's front door.

I changed the locks.

Friday evening, I turned the bookshop signed to closed and locked the front door. I slumped against the glass, my back to Gretel's angry gaze. It had been a good day for sales, but I was glad it was over.

Gretel's fury burning twin holes in my side, I removed the cash tray from the register. I hurried into the storage room and closed the door behind me, locking that as well.

The work day wasn't over. I still had to do a cash count, organize the sales receipts, do a quick inventory check.

The bookstore was too much for one person. I needed help, but I hesitated on setting out a HELP WANTED sign. Mike had been able to employ me, but he'd had a second income stream. I knew the bookstore business well enough, but uncertainty niggled at me.

Someone banged on the rear door, and I jumped in my chair, slamming my knees on the underside of the desk. "Ow."

"Lenore? You in there?" Jayce shouted.

Relaxing, I went to the alley door, unlocked it. "Hey, what's going on?"

"Your phone's dead." She strolled into the storeroom, shoved aside the cash tray, and plopped onto the desk. "And Brayden's bailed on me for the concert tonight. Want to come?"

"I'm kind of busy."

She fixed me with her gaze. "Lenore?"

"Ye-es?"

"You need to get over your thing about crowds."

"Why? I live in a small town. Crowds are easy to avoid."

She sighed. "Because it's good for the soul. Besides, this is one of your favorite bands."

"I don't have a favorite band."

"Well, it's one of my favorites, and you need a break." She grasped my hand and tugged me toward the door.

Laughing, I resisted. "Jayce, I can't just leave."

"I'll do the cash count."

Maybe she was right. Maybe I did need to get over it. "All right. You take the cash. I'll do the receipts."

We finished in under an hour, and I followed Jayce home. She changed into her concert style — extra makeup, wild, blown-out hair, an emerald tank top over cut offs, and wedge sandals. I stuffed an Agatha Christie in my purse and went as is. I had no one to impress, and I wanted to relax. Dressing up wasn't relaxing.

Jayce nominated me designated driver, and I drove us both down the highway and lower into the foothills. The pines made way for rolling hills carpeted with tall golden grass and twisted oaks.

I followed a line of cars into a dirt parking area. Vineyards climbed the nearby hills. Triangular flags fluttered above the arched, wooden entrance to the concert grounds.

We joined the mass of people, and I pulled in my psychic antennae, dampening my aura so I wouldn't feel as much of the crowd's energy. Unfortunately, this had the dual effect of making me less noticeable. Shoulders hunched, I stood in line for wine and snacks, and got bumped and jostled from every direction.

Finally, we escaped the whirlwind of people and strolled into the natural bowl that made up the stadium.

Jayce unfurled a soft, plaid blanket on a spot on the hill, and we sat, our territory marked.

"Why couldn't Brayden come?" I asked, pulling my book from my purse.

She glared. "Seriously? You brought a book?"

"The light's still good enough to read."

"Put. It. Away."

I did.

Jayce popped a cheese-covered nacho into her mouth. "And to answer your question, Brayden's shift was changed. One of the other paramedics is having a baby."

"Who?"

We gossiped about our fellow townsfolk, and for a time the world seemed normal. The deepening dusk turned the distant mountains cobalt. A red-tailed hawk wheeled above the crowds. The band set up onstage to the occasional clatter of cymbals and thrum of a base guitar.

The venue attracted people from all over – but it was easy to spot the folks from Doyle. First, because I knew them – it was a small town. Second, because we all had a faint gleam about us, a shimmer, dulling around the edges, and that strange, too-perfect skin. No sun spots or blemishes or dark circles beneath the eyes for us. The fairy's glamour enforced perfection.

No one else seemed to notice our oddness though. Or maybe they did, I thought uneasily. The people from Doyle clustered in small groups on the lawn. No one encroached on their space. I looked around. No one encroached on our blanket either. Other concertgoers jammed ass to elbow against each other, blankets overlapping.

Jayce stretched out her long legs and crossed her ankles. "What's wrong?" She waved at a group of men I didn't recognize, and they waved back. One made his way toward us.

"Nothing." I didn't want my mood to ruin the concert for Jayce. Burnt out of house and business last winter, she needed fun more than I did.

The man dropped down on the blanket, and he and Jayce engaged in easy conversation.

I watched them out of the corner of my eyes. He was into her, but she had a boyfriend and maintained a pleasantly neutral air. I doubted he caught the subtlety. Men rarely did when it came to Jayce.

The opening act stormed onstage. Anything I might have added to the conversation was obliterated in the twang of guitars and clatter of drums. The band was good, and I relaxed back on my elbows.

Half-way into the set, I jolted upright.

In his usual button up shirt and slacks, Heath Van Oss trudged up the narrow trail toward the concession stands. The bookdealer paused, his dark head turning as if he was searching for someone, and then he continued on. What was he doing here? Meeting someone? Did he know someone in Doyle aside from Mike?

I touched Jayce's arm, and she turned.

"What's up?" she said. At least, I think that's what she said. Her mouth was moving, but her words were lost in the roar of sound.

"Heath Van Oss is here!"

"What?"

"Heath Van Oss!"

"Something to eat?"

"NO, Heath!"

She shook her head. "Chili fries!" And she turned back to the concert.

I lumbered to my feet.

Van Oss crested the grassy hill. Soon he'd disappear from sight.

I hurried after him.

He vanished over the rise.

I ran. Panting, I reached the top of the hill and raced down the dirt track to the concession stands. The hill behind me muted the sounds of the concert. People milled the grounds chatting, standing in line for food and wine. "Where are you?" I muttered.

And then I saw him, striding toward the exit. I trotted after Van Oss, not much worried about being seen. There were too many music fans moving between us.

He held a cell phone clasped to one ear and walked behind a blue-painted popcorn stand. I edged past the food line and around the corner of the stand.

The bookdealer was speaking, but his words were obscured by the music and babble. I tiptoed to the rear corner of the stand and pressed my back against its peeling paint.

"...think I gave the old guy a heart attack," Heath was saying.

I froze, my heart thumping. Was he talking about Mr. Pivens?

"...This is taking too long, and I'm tired of getting jerked around. You told me you'd be here... I've searched the store and the house. If he's put it somewhere else..." His voice hardened. "That's your problem. You want me to do the job, the price is going up... Fine.... Fine." He hung up and swore.

I edged backward and stepped on a plastic cup. It cracked, brittle, making a sound like a whip.

He cursed again.

I scuttled toward the back of a food line.

He grasped my arm and yanked me to a halt. His smooth skin was an angry mask. "What are you doing here?"

"I thought I saw you," I stammered. The people in line either hadn't noticed he'd grabbed me or were pretending not to see. "I came to speak to you, but then I saw you making a call, and I didn't want to interrupt."

Abruptly, he released my arm. "Speak to me about what? Did you find the book?"

"You never told me the title of the book, but I haven't found anything yet to do with American folklore."

He stared down at me, his classically handsome features marred by disdain. "The Folk and Fairy Tales of America," he finally said, "by Ichabod Langley."

"I did see mention of that book in Mike's records. According to the ledger, you sold him that book two years ago?"

"That was a different edition."

"I thought it was a vanity printing. I'm surprised there was more than one edition."

He sneered. "If you knew anything about the business, you'd know Mark Twain vanity published. Where have you looked for it? I heard the old man kept his best books locked tight in a secret location."

My face heated. "Did he tell you that?"

"He didn't have to. He collected rare, occult books. Of course he's got a hidey-hole. All rare bookdealers are nuts, haven't you heard?" He smiled wickedly, a smile that almost made me like him. "And yeah, that includes me. He's probably got it hidden beneath a loose floorboard or in a secret desk drawer."

"I'll keep looking," I said.

"Do that." He turned on his well-shod heel and strode away.

I slumped against the stand. He was working with someone, someone most likely in Doyle. I didn't believe him about the two books, but it should be easy to check if there was more than one edition of The Folk and Fairy Tales of America.

Deep in thought, I walked through the concession stands toward the arena. "Lenore!"

I turned at the crest of the hill. The music pounded, rolling through me.

Connor jogged to my side, his smile wide, his teeth brilliant white against his olive skin. "Hey," he shouted. "I didn't think you were going to come." The v of his band t-shirt revealed a muscular chest covered in crisp, black hair. A navy, fleece jacket was slung over one shoulder. His battered jeans hung loose about his lean hips.

"Jayce talked me into it," I said, unable to stop myself from smiling. "Connor, I just saw Heath Van Oss—"

"Who?" He put his hand to his ear and shook his head. "Sorry." He motioned me down the hill, away from the band.

Beside a cart selling red plastic cups of wine, he paused. "Sorry, I couldn't hear you. What were you saying?"

"Heath Van Oss. The bookdealer. He's here."

"Everyone's here." He motioned toward the milling crowd.

"I overheard Van Oss talking to someone on the phone. He said he nearly gave the old man a heart attack. I think he was the one who broke into Mike's house."

His eyes darkened. "What exactly did you hear?"

I closed my eyes, remembering. "He said, I think I gave the old guy a heart attack. And then he said it was taking too long. He was tired of being jerked around. He'd searched the house and store, and if the person wanted him to keep looking, the price was going up. He was angry. Or at least annoyed."

Connor's mouth compressed. "All right. It's not enough for me to take to the sheriff or bring him in for questioning. But I'll talk to him tomorrow."

Relieved, I pressed my hand to my heart. He was taking my information seriously. "Thank you."

"Don't thank me yet. Even if he did break in, he'll deny it, and I won't be able to do anything without evidence."

"Can't you take his fingerprints?"

"Didn't you tell me the burglar wore gloves?"

I slumped. "Oh. Right."

"But I'm curious about this guy now. It will give me an excuse to talk to him." He looked around. "So where's Jayce?"

I smiled tightly. I wasn't jealous. Connor could like whoever he wanted. But even when Jayce had a steady boyfriend, Karin and I stood in her shadow. It wasn't Jayce's fault. It was just who and what she was. "On our blanket. Do you want to join us?"

"Why not? Lead the way." He grasped my hand, and I started at his touch.

Warmth flowed up my arm and into my heart. Wordless, I led him to our blanket, and we sat. The stranger was still stretched beside Jayce but focused on the band. She wasn't paying attention to him. The band waved, and the crowd applauded. Blessed quiet fell.

Jayce turned and smiled when we sat on the blanket. Her smile reversed. "Where are my chili fries?"

I rolled my eyes.

"What?" she asked. "I thought you were getting food."

"I can grab something," Connor said.

She eyed us. "No, I'll go." Jayce sprang to her feet. "Come on," she ordered her acolyte, and he followed her up the hill.

Connor lay on the blanket and stared at the sky, dimmed by the concert lights. "I finished that book you suggested. I liked it. The writing didn't get in the way of the plot."

"It's not supposed to." But I liked that he'd noticed.

He shrugged. "You know what I mean. So when's your next chap book of poetry coming out?"

"I'm not sure." Since we'd first heard the words "Rose Rabbit," ideas had been bubbling in my head and pouring out my pen. I wasn't sure when they'd stop. I had enough for a chap book now – you only needed nineteen poems or so. But how had one of those poems found its way into Mike's ledger in my handwriting? A chill rippled my skin.

"Are you cold?" Rising, he shrugged out of his jacket and handed it to me.

Our gazes locked, and I tried to stamp down the dizzying current that rushed through my core.

"Thanks," I said roughly.

He watched me slip into the jacket, still warm from his body heat, and my stomach fluttered.

"So what's it called?" he asked.

"Tales of the Rose Rabbit," I said promptly and blinked. The title had popped into my head as if I'd given it thought before, and I hadn't.

"Rose Rabbit? What are the poems about?"

"They're kind of surrealist," I said, unsure how much he really wanted to hear. "I'm doing a mix of styles – from prose to sonnets."

"Makes sense," he said. "You can match the rhythm and structure of the poem to its theme."

"Right," I said, surprised.

He grinned. "I'm more than just a beat cop, you know."

Delighted, I laughed. "I guess you are. Do you write?"

His skin turned a shade darker. "Took creative writing in college. I never got a degree in it or anything, but I like to write when I travel, sometimes to just get ideas out of my head. Nothing worth publishing." He lay back down.

After a moment, I stretched out beside him.

Unspeaking, he grasped my hand, and unspeaking, I let him. And even though our relationship could never go anywhere, in that moment, this was enough.

CHAPTER 16

I shouldn't have done it.

Connor had told me he would talk to Van Oss. And yet, Saturday morning, when I should have been prepping to open the bookstore, I stood in front of the Historic Doyle Hotel. It looked like something out of New Orleans's French Quarter. Opened in the 1850s as a stopover on the stagecoach road, the walls were square blocks of stone. People believed the stone walls and iron shutters had been designed to protect Doyle from forest fires. But no mountain fire had ever done more than scorch the edges of Doyle's borders. I suspected we had a certain fairy to thank for that.

I glanced down Main Street. Most of the old buildings had iron shutters, and iron was a protection against the fae. Had the early townsfolk suspected, even then, that an unseelie was at work?

A wedding couple posed for photos on the hotel's second-floor balcony, swagged with red-white-and-blue bunting. The bride wore a wedding dress, her bouquet in one hand. Her fiancée, in an untucked, loose white shirt and khaki slacks wrapped his arm around her waist. From the middle of the road, a photographer snapped pictures. Even the photographer looked happy.

My heart clenched. If we failed, Jayce and I would raise Karin and Nick's daughter. I didn't want to think about losing either of them.

And that was why I'd come on a hot morning to see the arrogant bookdealer. Van Oss was obviously connected to Mike's murder. I didn't care what the police said or what the coroner would say. Someone had pushed Mike off that ladder or laid his body beside it to make his death appear an accident. It was the only explanation for his tortured spirit. I couldn't wait for the police. Not with my sister so close... My throat tightened, and I blinked rapidly.

Squaring my shoulders, I walked through the high front doors. I paused, scanning the reception area, cobalt blue with white wainscoting.

The receptionist, Erica, looked up from behind the reception window. She came into the bookstore often – historical romance was her game, and if it involved a vampire, so much the better.

She smiled, her brown eyes crinkling. "Hi, Lenore. When's your sister going to write a historical?" My age, she was tanned and slim, a whimsical pattern of freckles dotting her nose and cheeks.

I laughed. "Probably never."

"So what brings you to the hotel?"

"I'm here to see Heath Van Oss."

"Let me call up for you." She picked up the desk phone's receiver and dialed, smiled at me, frowned. "I'm sorry, he's not answering. He might be in the breakfast room."

"Mind if I check?"

"Go right ahead. Oh, Lenore?"

I paused.

"I'm sorry about Mike," she said. "He was a great guy."

"Thanks." I nodded to her and strolled into the breakfast room. The same color scheme dominated here – blue and white. Couples sat in antique, wooden chairs at tables covered in white cloths.

I ignored the ghosts sitting beside them.

Morning light streamed through the high, paned windows and was diffused by sheer curtains. The room smelled of sausage and eggs and pastry, and my stomach growled. I laid my hand across it and scanned the room again. No Heath Van Oss. He hadn't checked out, or Erica would have told me.

Maybe he'd gone for breakfast somewhere on the street. Or maybe he'd gone to meet whomever had brought him to Doyle to collect the book.

My plan had only been to find Heath at the hotel and confront him. Without any further ideas in mind, I wandered into the reception area. Erica had vanished from behind the desk.

Behind me, something croaked.

I turned, hair prickling the back of my neck.

A blue-carpeted stairway led to the second floor. The turkey vulture perched on the top step.

I froze, rooted to the carpet. "Oh, no," I said beneath my breath.

It hopped in an ungainly flutter of wings and disappeared around the upstairs corner.

I cursed softly. So it wanted me to follow. I didn't have to comply. There was no law against ignoring an animal spirit's call. But when you started ignoring them, they started ignoring you.

Legs wooden, I climbed the stairway. They creaked beneath my feet.

An apparition of a maid, in a long, black dress and white apron, brushed past me on the stairwell, and my flesh pebbled from the chill.

I turned to her. "Miss?"

She turned on the steps, a stack of towels pressed against her chest.

She was young, with black hair piled in a loose bun and serious brown eyes. I guessed she'd died in the late nineteenth century, perhaps the early twentieth.

"Yes, Miss?"

"I've come to see..." I stumbled to a halt, numb. Maybe Van Oss wasn't dead. Maybe someone else had died. Maybe no one had died, and the vulture wanted me to see something else. But he only showed up when death had paid a visit.

She nodded. "Yes, Miss. He told me you'd be coming." She climbed the steps, passing me.

"He?" I asked sharply.

But she didn't respond. At the top of the steps, she whipped around the same corner the vulture had vanished behind. I hurried up the stairs.

She strode down the hallway, past a modern maid's cart and a wedged-open door.

Rubbing my arms, I forced myself not to look at the photos of old Doyle lining the walls. I'd met too many of their ghostly subjects.

Lengthening my strides, I caught up with the maid's ghost in front of a white, wooden door.

She angled her head toward it. "In here, Miss."

"Who told you I'd be coming?"

"The Rose Rabbit, Miss."

"The Rose..." I reached to grasp her arm, my movement quick and erratic, and realized at the last moment what a useless and rude gesture that would be. My hand dropped to my side. "You've seen the Rose Rabbit?" In my mind, the name deserved capital letters. "What is it?"

"It's a he, Miss. Very good looking, with shining blond hair. But I think he's had a difficult time."

"What do you mean?"

"He's a bit beaten up."

I stilled. He sounded like the blond man I'd been seeing, the one who'd watched while Mr. Pivens had the heart attack. The one who'd appeared on the highway before I'd blipped to the wellhouse. If the ghosts could see him, what was he? Because he wasn't dead. I knew dead. I sensed it nearby now, an icy, empty presence on the other side of the door.

The ghost motioned to the closed door. "Aren't you going to see him then? Go inside?"

"I don't have a key."

"Oh, that's no problem." She reached into her apron pocket and withdrew an old-fashioned skeleton key. It shouldn't have fit into the modern lock, but it did, because the spirit believed it would. The lock clicked, and the door drifted open an inch.

Dread twisted my stomach. I lifted my palm to the door and paused, hand raised. "What's your name?" I asked, remembering myself. I had a duty to aid the dead, and she was here for a reason, and I really didn't want to know what was on the other side of that door.

"Miss O'Shea, Miss."

"Why are you here, Miss O'Shea?"

"I work here, Miss. Will that be all?"

"The Rose Rabbit, who is he?"

"Oh, he's something special, Miss." She bobbed a curtsy and strode down the hall, her long skirts flapping.

"But what? How is he special?"

The ghost vanished through a wall.

Shit.

I stared at the door. I could smell the death now, fetid with a base note of overripe strawberries. "Mr. Van Oss?" I called and knocked on the cracked door. It swung open.

"Mr. Van Oss?" I called more loudly, on behalf of any neighbors or maids who might hear. Pushing the door wider, I stepped into a short, narrow hallway. The bathroom door stood open, and Heath was not inside.

Cautious, I crept further into the room. "Mr. Van Oss? Your door was open. Are you all right?" I asked, knowing he wasn't.

I edged around the corner. A king-sized bed with a rumpled white duvet. Beige pillows propped against the headboard. A rustic, barn-door wall behind metal art cutouts. A suitcase, open, lying upon a stand.

He was here. The bookdealer hadn't checked out, and death coiled around me, cold and cloying.

"Mr. Van..." I trailed off. Two feet in coal-colored socks stuck out from behind the bed, and my breath caught. I know the body is just a shell. Van Oss was gone, and the man had been a rude jerk in life. But there was something achingly vulnerable about those socks.

I went to the phone by the bed and called reception.

"Hello, Mr. Van Oss, this is Erica at reception. How can I help you?"

"Erica, this is Lenore."

"Lenore? So you found him after all."

"No. I came upstairs. His door was open. Something's wrong. Please call nine-one-one."

"Wrong? What's wrong?"

He was dead, but how? Stretching the cord to its limit, I rounded the bed.

He lay on his stomach, his arms a loose sprawl, and his head...

I gasped. "Oh, God."

"Lenore, what's wrong?"

"He's dead." I had to force the words between my lips, remember to breathe. I dropped the receiver and backed, stumbling, from the room.

I shouldn't have come. I shouldn't have gone in. I shouldn't have seen this, would never forget it.

Heath Van Oss lay on his stomach, his arms outstretched. His corpse stared at the ceiling. His head had been twisted one hundred and eighty degrees.

CHAPTER 17

"The receptionist told you he hadn't answered his phone." The sheriff's gaze was arctic. She laid her hat on the hotel conference room's small meeting table. It was wooden and round and as antique as the rose-print wallpaper. "Why were you in his room?"

I glanced at the closed door. "I told you, the door was ajar."

"But you didn't tell me why you went upstairs in the first place."

"I thought I'd put a note under his door."

She folded her arms, the cheap fabric of her uniform crinkling. "A note about what?"

"He told me that he'd given Mike a book to value, but he didn't have a receipt and I couldn't find the book or any records of it in Mike's files. It had to be important to Mr. Van Oss, or he wouldn't have stayed so long in Doyle."

Her blue eyes narrowed, skeptical. "And so you were leaving him a note saying nothing?"

"I overheard him talking to someone at the concert last night. It sounded like he might have been the one to break into Mike's house, when Mr. Pivens had his heart attack."

"You didn't believe him about the book he'd lent to Mike."

"No, I didn't. Not after I discovered Mike has a different book worth over a million dollars."

Her lips thinned. "And so you decided to break into Van Oss's room."

"No! I wasn't... I told you, the door was open. How could I have broken in? How could I have done... that?" My voice cracked. I looked at the rose wallpaper and tried to blank out the image of his head twisted backwards.

"All right, you can go."

I drew in a quick breath to argue, then realized I was being released. Leaping from my chair, I scuttled out the door.

Connor stood in the reception area talking with a group of deputies. He looked at me, his expression hard and angry.

I hurried from the hotel. A wave of heat off the macadam slammed into me, and I slowed. Sheriff's vehicles lined the street outside. The sun glittered, blinding, off their chrome.

Alba stood on the opposite side of the street in her sandwich board. "Justice! This is God's will. The evil shall be punished!" She shook her sun-darkened fist at the hotel.

Tourists paused, staring at the black-and-white SUVs. Noticing Alba, they hurried on, their heads bent, their voices low.

Councilman Steve Woodley strolled past gnawing on a paperclip. He nodded and smiled, his blue-and-white striped shirt impeccably pressed. Woodley smoothed his hand over his tonsure of silver hair. "Lovely day, we're having, Lenore."

"Yes," I choked out.

He shook his head, "Oh, that Alba. I'd better speak with her." He crossed the street. "Alba!"

A look of black terror crossed her face, and she scuttled down the road.

On the other side of the street, he paused, his hands on his hips, staring after her.

I walked on. When I reached the bookstore, I was shaking so badly I dropped the keys. But I managed to unlock the door and hurry inside. Locking it behind me, I turned on the ceiling fan, walked to the window behind the register and flung it open. I called Jayce.

She answered on the fourth ring. "Lenore?" Her voice was indistinct, fuzzy, and I guessed I'd woken her up. "What's going on?"

"Heath Van Oss was murdered."

"Who?"

"The bookdealer, the one who claimed he'd given Mike a book of folklore to value. He's dead. Someone killed him. Someone..." My breath hitched. Who could have had the strength to break his neck like that?

"Are you all right?" Her tone sharpened.

"I'm fine. I'm at the bookstore. I found him, Jayce, at his hotel."

"The police didn't arrest you, did they?"

"Of course not."

"Call Karin. I'll be right there." She hung up.

I called Karin, and we repeated the conversation.

"Did Van Oss have any connections in Doyle, aside from you and Mike?" she asked.

"I'm not sure," I turned and my hip struck the counter. "Last night, I overheard him talking to someone on the phone. He said he nearly gave the old man a heart attack. It sounded like he was the one who'd broken into Mike's house, and he was working with someone nearby."

"Have you found any evidence of this book of folklore he claimed he lent Mike?"

"No, none. I think he made the whole thing up and was after the million-dollar book." But he had sold Mike a book like the one he'd described. The folklore book wasn't a fiction. So where was it?

"More than a million," Karin corrected. "But how would he have heard about it? Could he work for the auction house Mike had contacted about the book?"

"It's possible," I said. Van Oss had been working with someone, and if that someone had killed him, then it was someone from Doyle. Peter or Gretel? Sweat dampened my forehead, and I wiped it away with the back of my hand. I couldn't imagine Gretel twisting a man's neck like that. But Peter might be able to manage it.

Karin agreed to come to the bookstore, and we hung up.

I checked the clock over the door. Ten o'clock, time to open. I paced, restless. I didn't want to open the store, but I had bills to pay and didn't like the idea of being alone with my thoughts. Finally, I flung open the door, hooking the top so it wouldn't drift shut.

The temperature dropped. Something shifted in the corner of my eye, and my head whipped toward the closed storage room.

Nothing was there, but I walked to it anyway and opened the door.

The storage room was as I'd left it, boxes restacked, the computer with its cracked monitor on its desk, books on metal shelves. A breeze stirred my hair.

Voices murmured behind me, and I turned, jumping a little.

A middle-aged couple browsed the shelves.

I pasted on a smile. Live people – tourists – not ghosts. "Hi! Let me know if I can help you find anything."

I moved to the counter and turned on the cash register. An elderly man I knew walked in and headed straight for the history section. And then the floodgates opened, and people strolled into the bookstore in ones and twos. The desk phone rang.

"Hello?"

It clicked, went to a dial tone.

Faintly, a second phone rang in the storage room. One ring, and it stopped.

The desk phone rang. Eyeing it warily, I picked it up. "Hel—"

Dialtone.

The storage room rang, hollow and echoing. Once. Done.

The desk phone rang. A teenager stepped up to the desk with a graphic novel.

I ignored the phone. It stopped after one ring.

My hands fumbled the teenager's change, ripping the receipt too high on the register. A line formed behind the teen.

The phones kept ringing, disconnecting.

My movements were clumsy. Paper bags stuck together. The register refused to open. And still the customers came. They asked questions, bought books, kept me running from the counter to the storeroom to the bookshelves. I clambered down the ladder and handed a young mother a book on the terrible twos.

"I can't believe you have it," she said, smiling. "I've been looking for it everywhere. I'll take it."

I rang her up and glanced at the crowd milling in the store. It was a crowd, a real crowd. I couldn't remember seeing so many people in the store outside of a book signing. The customers didn't give me time to think, much less worry about Van Oss's murder.

Karin walked inside. The baby weight had already changed the way she moved, and my chest squeezed, a shroud of worry wrapping around me.

She frowned in her lightweight blue, knit top and white slacks. Her expression grew abstracted, and I knew she was using her powers of sight on the bookstore.

"Thank you, come again." I handed the bag to the woman and slammed the register shut. I hurried around the counter to my sister. "Do you see anything?" I asked in a low voice.

"Have you done something?" she murmured out of the side of her mouth. "There's magic here. And what's with the phones?"

I went cold. So I'd been right, and this swarm of customers was not natural. "I have no idea what's going on."

"Excuse me?" An older, jowly woman waved a book toward me. "Do you have book three in the series?"

"In the storeroom," I said. "I'll get it." And to Karin, "I'll be right back." I hustled to the storeroom and located the book, the third in a romance trilogy.

When I returned, Karin stood behind the counter and was signing one of her romance novels for the older woman.

"...getting married?" the woman exclaimed. "But that's so romantic, just like something out of one of your novels. How far along are you?"

"Six months." Karin pulled the cord from the counter phone. Both front and back phones fell silent. "Fingers crossed the wedding happens before the baby comes."

"Here's that book you wanted," I said.

"Imagine running into you in a bookstore," the woman said to Karin. "I can't wait to tell my friends."

Karin and I shared a look. She was about as comfortable around fans as I was in crowds. Karin didn't believe she deserved the fans, and couldn't quite believe it when someone recognized her.

I sold the fan the books. Three more people lined up to exchange cash for fiction. This should have made me happy. It didn't.

"I'll take the register," Karin said, pulling up a stool.

"Excuse me?" a customer waved from the back of the store.

"Thanks," I said and hurried to help the man.

At some point, Jayce wandered in, left, and returned with lunch for the three of us. Karin ate at the register. I grabbed bites in the storeroom whenever I was sent there to retrieve a book.

Jayce watched, bemused. She wasn't a book person, but I loved her anyway.

Finally, the wave of customers ebbed. By three o'clock. the store had cleared out.

I sagged against the counter. "Wow."

"So, little Miss magic-on-people-is-unethical finally broke down," Jayce said.

"It is unethical," I said. "And it wasn't me!"

Arching, Karin massaged her lower back. "Then who?"

A quiver of unease rippled my spine. "And why?" Had someone been trying to keep me here, out of the way?

We stared at each other, consternation on my sisters' faces.

"Toeller?" Karin asked.

"It has to be," I said. "She's the only other person in town with that kind of power."

"What happened this morning?" Karin asked. "Tell us everything you can remember."

I did, starting with my arrival at the hotel, the vulture spirit, the ghost.

"The Rose Rabbit told her you'd come?" Jayce asked, her mouth slackening. "What the hell is this thing?"

"Whatever he is, he looks human," I said, "even if he is terribly scarred."

"But he's not human," Karin said. "You said Heath's head was twisted all the way around. That would have taken a lot of strength or skill, I'd say almost preternatural strength."

"You think the Rose Rabbit may have killed him?" My brows drew together.

"He was there," she said. "He knew Heath was dead, and he somehow knew your connection to him. If he was a human, the police would be questioning him now."

"But he's not human," Jayce said. "And what reason would he have to kill a rare bookdealer?"

"It sounded like Heath was working with someone," I said. "If that person is here in Doyle, he may have killed him."

"I suppose that makes more sense than a rabbit doing it," Karin said.

"He's not a rabbit." Annoyed, I flapped my hands, skimming a low display. It wobbled, and I grabbed it before it could topple. We were no closer to understanding what the Rabbit was. And, I realized, I didn't know anything about Van Oss either.

It was time I found out.

CHAPTER 18

I sat at an outdoor wine bar, my foot swinging restlessly. Main Street's iron lamps glimmered in the darkness, a picturesque, fairy-tale scene. A ghost carriage clopped down the street. A Jeep zipped through it, and the apparition vanished.

Couples sat nearby, holding hands. They were a little too close for comfort, but I needed a place that was public and busy on a Saturday night.

I sipped my hard cider, cool and tangy with a hint of cinnamon. Yum.

Nervous, I shifted, and the ivory tablecloth brushed the tops of my thighs, tickling.

Peter and Gretel walked down the street toward me, and I wondered again at how different the two were. He moved at an amble, his top half angled backwards as if he didn't really want to get where he was going. His loose t-shirt and board shorts sagged around his hips.

Three steps ahead, Gretel pumped her arms and leaned into a non-existent wind. Even her jaw jutted forward, her sandaled feet making light slapping sounds on the walk. She wore tight, green cargo shorts and a tank that accentuated every supermodel-esque curve.

I waved.

They changed direction, angling toward me, but neither changed their pace.

Gretel arrived first. She jammed her hands on her hips, her chest heaving. "So? We're here. What do you want?"

"Do you want anything to drink?" I'd already drunk half my cider to calm my jitters. It seemed to be working. The waves of red-hot annoyance rippling off her didn't phase me one bit.

Peter scraped back a metal chair and dropped into it. "You buying?" He eyed me hopefully.

"Sure," I said, magnanimous after my half bottle.

Gretel snorted and clattered into her chair.

I handed Peter the wine list, but Gretel snatched it out of his hand.

He shrugged. "I'll get the usual."

Nose twitching, she scanned the menu, then returned it to her husband.

I motioned for a waitress wearing a short apron low about her hips.

The two ordered, Gretel managing to find the most expensive wine on the menu. Fortunately, Peter got a local beer.

Gretel folded her arms. "So? What do you want?" She enunciated each word, speaking slowly as if I were stupid.

"Did you hear Mr. Pivens was in the hospital?" I asked.

Peter started. "The hospital? What happened?"

His surprise seemed genuine. Either he'd broken in and was doing a good job faking it, or he hadn't heard. The latter was most likely. Van Oss had probably been the burglar. And Peter and Gretel had never made much effort to integrate into our small town. Even if they had, Pivens, from Angels Camp, wasn't one of us. I guessed that made him lucky.

"Someone broke into Mike's house while Mr. Pivens was inside," I said. "He had a heart attack." I hoped they wouldn't ask for more details. Mentioning I'd been inside with the lawyer wouldn't make them any happier.

They didn't ask.

"So what does that mean for us?" Peter asked.

"As long as there's a cloud over Mike's death, no one will get their inheritances." I wasn't sure if this was true, but my words had the predicted effect.

Gretel jerked forward in her chair. "Cloud? There's no cloud. It's all in your head that anything's wrong with his death."

"I didn't imagine the break-in at Mike's," I said. "There was a break-in at the bookstore as well. Now that bookdealer, Van Oss, is dead too, murdered."

The waitress returned and set the drinks in front of Peter and Gretel. "Can I get you anything else?"

"Yeah," Peter said, "the bruschetta plate. Gretel? You want anything?"

"I'll take the mushrooms," she said.

I ground my teeth. These two were determined to milk me for everything they could, but I was only a bookseller and poet... One who might have a million-dollar book on her hands.

Swallowing, I smiled, nodded.

The waitress disappeared into the wine bar.

"How much longer do you think it'll take?" Peter asked me.

"I don't know," I said. "The hospital expects to release Mr. Pivens soon." But worry gnawed like a mouse. This morning I'd learned he'd contracted pneumonia. It's the sort of thing that happens to old people in hospitals, but had Doc Toeller played a role? I sipped my cider to calm myself, enjoying the lassitude stealing through my limbs. "He would have hired someone to investigate, but he can't now. So it's up to us."

Gretel crossed her slender arms. "We don't have the money for a P.I. If you want one, you hire him."

"I don't have any either," I said. "You know what my salary was."

Peter's mouth twisted. "And I don't guess you make much as a poet."

"I thought it would be helpful if we could retrace the twenty-four hours leading up to Mike's death," I said. "I was off the day before he died. When did

Mike get to the bookstore that Wednesday? What do you remember from the day before he died?"

They looked at each other for a long moment. Gretel's brow furrowed.

I held my breath. Had I miscalculated? Had my appeal to their greed been too obvious?

"He got to the bookstore before I did," Peter said, and my breath released.

"What time did you arrive?" I asked.

"Around noon." He rolled his eyes. "You know the bookstore doesn't get busy before then anyway."

I knew Peter was supposed to be there when the bookstore opened at ten. "Did he talk to anyone? Were there any unusual customers or events?"

Gretel made a noise of disgust. "That Alba came in, crazy as ever, ranting about the government and Britney Spears. She knocked over one of our displays with her damned sign."

"Intentionally?" My eyes widened.

"No," she said, "but what did she expect would happen when she dragged that huge sandwich board into the bookstore?"

"Did she talk to Mike?" I asked.

Peter grinned. "Alba never talks to people. She talks at people. Mike managed to finally get her out. I don't know what he said to her."

"He told her he was working on it." Gretel shook her head. "Humoring her."

"Working on what?" I asked.

"Does it matter?" Peter drawled. "He was humoring her. And then..."

The waitress bustled to our table, a tray in her arms. She set three small plates and the mushrooms and bruschetta between us. "Can I get you anything else?"

"I'll have another glass of wine," Gretel said.

My fingers twitched on the tablecloth. Did Gretel have to be such a fast drinker with the most expensive wine on the menu?

"I'm good," Peter said. "You Lenore?"

I blinked, surprised by the courtesy. But he was ordering with my money. "Nothing for me, thanks."

The waitress left, and the couple got busy with the food.

"You were saying, Peter?" I asked.

"Huh?" Chunks of tomato slid from his bruschetta and plopped onto the ivory tablecloth.

"After Alba left," I said, swallowing my impatience, "did something happen?"

"Oh, right." He chewed noisily, bread crusts snapping and crunching. "That bookdealer showed up."

"So Thursday wasn't the first time they'd met." That made sense. If Heath really had given a book to Mike to value – which I doubted – that must have happened on Wednesday. And if he hadn't...? "Did he have a book with him?"

"I didn't see one," Peter said.

"Did it look like they knew each other?" I asked.

Peter tilted his head, his brow scrunching in thought. "I wouldn't say so. What did you think, Gretel?"

"They didn't know each other," Gretel said. "Mike looked confused, kind of wary, when the guy held out his hand to shake."

"Did you see Van Oss with a book?"

"Nope," she said.

Van Oss had sold Mike a book of American folktales years ago. Gretel and Peter had to be wrong wrong. Or lying. I leaned back in my chair, putting more distance between us.

"Mike didn't like him." Gretel popped a buttery mushroom into her mouth.

"What do you mean?" I asked.

"I could just tell," she said. "He was leaning away from the guy, like you are from us now."

My face warmed, and I laced my hands over my stomach.

She laughed, a harsh, unpleasant sound like the cawing of crows. "There's no sense in pretending. You don't like us, and we don't like you." She tapped her index finger on the table. "But we deserve our inheritance." She raised her finger, leaving a faint blot of oil on the white cloth.

"What happened next?" I asked.

Gretel shrugged her narrow shoulders. "That sexy bald councilman came in—"

"Steve Woodley?" I asked.

"I guess so," she said. "Silver hair? Goatee? Looks like that Star Trek guy, Patrick Stewart? Anyway, Van Oss left, and Mike went to lunch with the councilman while we got stuck at the bookstore."

"So that must have been, what?" I asked. "Around one o'clock?"

"I guess," Peter said, negligent. He stretched his long legs beneath the table and bumped into my ankle.

It had been a busy noon hour for Mike – crazy Alba, the bookdealer, and then Steve Woodley to the rescue.

"What time did Mike return?" I asked.

Gretel's brows slashed downward. "He came back at two-fifteen. We had to wait before we could go to lunch."

They'd had to work an entire two hours and fifteen minutes before taking their lunch break. Poor Mike. I didn't know how he'd put up with them.

"Don't look at us like that," Gretel snapped.

"Like what?" I asked.

"Like you're better than us."

"I wasn't—"

"Oh, yes you were. We put up with your high and mighty attitude for years, and I for one am glad we don't have to anymore."

"Gretel," Peter said in a low voice, and she subsided. "So we got back from lunch around three-thirty," he continued. "Mike took an extra fifteen minutes, so I figured we deserved it as well. And then we sold a few books, and closed up at seven."

"Who did you sell books to?" I asked.

"A couple tourists came in. That guy your sister's engaged to–"

"Nick?" I asked, surprised.

"He had a book on order. Mike took care of it."

"What was the book about?"

He raised a lazy brow. "How should I know? Why don't you ask him?"

Annoyed, I jerked down the hem of my white, cotton top. "I will. Anyone else from Doyle come in that you recognized?"

"Some guys from the high school buying their gaming books," he said. "They dropped a load of cash – all sweaty, crumpled bills. Must be nice to have an allowance."

"Maybe they have a job?" I motioned to the waitress, and she wove through the packed tables.

"Yes?" she asked.

"May I have the check please?"

She consulted her small, black leather folder and drew out a bill. "Here you go."

"Thanks." I scanned the bill and my stomach plunged. I hoped the information the Gallins had given me was worth the price.

Nine o'clock. Saturday night. I should have just gone home after meeting with Peter and Gretel, but a sense of urgency drove me. So I strode down Main Street's uneven sidewalk, careful to lift my feet so I didn't stumble in the darkness. Doyle was a small town. If Mike and Steve had eaten here, their lunch possibilities were limited.

I darted into Antoine's Bar, packed to the gills. The juke box blared a country tune. I hunched my shoulders against the crowd.

Raucous drinkers brushed against me, stood in my path. Karin was the sister who saw auras and connections, but even I could sense the dark hunger of the bar's patrons.

Jayce and her boyfriend, Brayden, sat holding hands across a small, wooden table in the old-west bar.

Fractionally, my muscles relaxed. I'd found allies. I squeezed through the crowd to their table.

Brayden leapt to his feet, towering over me. He swept his dark hair off his brow, and he smoothed the front of his green t-shirt, taut against his broad chest. "Lenore! Can we get you a chair?"

I looked around. "Good luck finding one."

"Take mine," he said. "I was about to get another beer. Jayce? Lenore? You want anything?"

We shook our heads, and he vanished into the sea of people.

"What are you doing here?" Jayce shouted over the roar of the crowd.

I took his wooden chair and sat. "I need to find the waitress who was here Wednesday at lunch, a week and a half ago."

"Why?" Jayce asked.

"Mike may have had lunch here with Steve Woodley. I'm trying to retrace his steps, find out who he talked to, the day before he died." I looked to the bar, and my shoulders sagged. It was hopeless. I'd have to return tomorrow, during the day, or maybe even on Wednesday. But I could feel the clock ticking down. We were running out of time.

"Maybe I can help." Jayce closed her eyes, lowering her head and smiling, and I felt it. A subtle, sensual energy flowed from her and flooded the room.

A handsome young waiter pushed through the crowd. "Hey, Jayce. Can I get you anything?"

Her eyes slanted away, coy. "Maybe." She cocked her finger, and he drew closer. "Who works here lunches on Wednesdays?"

"Me. Sal. Why?"

She glanced at me.

"Do you remember Mike Gallin, the bookstore owner, having lunch here with Steve Woodley?" I asked.

"The councilman?" he shook his head. "I didn't serve them. Want me to ask Sal?"

"Yes, please," Jayce said.

Dazed, he wandered off.

"That was a little mean," I said.

"Just some harmless flirting."

"I meant the magic."

"What's the harm?" Her expression sobered, and she leaned toward me. "He's one of Toeller's boy toys."

"Really?" I blinked and looked toward his departing back. But he'd already vanished into the crowd. Toeller liked younger men. Lots of younger men, though she always kept them on the right side of legal.

"I've seen them here together and at other places too."

I twisted my necklace, adjusting my Saint Michael's charm. "Can we trust him?"

"To tell us if Mike and Steve were here for lunch? I think so."

The waiter returned with a harried looking waitress, Sal. Her smile was weary, but I knew her from the bookstore. Cookbooks and feng shui. A tattoo of an om symbol decorated the inside of one wrist.

"Hi, Lenore," she said. "You wanted to know about the Wednesday before last?"

"Was Mike here with anyone?"

She shook her head. "No. It was a quiet lunch. I would have remembered him." Lightly, she touched my arm. "I'm truly sorry about what happened."

"Thanks."

Someone shouted for beer, and she and the other waiter hurried off.

Brayden returned and set two mugs of beer on the table. "It's a disaster at the bar. I don't want to face that again anytime soon."

I rose. "You can have your chair back."

A man bumped into me, his energy aggressive, his stained t-shirt reeking of cigarettes. My neck corded.

"Please, Lenore," Brayden said, "stay."

If I didn't get out soon, I'd scream. "It's okay, I was leaving anyway. Thanks, Jayce."

She frowned. "Sure."

I pressed through the crowd, emerging onto the sidewalk and gasping in the cool night air. The temperature had dropped at least ten degrees since I'd gone inside, the way it can in the mountains.

I hurried to the next restaurant on my list. The owner said he hadn't seen Mike in there for weeks. The next restaurant was also a bust. I found people who'd worked there that Wednesday, but no one remembered Mike.

The last restaurant on my list, Alchemy, was the farthest from the bookstore and the least likely place for Mike to go to. But if he'd come here, that might explain why he'd returned late from lunch.

I checked my watch. It was after nine o'clock, and Alchemy's patio tables were emptying.

I walked inside the Spanish-tiled entry. The restaurant was chic, modern, with a tiled fireplace inside and one on the patio.

The hostess, Jenny, looked up from her stand and smiled. "Hi, Lenore. Can I help you?"

"Mike might have been here two Wednesdays ago, the day before he died. I think he might have left a book here," I lied.

She shook her head. "You can check the lost and found, but I don't remember seeing a book inside it."

"Actually, I'm not even sure if Mike was here that day."

"He was," she said. "I sat him and Steve Woodley at that table over there." She nodded to an empty table by the bar. A ceiling fan spiraled above it.

"You remember them?" I asked, giddy with my success.

"How could I forget? He died the next day. I'm so sorry for your loss, Lenore. Have you heard anything about the funeral?"

"Not yet." Unable to meet her gaze, I stared at my hands. "Do you remember anything about that lunch? Was he in a good mood? Bad mood?"

"They seemed okay when they arrived," she said, her voice uncertain.

"But when they left?"

"I think they'd been arguing. I couldn't really hear them. They kept their voices low, but they were intense, you know?"

"Who was their waiter?" I asked.

"Jim." She motioned to a tall, wiry waiter in black slacks and a white shirt leaning on the bar.

"Is it okay if I...?" I canted my head toward the bar.

"Sure. And let me know when you hear about the funeral, will you?"

"I will, thanks." I made my way through the tables to the marble-topped bar.

Jim drummed his long fingers on it, watching the bartender mix a drink.

"Hi, Jim."

He turned and smiled, his shock of dark hair falling across his right eye. "Lenore. How's it going?"

"It's going. I heard you waited on Mike and Steve Woodley two Wednesdays ago, the day before Mike died."

His mouth pulled down. "Yeah, my condolences. Mike was a good guy."

"I'm trying to retrace his steps that day," I said, hoping he wouldn't ask why.

He didn't. "Oh?"

"Did anything unusual happen while they were here?"

"Unusual?" He tossed his head. His hair shifted, then fell back into place over his eye. "They seemed kind of tense, and that was weird."

My pulse quickened. "Tense how?"

"They seemed to be arguing, but I was trying not to listen."

"Did you hear anything?" I asked, leaning closer.

"Woodley was saying something about the importance of maintaining the status quo. Mike didn't seem to like it."

"That's it?" I asked, disappointed. That could have been about anything. "Anything else?"

"Sorry. Why do you ask?"

"I guess I just want to know what happened to him. There's a book that's missing," I said, spinning out the lie, though I wasn't sure why I bothered. "I thought maybe it had landed here."

"I didn't find anything at his table. If I had, I would have returned it."

"Okay. Thanks."

Pensive, I wandered outside. The same ghost horse and carriage rattled down the street. Oblivious, a tourist couple walked into its path. The carriage ran through them, and the woman shivered. Her companion draped his sports coat over her shoulders.

I was as oblivious as the tourist couple, and my so-called investigation had left me with more questions than answers.

CHAPTER 19

Sunday morning, a fire burned at the top of the valley. I awoke, my eyes dry and hot. The people of Doyle took mental inventories. Which of their precious belongings could they throw into their cars should the wind shift, and the fire turn towards our town?

By the afternoon, the acrid scent of burning pine and brush had thickened. From my perch behind the cash register, I glanced up from my mystery novel and looked out the bookshop window.

An SUV loaded with kayaks drove past. The fire was driving the wiser tourists away. But I couldn't leave, and so I took shallow breaths, tasting smoke and burnt sap and anxiety.

Two people wandered the bookstore's aisles, one a regular, one a tourist. By my elbow, the radio crackled. We all had our radios on, waiting for word on the blaze. But I suspected Toeller would keep Doyle safe. No fire had touched Doyle yet.

On impulse, I picked up the phone and called Karin's boyfriend, Nick.

"Hey, Lenore," his voice rumbled, warm, over the line. "What's up? Has the wind shifted?"

I smiled. Lenore had picked a good one with Nick. "No. We haven't gotten an evacuation order. You?"

"Nothing here, but I've got my go-bag packed."

"Quick question. Have you been special ordering books from Mike?"

There was a pause. "Yeah. I thought learning more about local history could help with our problem."

"Why didn't you come to me?" Maybe I was overreacting, but had he been trying to hide something?

"You were never around when I called. He was great - even found some books that are out of circulation."

"Did you find anything worthwhile?" But he couldn't have. If he had, Karin would have told us. But I was desperate for good news.

"We're not sure. Look, I'm not far from you. I was just headed into town to check on Karin. Why don't I stop by the bookshop, and we can talk?"

My two customers were still pondering their reading choices, and I didn't envision a wild surge of shoppers. "Sure. Stop by."

"See you soon." He hung up.

I tidied the counter, checked email, glanced at the door, the clock, rubbed my stinging eyes. My regular bought a sci-fi novel. The tourist wandered out.

Finally, Nick strode into the bookstore. Tall, tanned and athletic, his blue t-shirt stretched across his muscular chest. He wore khaki slacks and hiking boots, and I wondered if they were his evacuation clothes, because I knew he wasn't hiking today.

Catching sight of me behind the counter, he smiled broadly. "Hi, Lenore."

"Nick." I hurried around the counter and gave him a quick hug.

"How are you doing?"

"Good." I studied him. "Except for the secrets Mike kept from me. I didn't know he was special ordering books for you."

"I didn't know that was a secret."

"What did you learn?"

In answer, he pulled a small, leather-bound notebook from his pocket and handed it to me. "This is a list of all the Doyle fairy references Karin and I've found and their citations."

I flipped through the first five pages. Everything after that was blank. I lowered my head. "No offense, but it doesn't look like much."

"Take your time and read through it," he said. "I'll browse the history section." He strode to the military history shelf and studied the book spines.

The first two pages of the notebook were covered in fairy references – mainly mentions of the fairy spring in the woods. But Nick had captured references to other nearby springs reputed to have healing waters. I gasped.

He looked up. "So you found it."

"The Bell and Thistle pub used to be over a spring?"

He tapped a hardback on the Battle of Dunkirk against his chest. "A spring with healing waters. They used the water in the beer they brewed. And then the spring dried up. When I couldn't find anything on the fairy, I decided to start researching the spring itself. There are springs all over the world reputed to have healing properties. Maybe there's something to drinking fresh spring water. But I wonder if the rumors are true here. Something has to explain the way you people look."

I ignored the "you people." "Why didn't I know this? It could explain why the pub was taken. If the spring it was built over belonged to the fairy..." I frowned. If it had belonged to the fairy, why had she waited nearly a century to remove the pub?

Nick strolled to the counter. "You're thinking the bar itself should have been offensive to her, so why did she wait so long? Normally, when humans interfere with something sacred to the fae — a tree, a spring — trouble follows." His face creased, and I knew he was thinking about his missing sister, Emily. He cleared his throat. "But it didn't in this case."

"No," I said slowly. "Up until its disappearance, I never heard of any problems at the pub. Do you know when it was built?"

"In the eighteen nineties."

"So sometime after the doctor came to Doyle. Maybe she didn't mind the pub. Maybe she wanted the spring covered."

"Why would she?" He braced his sun-weathered hand on the counter.

"Well, she didn't lose access to the waters, did she? They were using it to make beer, you said."

"All through Prohibition, if the rumors are true. But she couldn't use it as a portal anymore."

I nodded. "If it ever was a gateway." We'd assumed the fairy spring in the woods was a door to her true home in the other world. "The well," I muttered.

"You mean the one beneath the wellhouse?" Nick nodded. "That was believed to have healing spring waters too. But it dried up in the nineteen fifties."

"When was it covered?"

"In the sixties." He reshelved the hardback.

"But building a well would have affected it too. Would it have damaged the spring, or made it easier for her to access?"

He cocked his head. "You're asking the wrong guy."

I smiled. "You were one of the first to figure out there was magic affecting Doyle. I can't imagine a better person to talk to."

He ran his hand over the top of his black hair, ruffling it. "Yeah. Well. Necessity is the mother of invention. People have returned from the forest. I have to believe..." He trailed off and looked out the front window.

I coughed. The smoke was seeping into my throat and lungs now. "Were there any more springs or wells you found associated with healing waters?"

He shook his head. "No. Just those three."

"And two were covered, essentially blocked." I straightened, my head spinning. Was it possible? "And she didn't mind. In fact, she's been fighting to preserve the wellhouse. She wanted those two springs covered."

"What are you thinking?"

"If we're right, and the springs are portals—"

"Which is typical in the mythology"

"What if she's been keeping something out of our world?"

We stared at each other.

"The Rose Rabbit," we said in unison.

"We're making some big assumptions," Nick said quickly. "This is all guesswork. And we don't even know what this Rose Rabbit character is."

"But if she's keeping him out, then they're not allies." I paced behind the counter, and spoke more rapidly. "They're enemies."

"And the enemy of my enemy might be my friend."

"Or not," I said. "When the Bell and Thistle vanished, it left its spring uncovered." Once the law enforcement teams had left, I'd returned to that site over and over, studying it, trying to feel its magic. All I'd gotten for my pains were some deep meditation sessions and thistles in my butt. It was hard to believe that barren crater had once been a live spring. "But I've been seeing him."

"Seeing who?"

"A man with a scarred face, but he seems to... shine. He's got to be the Rose Rabbit."

"You can't be sure," he warned. "These are guesses."

My jaw tightened. "I can. I know it. And the ghost at the hotel described the Rabbit perfectly."

"You think this Rose Rabbit made the pub and all those people disappear?"

"I don't know. If the doctor's worked so hard to keep those two springs covered, it doesn't make sense that she'd remove an entire pub from one of them." My insides twisted. I'd hoped the Rose Rabbit would be an ally. But if he'd made the pub vanish, then he was as bad as the doctor. Maybe worse.

"Dammit," he said, "I should have shown you this sooner."

"Does Karin know?"

He made a wry face. "She does, but I think she's got baby brain. And please don't tell her I said that."

One corner of my lips curled. "That's what she's been telling me."

Doctors still argued whether the pregnancy-induced mental fog was real. But if logical Karin hadn't picked up this connection... Or maybe the problem was that she was too logical to see it. I'd just gone off on several intuitive leaps. "We need to talk to Jayce and Karin together. We may be right about the springs, but I don't see how it helps us. Did Mike know you were interested in the fairy legends?"

An odd look crossed Nick's face. "I don't think so."

"Don't think?" I asked sharply. "But you're not sure?"

"I told him I was interested in anything historical on Doyle, including legends. But there was one night... You weren't here. The bookstore was nearly empty. He said something to me that seemed odd."

"What?"

"He said there was more to Doyle than met the eye, and I needed to take care. Then he said something, a quote, I think. '...If you gaze for long into an abyss, the abyss gazes into you.' Mike laughed it off and told me not to get obsessed with the past, but there was something in his eye that told me he was holding back. And then it was gone, and I thought I'd imagined it."

I felt the blood drain from my face. "It's from Nietsche. And that isn't the whole quote."

"What's the rest?"

"'He who fights with monsters might take care lest he become a monster... If you gaze for long into an abyss, the abyss gazes also into you.'"

He angled his head. "That's... interesting."

Interesting? It was terrifying. Mike may have known what we were up against. Had that knowledge gotten him killed?

At six o'clock, I locked the bookstore and flipped the sign in the door to CLOSED. Outside the window, the sunset flared in bands of fuchsia and blood orange and violent purple, the colors intensified by the smoke. How could something so destructive create so much beauty?

In the storeroom, I had to count the cash three times before the number came out right.

My thoughts tangled. Finding out if there were more than two editions of The Folk and Fairy Tales of America was proving harder than

I'd thought. I couldn't even find mention of one edition. But that book had to exist, because Mike had listed it in his ledger.

What had Mike known? Had he been warning Nick off from looking too closely into Doyle's magic spell? Mike's interest in occult books now took on a new light. If he'd known about the unseelie who ran Doyle, had he been gathering information on her as well? Did others know the truth?

I pushed the vacuum around the front room, its mindless roar the perfect counterpoint for my useless theories.

Finally, I turned out the lights and left, locking the front door. The sky had darkened to the color of a bruise. The bookstore's exterior light had come on automatically and attracted a crowd of insects. They buzzed and fluttered and pinged off the glass lampshade.

"Lenore?" a man asked from behind me.

I gave a little jump and turned, an ungainly ballerina, squeezing the keys in my palm hard enough to wince. "Councilman Woodley."

"I told you, call me Steve." He blotted the top of his skull with an old-fashioned handkerchief, then slipped it into the inside pocket of his navy blazer. In spite of his age, his skin had that same, waxy perfection we all had, and I shivered.

"Were you looking for a book? I've just closed, but—"

"I was looking for you, Lenore," his deep voice boomed.

"Oh." I shuffled the keys between my fingers and glanced down the street. "How can I help you?"

"I understand you've been asking about the lunch Mike and I had the day before he died."

My cheeks heated. "I was trying to reconstruct Mike's—"

"Why on earth didn't you just ask me?"

"I was going to," I stammered. "But…"

Two teenage girls in shorts and tanks raced toward us, their sandaled feet loud on the concrete sidewalk. Coltish, they swerved and darted around the corner of the bookstore.

His blue eyes crinkled. "Why don't you tell me what you want to know?"

"I was trying to reconstruct Mike's last day. I heard you and Mike had an intense conversation at lunch."

"We were arguing politics." He scratched his goatee. "Mike was quite libertarian in his outlook."

I bit back a smile. Mike's railing against taxes and regulations had been passionate, colorful, and often hilarious. "I heard he wanted to change something?"

"Reduce the local sales tax," Steve said promptly. His gaze shifted to the bookstore's darkened windows. "But even if I agreed with that, it would take more than one person to make that change. That's a job for the voters. I'm sorry now our words grew so heated over something so trivial. I didn't know it would be the last time I'd see him alive."

"Of course not. How could you have?" I asked, shamefaced. I should have stopped then. If I was as shy as my sisters thought, I would have. But I plowed onward. "Was there anything else you remember from lunch? Did Mike take any calls? Speak to anyone?"

His silvery eyebrow rose. "Take calls? Mike barely knew how to use his cell phone. He only turned it on when he wanted to call someone. But it was an ordinary lunch. Why?"

"Only because I'm trying to reconstruct—"

"But why? Mike's death was the result of a fall. It was tragic, but how does retracing his steps change anything?"

"It doesn't, but—"

"Do you think his death wasn't natural?"

My jaw shifted forward, and I worked to tame my irritation. "I don't know what to think."

"Lenore." He grasped my shoulder. "It was a terrible accident. Let it go."

I blinked. "Right. Yes. Of course."

"Good. I'm glad we had this chat." He left, striding down the street toward the town hall.

Thoughtful, I walked up the hill to Mike's Victorian and let myself inside. The high-ceiling foyer was sunk in gloom, and I flipped on the lights, locked the door behind me.

Turning on lights as I went, I crept into the library. A sliver of light from Alba's house shined through the ivy covering the arched windows.

I pulled the fake book from its spot on the shelf. The bookcase swung inward, and I walked inside the secret room.

I studied its glass-fronted shelves. None of the books leapt out at me as fairy related.

Slipping on the cotton gloves lying atop the Wooton desk, I opened the glass cases. I pulled each book from its shelf and scanned the pages. In spite of the urgency of my mission, I felt drawn to linger. Magical rituals and tales of occultists gone wrong – of course Mike had been fascinated. Who wouldn't be?

I sighed. It would take months to read all these books. I turned and stared at the folding desk. Had Mike hidden answers inside?

I checked my watch. It was eight o'clock, and I'd promised Nick I'd meet with him and my sisters. I was late.

Returning the Lovecraft novel to its place, I hurried from the house, careful to lock the front door.

The smoke was thicker, making me rasp, and the darkness oppressive. A shade shifted in the garden, and I froze, my eyes widening. But if it had been Mike's spirit, it had already vanished. I let myself out through the front gate.

A door slammed.

I looked toward the sound. Alba stood on her front porch and scowled at the female FBI agent. The agent walked slowly down her steps, her long legs picking her way through Alba's untamed front yard. The collar of her navy blazer was turned up.

"Corporate shill!" Alba screeched. "Get off my property!"

Agent Manaj caught my eye. "Miss Bonheim, fancy meeting you here."

"I didn't kill that liar," Alba yelled, her neck cording. "Even if he did deserve it, poking his nose where it didn't belong."

"Hello, Agent Manaj."

From her porch, Alba shook her fist at me. "Stay away from me, witch!"

"I'm glad I ran into you," the FBI agent said. "I understand you found another body. You're lucky. If it had been up to me, you'd still be answering questions."

"Why?" I asked, unnerved.

"You found two bodies under suspicious circumstances." She stepped onto the sidewalk.

"At least the police think Mike's death was suspicious. I've been telling them that since I found him."

"Is that why you were in Heath Van Oss's hotel room?"

"Like I told the sheriff, I wanted to talk to him about a book he claimed he'd lent Mike to assess."

"So she tells me. Has the book turned up?" She craned her neck toward Mike's house. The Victorian's gables and turrets, silhouetted against the darkening sky, had a haunted look.

"Not yet," I said.

"You said 'claimed.' Do you think Van Oss was lying?"

"He never showed me a receipt for the book. He'd sold Mike a book with the same title a couple years ago. He told me the book he lent Mike was a different edition, but so far I haven't been able to find any evidence for it. I think Van Oss made up the story of the second book. I think he wanted the book he'd sold to Mike back for some reason, and he didn't want to pay for it."

She smiled thinly. "The Folk and Fairy Tales of America must be some book."

My pulse jumped, and I shifted my weight, putting a few more inches between us. I hadn't told the sheriff the name of the book. How had the agent learned about it? And what was she really doing here? Van Oss's murder and an old man falling off a ladder didn't seem to fall into the FBI's purview.

A black-and-white patrol car rolled to the curb. Its tires crunched on loose gravel.

Alba darted into her house, her screen door banging shut behind her.

Connor stepped from the patrol car, and warm relief rolled through me.

"What's going on here?" He strode up the walk, his movements sure and purposeful.

"Nothing for you to worry about," the agent said. "I'll see you soon, Miss Bonheim." She turned on her heel and strode to her gray sedan.

Silent, Connor and I watched her get inside and drive off.

"She'll see you soon?" His gaze met mine, and my heart gave a small lurch. "About what?"

"I'm not sure. She was talking to Alba about something."

His expression flickered. "What are you doing here?"

"I came to take another look at Mike's private collection," I said. "But I didn't find anything."

He blew out a weary breath. "Are you coming or going?"

"Going. Why?"

"We got a call that lights were on in Mike's house. The neighbor thought it might be another break-in."

"It was me," I said. "I had all the lights on. The place is spooky at night. Mr. Pivens gave me the key and permission to be here. You can ask him." But I hoped Connor wouldn't, because I'd sort of implied I wouldn't visit Mike's alone.

"Then that's one mystery solved." He shot me a rueful look. "You heard the bell, didn't you?"

I nodded, wanting to apologize for his disappointment.

"I really thought I'd figured that out," he said.

I motioned toward Alba's overgrown yard. "You didn't seem

surprised to hear Agent Manaj was interviewing Alba."

"Alba was lurking around the hotel the night Mr. Van Oss died. And I didn't tell you that."

But he had told me, and the admission almost made me smile. "Why would Alba kill Van Oss?" I asked. "And why is Agent Manaj involved in Van Oss's murder investigation?"

"Alba wouldn't kill Van Oss, but she might have seen something. And the FBI's involvement is above my pay grade. Did Van Oss give you his card?"

"Yeah, he did."

"Can I see it?"

"Sure." Perplexed, I rummaged through my purse and located the card inside my wallet. I handed it to him.

Our fingertips brushed, and my pulse went into overdrive again. I jerked my hand away.

Connor's expression sent pinpricks of heat flurrying across my chest and neck.

He looked... pensive.

I cleared my throat and tried to pretend I hadn't noticed. "Why do you want to see his card?"

He stared at the thick, embossed card, then pocketed it. "Because there is no Heath Van Oss."

CHAPTER 20

I parked in my aunt's driveway and cut the headlights. Light streamed through the windows of the shingle and stone house. The beams illuminated lazy whorls of smoke that had been invisible during the day. The acrid fog drifted low along the ground.

Nick's SUV and Jayce's pickup were coated in fine ash. I grabbed my purse from the passenger seat and hurried up the porch and inside.

Voices drifted to me from the rear of the house. Not bothering to kick off my shoes, I strode down the hall and into the kitchen.

Drinks in hand, Nick, Karin and Jayce turned to me from their posts. Jayce and Karin leaned against the counter. Nick stood by the refrigerator.

"We were just arguing if the fire was natural or not." Jayce pressed the glass to her forehead, and the ice tinkled.

I set my purse on the butcher block work island.

Dead Hex perched on top of the refrigerator and studied Nick with a disturbingly intent expression.

I tore my attention from the dead cat. "Have you sensed anything?"

Jayce shook her carob-colored hair. It fanned out around the shoulders of her ruby knit top. "No magic. As far as I can tell, the fire is just a fire."

I looked to Karin, and she nodded, one hand resting on the swell of her abdomen. "I don't see any magic either, but it doesn't feel natural, does it?" She set her glass on the counter and tugged down the hem of her loose, navy top. The blouse was an old favorite of hers, but not being designed for pregnancy, it rode up.

"Then what?" I asked.

"The timing seems ominous," Nick said. "Two suspicious deaths and now a fire. Could the doctor have caused it for some reason?" Nick had left his hiking boots at the door. He wore thick, gray socks with red griffins on the ankles – a whimsical touch I wouldn't have expected from the lawyer.

The cat hunched closer to the edge of the refrigerator as if readying to pounce. He could jump on Nick all he wanted, and all Nick would suffer was a chill. But I didn't like Hex bothering my family.

The cat reached out a paw and batted at a lock of Nick's hair that stuck up at an unruly angle.

"It's possible." I walked to the refrigerator and reached for the cookie jar atop it, nudging the cat with one hand.

Though my hand passed through the ghost, the cat hopped to the floor and scowled. Tail high, he stalked from the kitchen.

I pried open the cookie jar and removed an iced, oatmeal cookie. "Though I don't know the fairy would resort to arson. Fires have a habit of skipping Doyle. Maybe the fire is just a fire." I bit into the cookie and looked a question at Nick.

He nodded. "I've told them about the link between the wellhouse, the spring at the Bell and Thistle, and the fairy spring in the woods."

"I should have figured it out sooner," Karin muttered.

"Even if it's true that the springs are connected to her," Jayce said, "we don't know what it means."

"But it must mean something," Karin said. "It can't be a coincidence that the Bell and Thistle, a pub that happens to be sitting on top of a dried magic spring, disappeared. Or that the doctor has been fighting to declare the wellhouse a historic landmark so developers can't touch it. These places are important to her somehow. And we know the fairy spring is part of her magic." She shared a look with Nick. They'd both had disastrous experiences at that spring in the woods.

"I saw that FBI agent outside Alba Pollard's house," I said. "She's interested in Heath Van Oss's murder."

Nick's brow furrowed.

"And there's more," I said. "Heath Van Oss is an assumed name. He doesn't exist."

"That could explain why the FBI is interested," Nick said. "They take identity theft seriously."

We stared at him.

"I've got a buddy in the FBI," he said. "We talk."

"Has he mentioned the Bell and Thistle?" Jayce asked.

"He's asked me about it. It's not his case, but he's curious like everyone else. If Heath was a person of interest in another FBI investigation, that could explain why the agent is hanging around."

"Wait." Karin turned to me. "Didn't you check up on this Van Oss guy when he was bugging you about this book he supposedly lent Mike?" she asked.

"I did," I said, bridling at the implicit criticism. "Just a minute." I hurried to my office and grabbed my laptop computer. Returning with it to the kitchen, I set it on the work island and woke it up. I typed in Heath's name, and clicked on a link. "There. He has a website."

Karin gave me a pitying look. "Anyone can set up a website." But she crowded around the computer with the others.

His website was an elegant black page with white script proclaiming Heath Van Oss, Rare Books.

Dealers in rare and antiquarian books for over fifteen years, our office is based in San Francisco (by appointment only). We work with a large number of important collectors worldwide, as well as rare book libraries and other institutions. If you have a rare book or library, we can offer you immediate and top payment. We'll travel globally for important and interesting materials.

Beneath that three headings: Free, Twenty-four Hour Evaluations; We Buy Old and Rare Books; We Buy Entire Libraries.

"Is it only one page?" Karin asked.

"Yes, but there's a contact link," I said and clicked on it. An email address appeared in the browser.

"Who's we?" Jayce asked. "Does Van Oss have a partner?"

"If he does," I said, "there's no name."

"There's one way to find out." Jayce pulled the computer toward her and typed quickly, pressed send.

"What did you do?" Karin shrieked.

"I sent him an email saying we had an old book on American folktales that needed valuing," she said.

Karin gaped. "But–"

"What's the worst that can happen?" Jayce asked.

I winced. "I wish you hadn't said that."

The fire was under control when I woke up Monday morning, leaving a cloudless, blue sky scented with burnt pine. I dressed in white linen shorts and a matching, loose short-sleeved top. I didn't need to step outside to know it was going to be hot. I knotted my hair into a loose ponytail.

Grabbing Mike's ledger listing his collection and my purse, I stepped onto the front porch.

Picatrix wove through my ankles and gazed hopefully through the open door.

"It's okay," I told Jayce's cat. "He's not home."

The cat nodded and trotted inside and up the stairs.

I rubbed my eyes. Surely I'd imagined that nod?

Shaking my head, I got into my Volvo and drove toward Mike's Victorian. I was getting paranoid about the ledger, even though I hadn't found anything special in it aside from my own poetry. But that was odd enough, and I didn't like having the ledger out of my sight. I hadn't fully explored Mike's mysterious desk in the secret room. But the last time I'd searched it, I'd been hunting for inventory information. Now I wanted more.

Who was Heath Van Oss? How had Mike gotten my poem in my handwriting into his ledger? And how had he gotten his hands on our family curse story? Mike's interest in the occult was seeming less random and more personal. If he'd known about our curse – the real story – then he may have known about Doyle's fairy problem.

Shrugging my shoulders, my grip tightened on the wheel. I was starting to hate the word "fairy." It sounded fun, even innocent. But what was happening to the people of Doyle, to my sisters, was anything but. The doctor was dangerous.

Had Mike known?

Driving up the steep hill, I parked in front of his house, curbing my Volvo's wheels. I flipped through my key ring and pushed open the white picket gate with my hip.

"Oh, no you don't!" A hand grabbed my arm and yanked me around.

I gasped. Keys, ledger and purse tumbled to the sidewalk.

Alba's grip tightened on my bare arm. Her blue eyes blazed. "Stay away from us, witch!" Her army green tank top hung loose above her dingy, gray shorts. Its deep arm holes and collar threatened to expose her sagging breasts.

I shook myself free. It was as if she'd emerged from a crack in the sidewalk. "What are you talking about?"

"This isn't your house," she snarled. "You don't belong here."

I sighed. "Alba, I have a key from Mike's executor. He asked me to go through some of Mike's things."

"Lawyers are all vultures. Now get out of here and stop bothering us."

A swiftly moving shadow passed above our heads, and I glanced up, half expecting to see my turkey vulture. But it was only an airplane.

"I'm sorry you're upset," I said. "I miss Mike too."

She deflated. "Mike was an idiot, getting himself killed."

"Getting himself?" Beads of sweat formed on my arms and chest. "Do you think someone killed him?"

"Of course someone killed him. Do you think he just fell off a ladder and died? He was nimble as a squirrel and always sticking his nose where it didn't belong."

"Do you know who hurt him?" I asked too loudly.

She leaned closer, stale coffee on her breath. "The government," she whispered. "It's a conspiracy. That's why the FBI was here yesterday, trying to figure out what I knew. But I'm too smart for them. I didn't tell that agent anything." She jabbed me in the chest. "And you'd better not say anything either, if you know what's good for you."

I rubbed my chest. Dammit, did I have a target there? This is what I got for questioning a schizophrenic. But Alba had lived next door to Mike for decades. Maybe there was some mindfulness in her madness. I said a silent prayer for patience. "Why would the government be after Mike?"

"They've lulled us into a dream – all this technology and television hypnosis has stopped us from feeling the truth." Her words were a hiss, and I swallowed, my mouth dry.

"What's the truth?" I asked.

"None of this is real. Mike knew. He was trying to fight it. I was helping."

"How?"

"By telling everyone!" She thrust a bony finger toward her front porch. Her sandwich board lay at an angle against the railing.

"How did Mike find out?"

She tossed her lank, gray hair. "He listened to me."

"I thought the FBI agent was asking you about that man who was killed the other day – Mr. Van Oss, the bookdealer."

Her suntanned face twisted in a sneer. "He was no bookdealer. He was a common criminal."

"Oh?" Did she really know something? Or was I clutching at slippery straws?

Turning, she marched into her yard and struggled into her sandwich board. "Don't trust the government!" She stomped down the steep road, the board banging against her knees.

Unsettled, I collected my things. The ledger had fallen open, wrong-side down on its spine. Dirt specked its creased yellowing pages. I brushed them off and trotted up the steps to Mike's house.

Stepping into the high-ceilinged foyer, I locked the door behind me. Slices of color, light filtering through the stained glass, painted the rug and hardwood floor.

The temperature plummeted.

My breath ghosted the air, and I rubbed my arms. The scent of Mike's cherry pipe tobacco thickened.

"Mike?"

I stood for a long moment, my head cocked, listening. Hearing and seeing nothing, I continued into the library and the secret room. The lights flicked on automatically. I closed that door behind me too, my skin pebbling in the air conditioning.

In front of the three-piece desk sat a cane-backed, rolling wooden chair. Determined to conduct a thorough autopsy of the desk, I sat and scooted closer. Mike would keep the most important things, the items he consulted the most, in easy reach. So I started with the closest drawers and worked my way outward.

In the top right-hand drawer was an old-fashioned card file. I flipped through it – contact names and numbers and notes. I sighed. Jerry Pringle – dealer. Arnaud Lecroix – collector. These were his fellow bookdealers.

Digging my cell phone from my pocket, I started calling.

My approach was simple – Mike had passed, and I had inherited his book collection. I was looking to sell – could they recommend an appraiser? And what about Heath Van Oss?

My approach turned out to be a little too successful. If I'd doubted the value of Mike's collection before, my doubts were erased now. Every dealer I called offered to appraise and buy the books. One man offered to buy the entire collection sight unseen. He named a price I would have considered extravagant before learning about the mysterious million-dollar volume. None had heard of Van Oss.

To one dealer, who'd expressed the most regret over Mike's passing, I confessed. "There are three books in particular I'm concerned about getting a proper valuation."

The man's chuckle was dry. "And you quite rightly don't trust any of Mike's fellow bookdealers. If you believe you have anything truly precious, then I suggest using an auction house. Let the market's demand determine the price."

"May I tell you about the books?"

"Of course." Another chuckle. "I've only been restraining myself from asking for details out of respect. He told me about you, you know."

My breath hitched. "He did?"

"He said you were too intelligent to be a mere bookseller, but you undervalued your worth. I believe he'd hoped he could bring you into his world of rare books. I suppose he has now."

"I suppose he has," I repeated sadly.

"Are you certain you simply want to sell it all? The book world needs more honest dealers like Mike."

"Right now, I'm not sure about anything." I braced my elbow on the desk. "His death, inheriting his business, has been such a shock."

"Then take your time. Mike's collection won't become any less rare. Now tell me about these three books you're concerned about."

I consulted the ledger. "A third edition set of The Golden Bough, a first edition of De Praestigiis et Incantationibus Daemonum et Necromanticorum – I'm not sure about the pronunciation. Sorry. But it's by Richard Argentine, and an illustrated William Blake – Songs of Innocence and of Experience. There's no note on the edition number here, only that it was printed in 1794."

There was a long silence. Then, "Good Lord."

"Do you recognize them?" I leaned forward. Roughly shifting aside a pile of receipts, I braced my elbows on the desk.

"Your Golden Bough – I presume it's the entire thirteen-book set?"

"Yes," I said, my excitement rising. "Is it valuable?"

"Not as much as you may be hoping. Its retail value is somewhere in the neighborhood of twelve to fifteen hundred dollars, depending on its condition. Your demonology book is a bit more challenging, but let's say around three thousand dollars. Again, it depends on the condition of the volume. It's the Blake I'm interested in. You said it was from 1794, and it's the Songs of Innocence and of Experience?"

"Yes. I'm going by Mike's notes on the date."

"How much do you know about William Blake?"

"He was a British poet who had visions," I said, thinking hard. "He wrote what his voices guided him to. Blake was a painter as well. He self-published his illustrated poems, creating the engraving plates, hand tinting the colors..." I went cold. "Wait. You don't think...?"

"I couldn't possibly say without examining the actual book. After Blake's death, unscrupulous dealers bound together mismatched copies of Songs of Innocence and Songs of Experience. They pawned them off as one of Blake's original bindings."

"Didn't Blake die in the early eighteen hundreds?"

"Yes. If you have a 1794 copy, one he'd bound himself, well, it would be quite remarkable. So remarkable, I have a hard time believing it."

I swallowed. "Then this could be one of Blake's original, handmade works?"

"Let's not get ahead of ourselves. I can't imagine Mike getting his hands on a find like that. The discovery of an original William Blake... Well, that's about as unlikely as the discovery of an unknown Van Gogh. It's most likely Mike found a reproduction, but even a well-made reproduction can have value."

But the auction house had authenticated one of the books, and said the bidding would begin at a million dollars. Could the Blake be it? Had Mike found an undiscovered original volume by William Blake? Good Lord indeed.

He chuckled. "Don't get yourself worked up, my dear. It's likely a fraud."

"Right." My mouth was dry, and I swallowed again. "There's another book in Mike's collection that's giving me some trouble. It's called The Folk and Fairy Tales of the Americas, by Ichabod Langley. Have you heard of it?"

"Not a whisper, but folk tales aren't my specialty."

Head cocked, I stared at the glass-fronted bookcases. "According to you, neither is William Blake, but you seem to know a lot about it."

"Ah, well. Bookdealers."

"Have you heard of a bookdealer named Heath Van Oss?"

"Van Oss?" His voice sharpened. "He's no bookdealer. If he's sniffing around, keep Mike's books locked up tight."

"Why?" I asked. "What do you know?"

He blew out a heavy breath. "Know? Nothing. Suspect? Everything. I was involved in a bidding war for a rather nice library of books of magic—"

"Magic?" My pulse quickened.

"Not real magic, of course. Stage magicians, magic tricks. That's how Mike and I became acquainted. Occasionally, our interests overlapped, but not so often that we were true competitors. I specialize in books and ephemera about stage magic, and he in the occult. We helped each other out when we found books that might work in the other's collection. At any rate, I had a buyer lined up – a wealthy one – and money was no object. Van Oss represented the other bidder."

"Who was the bidder?" My hand tightened on the phone.

"It was all anonymous. We bookdealers like to keep our secrets. It makes us more important. At any rate, all was going well, and I had the deal sewn up. And then someone broke into the house and stole the most valuable pieces."

"And you think Van Oss was responsible?"

"I could never prove it, but there was something about the man I didn't like. When I called my friends in the industry, no one knew a thing about the man. It was as if he didn't exist. Is he bothering you?"

"No," I said. "But he was here, and now he's dead."

"Dead?"

"Someone killed him."

"Not Mike?"

"No, Mike passed away a week earlier."

The air conditioning clicked on and hummed, a low drone. A strand of my hair whipped my cheek and stuck to the corner of my mouth. I scraped it free.

"Miss Bonheim, this sounds very suspicious. First Mike's death, and now the murder of Van Oss? It is a murder, isn't it? Not a simple accident?"

"No, it was murder."

"Then I strongly advise you to take care. The book world may seem dull, but where there's money, there are always people willing to kill."

CHAPTER 21

I returned the card file to the drawer in Mike's fold-up desk and studied the mass of cubbies. Untidy bits of paper and envelopes stuck from every one. I forced myself to continue my circuit of the Wooton desk and work my way outward.

File folders filled a bottom drawer. I pulled them out – tax information. A travel magazine from Canada. A folder marked HISTORICAL ASSOCIATION. Doc Toeller was its president. Had Mike been a member?

Outside the room, something creaked. I glanced at the door, still shut fast.

I flipped through the file. Faded brochures from the sixties on Doyle's history. A page torn from a yellow pad headed, BELL AND THISTLE.

I stilled. There was no date on the yellow sheet, so no way to know if he'd written this before or after the pub had disappeared. The page consisted of bullet points:

- *Opened 1855*
- *Sold to Patrick Doyle, 1887*
- *1920: Town boundaries shift – it becomes part of Arcadia Twshp*
- *1920: Prohibition – becomes a restaurant*
- *1921 - Doyle renegotiates town bndries. B & T becomes an "island" of Doyle inside Arcadia. Fy influence? Pwr ltd to Doyle?*

The air conditioner hummed.

Fy influence – that had to be fairy influence, right? I grimaced. Once again, I was jumping to conclusions. Mike couldn't have known about the fairy. But I gnawed my bottom lip. Or could he have? He'd been interested in the occult enough to build a respectable library on the topic. And fairies had played a supernatural role in human history since we began recording it.

Mike didn't have a bullet point for the date of the disappearance of the Bell and Thistle. If he'd made this list after it had vanished, he'd have included it, wouldn't he? It was the most interesting part of the pub's history, aside from the boundary change which returned it to Doyle.

I stared at another entry, Pwr ltd to Doyle? The fairy's power limited to Doyle?

That was the question. I wiped my palms on my linen shorts. I wanted to believe it, but I wasn't quite ready to. Surely the doctor had traveled outside the town at some point in her life. She had to leave Doyle to reach the Bell and Thistle, and we'd seen her at that pub. Karin was certain leaving Doyle wouldn't free us from her curse. But could other aspects of her power be somehow limited outside the town's boundaries?

I rose and paced the small octagonal room. If Mike had known the truth...

I paused and scanned the glassed bookcases. Were there answers on these shelves?

Something creaked outside the room, and my pulse accelerated. Old houses made noises. It could be nothing. But someone had broken in before.

I pressed my ear to the hidden door.

Above, a careful footstep.

Someone was in the house.

I grabbed my phone and inched open the hidden door.

Voices murmured upstairs – male and female.

I stiffened. Peter and Gretel, damn them. They weren't supposed to be in here.

I took the winding steps two at a time and emerged on the upstairs landing, my chest heaving. The hallway's wine-colored carpet was threadbare. Sepia photos of old Doyle lined the walls – wooden buildings and men in rough clothing and horse-drawn carriages.

Peter emerged from a room, his fists clenched. His hands loosened when he saw me. "Lenore? What are you doing here?"

"What are you doing here?"

His mouth worked silently, thought processes grinding forward. "I asked you first," he finally said.

"I'm inventorying Mike's library. Why are you here, Peter?"

Gretel emerged from another room. A gold pocket watch dangled from her delicate hand. "What's...?" Her eyes narrowed. "You! I should have guessed you'd be here."

"I'm supposed to be here," I said. "You're not."

She stepped closer to me, her neck cording. "How dare you. We were his family! This is our house."

"Yes, and it was also Mike's place of business. He ran his rare book business from here. The lawyer wants–"

"The lawyer is flat on his back in the hospital." Gretel jammed the watch into the pocket of her cargo shorts, and I'd no doubt she'd taken it from the room she'd just left. I'd never seen Mike wear the gold watch, but it had to be his. In the brief glimpse I'd gotten, it was likely an antique. But the watch belonged to them now, even if they weren't supposed to be here, so I said nothing.

"We're petitioning for Mike's other executor to take over," Gretel continued.

"Other executor?" I asked.

Peter cleared his throat. "That would be me."

"Oh." I blinked. Crap. "You're the executor now?"

He glanced apologetically at his wife. "Not yet. It's not official. Mr. Pivens feels—"

"It doesn't matter what he feels," Gretel said. "What matters is he can't do his job."

"But I thought he was getting better," I said. "He's been sending me emails, checking with auction houses."

"He's an old man," Peter said gently.

"And you need to leave," Gretel said.

My jaw tightened. "No. I won't." I was tired of getting interrupted and ignored and pushed around.

"I said, get out!" she shrieked.

"Gretel." Peter placed a hand on her arm. "She's right. Technically, we're not supposed to be here. Let's go." He tugged her down the stairs.

Swearing, she followed.

The front door slammed.

I exhaled a shaky breath. Of all the places to make a stand, this had to have been the stupidest. Peter and Gretel had always been grasping, but I think Peter, at least, had cared for Mike. I should have stayed more calm.

I glanced into the upstairs rooms. They didn't seem to be disturbed, so I returned downstairs. I jiggled the handle to the front door, making sure Peter and Gretel had locked it behind them, then walked to the hidden room.

At the desk, I sat in the cane-backed rolling chair and rifled through the remaining papers in the file. An organizational chart of the Historical Association dated this year. Doc Toeller, Sheriff McCourt, Steve Woodley, and other local luminaries were on the board.

And that was the last paper in the file. I flipped it over. In one corner of the page, Mike had drawn a spider web. A tiny fly was trapped in its center. I flipped the paper over, dropping it on the desk. It slipped to the floor.

Shaking myself, I bent to retrieve it. I was seeing omens everywhere. It was just a stupid drawing.

I flipped through the Canada travel magazine. It looked like it had been swiped from an airplane. An article on Anne of Green Gables and Prince Edward Island. As a child, I'd loved those books, and I paused to read the article. The island had seemed magical in the books, and the travel photos had me drooling. Maybe someday... I flipped the page.

A VILLAGE VANISHES: THE ANJIKUNI MYSTERY

Located along the Kazan River, the Anjikuni region is littered with legends of malevolent spirits and malignant monsters. The most controversial of these tales is of the thirty disappearing villagers who lived beside Anjikuni Lake.

On a frigid night in November, 1930, a trapper named Joe Labelle trudged into the lakeside Inuit village seeking shelter. But when he shouted a halloo, he was met with a wall of silence.

Wary, he continued into the village. The full moon illuminated shanties huddled on the lakeshore. But no people. No barking dogs. No smoke coiling from the chimneys.

Finally, scenting smoke, he found a dying fire, a blackening stew in its embers. He raced from house to house, yanking aside their caribou skin door flaps, but the village had been abandoned. Food lay half-eaten on tables. Half-mended clothing was discarded with needle and thread still inside. None of the supplies had been taken from the fish storehouse.

He searched for tracks indicating where the villagers had gone, but found none. It was as if they had simply vanished into thin air.

Rather than spend the night in the eerie village, LaBelle continued on to a telegraph office, miles away. There, half-frozen, he sent a message to the nearest Royal Canadian Mounted Police (RCMP). Convinced the villagers had disappeared due to supernatural forces, it took hours before LaBelle was able to calm himself and tell his story coherently.

The RCMP investigated. Its officers reported seeing strange, blue lights over the village, lights that did not look like auroras. Even more disturbing, the village cemetery had been emptied. In spite of the Mounties' investigations, the Anjikuni mass disappearance remains one of Canada's greatest unsolved mysteries.

Or does it?

The mystery was first reported in "Le Pas, Manitoba" on November 28, 1930 and then the next day in "The Hallifax Herald." After a flurry of speculative articles, interest in the story died and was not revived until 1959, when author Frank Edwards resurrected the tale in his book, "Stranger Than Science." The RCMP later accused Edwards of fabricating the entire tale. But if it was a fabrication, it was nearly thirty years in the making.

Uneasy, I checked the cover of the magazine. It was five years old. Had Mike found it after the disappearance of the Bell and Thistle? Or was this something he'd collected before, noticing our own pattern of disappearances? The Anjikuni tale wasn't exactly like the Bell and Thistle. The Inuit village had been left behind and only its people had vanished. But there were parallels. The proximity to bodies of water – Anjikuni beside a lake and Doyle surrounded by springs. Stories of dark spirits in the woods.

The blue lights in the sky implied UFOs. Stories of alien abductions and fairy abductions contained striking similarities, right down to the probing, tall figures, and weird lights. And stories of UFOs abounded in the Doyle region. We'd always assumed the tales were due to the saucer-shaped clouds that appeared over the mountains. What if there was more to it than that? What if the UFO abductions really were fairy abductions?

What if all of Doyle was doomed to disappear?

My scalp prickled, and I licked my lips. I couldn't discount the coincidences anymore. Mike's interest in the Bell and Thistle, his rare books on the occult, and now this article, filed within easy reach beside a folder on the Historical Association.

Mike had known. Or he'd suspected.

And Mike had died.

I shook my head. Everything we knew about our enemy told us she didn't act directly. She worked through influence. But the doctor had been suspiciously quick on the scene when I'd found Mike.

My stomach growled, and I checked my cell phone. It was eight o'clock.

Stunned, I stared, shook the phone. It blinked, unaffected and unbothered. Eight o'clock? At night? The day had passed since I'd been in here. How was it possible…?

I sucked in a breath.

I'd lost time.

No. No! I jerked to my feet. There was nothing alien or fairy about me getting lost in research. I was paranoid and tired, but I was not crazy.

I had to get out of here.

I unlatched the door, and the bookcase swung backward. Movements jerky, I walked into the library and closed the case behind me and fumbled for the light switch. The chandelier flicked on.

Something flickered in the corner of my vision, and I whipped my head toward the movement.

The turkey vulture perched atop the central, arched window. The bird's wrinkled, fleshy neck blended into the burgundy walls, making it appear decapitated. Ivy rustled against the glass.

I drew away, wanting to run.

But I couldn't. Not from my calling. The vulture was a messenger. A really ugly and creepy messenger, but it was a helping spirit.

"You again," I said, my voice flat. Feet leaden, I forced myself to approach the windows. "Please," I said. "No more people I care about. Just tell me what—"

Outside, Alba shouted something unintelligible. But she'd never been particularly intelligible, even on her good days.

I peered through a wide gap in the ivy. I couldn't see Alba, only her two-story house, its gabled roof silhouetted against the darkening sky. Lights streamed from the first floor windows, illuminating the home's peeling paint, dilapidated condition.

A woman shrieked. The sound cut off abruptly.

Silence rippled outward from her house.

Shocked, I took a step backward.

The quiet pressed in on me, a dull, thick, oppression.

I bent toward the glass.

Alba burst through her second floor window.

I felt, rather than heard, the thud of her body striking the ground, and I screamed.

CHAPTER 22

For a moment, I stood frozen at the window. And then I was running. Out the front door, down the steps, slamming through the gate, racing down the sidewalk.

A woman in shorts and a faded blue t-shirt stood amidst the weeds in Alba's garden, her hands covering her mouth.

"Carol!" Heart thundering in my chest, I raced into Alba's yard, dried weeds clawing my bare legs. The woman was one of Mike's neighbors, a reader of women's fiction and nineteenth-century gothics.

Married and middle-aged and soft around the middle, she turned toward me, her graying hair windblown. "Oh, my God. I was on the sidewalk. I saw her jump. She's killed herself!"

A chord sounded within me, faint and out of key. "Then she's—"

"Dead."

I saw Alba now, on her back, arms outstretched. Her dead eyes gazed at the stars emerging in the darkening sky. Her tank top twisted sideways, exposing her bra. Pity slowed my heartbeat, tightened my throat.

Hand shaking, I pulled my cell phone from the pockets of my linen shorts.

"I've already called," Carol said. "I can't..." She gulped. "I knew she was crazy, but I never imagined..."

A black-and-white SUV pulled up to the sidewalk. A deputy I didn't know stepped from the car and strode up the overgrown walk.

"I saw it all," Carol gabbled at him. "She jumped out that window." She pointed to the broken teeth of glass. "I came to see if I could help, but she was dead. And then Lenore arrived."

The grizzled sheriff's deputy knelt, pressing two fingers to Alba's neck. He shook his head and looked up at me. "Did you see anything?"

And for a moment, I wanted to deny it, stay out of it. I knew what would come next – this was the third body I'd found. I struggled for the right words. "I was in the house next door." I pointed to Mike's Victorian. "I heard shouting and came to the window. And then there was a silence – I don't know how long, maybe a minute or two. And then..." I motioned to Alba's broken body.

"What time was this?" he asked, rising.

"I called straight away," Carol said, checking her cell phone. "Eight-oh-six."

"She didn't kill herself," I said.

They stared at me.

I turned to Carol. "Don't you remember? She was shouting, as if she was arguing with someone—"

"I didn't hear anyone else." Carol darted a nervous look to the deputy.

"And then she screamed," I said, "and then everything was quiet. And then, a minute or two later, she came flying out that window. Remember?"

She scratched her fleshy cheek. "I don't... It all happened so fast." She turned to the deputy. "Honestly, I was trying to ignore the yelling. Alba's always shouting."

I stared at Alba, at the odd turn of her neck. "Her neck's broken, isn't it?"

"Wouldn't surprise me after a fall," the deputy said.

"But that man – Heath Van Oss – his neck was broken too, and..." I swayed, horrified. Mike. Mike's head had been at an odd angle. So the same person had murdered them all. But of course she had.

"Is everything all right?" a woman called from the sidewalk.

We turned.

Doctor Toeller rested one hand on Alba's gate and held a black doctor's bag in the other.

"Toeller!" Jayce stepped aside for a mother pushing a stroller. "What was she doing there?" Behind Main Street's false fronts, the sun glittered off the mountain peaks, still covered in snow. American flags fluttered from the wood and stone buildings. An electric saw whirred, and the thud of hammers echoed down the street.

"What do you think?" I asked bitterly.

"But what did she say?" Jayce asked.

"She said she was making a house call on Steve Woodley's aunt." I tugged on my purse strap, chafing my bare shoulder. Our footsteps clunked hollowly on the wooden walkway.

Jayce shook her head. Her hair cascaded over the shoulders of her short-sleeved, blue Henley. Her tanned legs moved smoothly beneath her matching blue shorts. "So she was right on the scene after Alba and Mike died."

"That's not the only coincidence. Alba's neck looked broken, and I realize now so did Mike's."

"Did you tell anyone?"

"I told the sheriff. She thought I was as crazy as Alba."

"Are you sure her neck was broken?" Jayce asked.

An aproned business owner set a dog bowl filled with water outside her open, blue-painted door.

"Of course not," I said, miserable. "It's not like I'm an expert, but it was definitely at an unnatural angle. So was Mike's."

"I thought he died from a blow to his head?"

The construction sounds grew louder. A breeze stirred my cream-colored tunic dress.

"I did too," I said. "But it's not like anyone's given me autopsy results. I don't know if there's even been an autopsy yet. Connor told me it could take weeks."

"I'm surprised the police didn't haul you into the station."

"Thank God Carol saw Alba's fall. She was able to confirm I ran out of Mike's house afterward." Connor hadn't been happy to find me there. Thin-lipped, he'd arrived later with Sheriff McCourt and hadn't said a word to me. It shouldn't have bothered me. But it did.

I scanned the street now, looking for him in vain.

"Then what happened?" she asked.

"More police. Steve Woodley turned up. Gretel–"

"Gretel? What was she doing there?"

"She said she was going for a walk and saw the police lights by Mike's house."

Jayce snorted. "Sure she was."

We came to a halt in front of Jayce's coffee shop. Brown paper covered the inside of the windows. The red-painted door stood open, and I smelled freshly-cut wood. Men's voices shouted over the roar of the saw and bang of the hammers.

Jayce frowned. "I really need to be in there today. Are you going to be all right?"

"Yeah."

"What are you going to do?"

"Talk to my friend at the hotel where Van Oss was killed. Maybe she saw something."

Jayce looked like she was going to object, then she smiled. "You know what you're doing. Call if you need any help."

"Thanks." I continued down the sidewalk, the morning air cool on my legs. Jayce's faith in me was touching, but I didn't know what I was doing. I only knew I had to do it.

The iron door coverings were hooked open against the hotel's painted, stone wall, and the wooden doors stood open. I walked beneath the American flag bunting and to the reception desk.

To my relief, Erica stood behind the window again. But this time when she looked up, her brown eyes were somber.

"Hi, Lenore." Beneath her tan, her slim face looked sickly.

"Erica, are you all right?"

She raked her hand through her caramel-colored hair. "Yeah. Sorry. It's the end of a long shift. How can I help you?" she asked formally.

I hesitated. "Were you working the night Mr. Van Oss was killed?" I'd assumed he'd been killed at night, but for all I knew, it could have been the morning.

She glanced past me, making sure the blue-carpeted reception area was clear. "I must have been the last person to see him alive. I gave him his key. I feel terrible."

"Because you gave him his key?"

"Because I thought he was such a jerk, and now he's dead."

"Jerk? What did he do?"

"He treated the staff like they were his feudal serfs," she said. "A real attitude. I hope that isn't what got him killed."

"You don't think one of the staff did it?"

"No, of course not." She shook her head. "I don't know what to think."

"What time did he come in that night? Do you remember? Was he alone?"

"Around nine, I think, and yes, he was alone. Why?"

"I think the same person who killed Van Oss also killed Mike," I said, feeling reckless. A real detective would have kept her theories to herself. But I wasn't a detective, and I didn't care. The more people who knew what I thought, the better – the safer? – I was.

Erica's eyes widened, and she sucked in her breath. "I thought that was an accident. Why would someone want to kill Mike?"

"Mike owned some valuable books. Van Oss was a rare bookdealer."

Her mouth slackened. "Rare? And you think...? Do the police know?"

"I've told them everything, but I don't think they're taking me seriously. I admit, it's a wild story for Doyle." I paused at that. Actually, it was a pretty boring story for Doyle. "But now Alba's dead, and it looked like her neck was broken–"

"Hold it." She braced her elbows on the counter. "You saw Alba?"

"I saw her fall. I think she was killed too. I was next door, at Mike's house. I heard her scream. And then everything went quiet. A few minutes later, she came flying out the window. I ran out of the house, but by the time I'd got there, it was too late, she was already dead."

"And you think someone... What? Threw her out the window?"

"I think someone broke her neck and then tossed her from the second floor to make it look like a suicide." The fall alone might not have killed her. She'd landed on soft ground.

"She was here, at the hotel, that night," Erica whispered.

A couple walked down the carpeted steps, their suitcases banging against the wall.

"Just a sec," she said.

I stood aside and tried not to dance an impatient jig while the couple checked out, asked about nearby wineries, gushed an ode to the beauties of Doyle. Finally, they left, their suitcases bumping out the open front doors.

"Sorry about that," Erica said in a low voice. "What were we saying?"

"Alba."

"Right. She was here. She followed some tourists inside, haranguing them about Britney Spears and government conspiracies and evil corporations. I tried to get her out, but instead of leaving, she went into the dining room." She made a face, as if she'd smelled something bad. "Fortunately, we'd finished with dinner, and no customers were inside for her to harass. I thought I'd have to call the police to remove her, but suddenly she just… left."

"Was that before or after Van Oss returned?"

Her brow furrowed. "It must have been after. The dining room closes at nine, but you know how it is. People come in at eight-thirty, and then they don't leave until nine-thirty or ten. It drives the wait staff nuts."

"And the dining room was empty?"

"Yeah, I remember how relieved I felt about that. The doors were open. The owner insists on always keeping them open, something to do with the fire code. But I'd put out the brass stand with the CLOSED sign and remember there was a couple still inside, eating dessert." She angled her head toward the door. "So it had to be at least nine-thirty when Alba came in."

"Do you remember anyone else? Anything unusual?"

"No. But…" She glanced around the empty reception area. "The police asked me the same questions. They kept asking about the period between nine and eleven p.m. That must be when they think he died."

"Did Van Oss say anything to you when you gave him his key?"

"No. Oh, wait. Yeah, he asked what time we locked the back door." She looked past my left shoulder.

Involuntarily, I tracked her gaze. On one side of the stairwell was a short hallway with an EXIT sign above it.

"Locked?" I asked.

"We lock that door at ten. Only people with a room key can get in through there after that time. It's a security thing."

"What did Van Oss say when you told him?"

"He nodded and said something like, 'That's okay then.' And then he went upstairs."

I puzzled over that. It sounded as if Van Oss had been expecting someone – someone who preferred coming in through the rear door. But even if they had, they still risked being seen by someone at the reception desk as they made their way around the corner to the stairs. It wasn't a huge risk though. Reception was behind a wall. Unless Erica had been standing at the window and looking out, she might not have noticed anyone. And she'd been distracted in the dining room with Alba. My stomach turned. But if Alba had seen someone…

"Did you see anyone come in that way?" I asked, pointing to the rear entrance.

She shook her head. "Nope."

"Do you have security footage of the back door?"

She made a face. "No, and none in the parking lot either. The cops asked the same thing."

"Asked what?" Connor said from behind me.

I turned, longing, embarrassment, and annoyance jumbling inside me.

He stood bareheaded in his deputy's uniform, his handsome face creased with tension.

Erica brightened. "Hi, Connor! You guys asked if we had security footage of the back door."

His brows lowered dangerously. "And why would you need security footage, Lenore?"

"I think the person who killed Heath Van Oss came in that way." I couldn't lie to Connor. "That Van Oss was expecting a guest, someone who came in between nine and ten p.m. the night he died. He did die in the night and not the morning, didn't he?"

His olive skin darkened. "Mind if I have a word?" He jerked his chin toward the front door.

I followed him outside, the sidewalk cool beneath my thin sandals.

"What are you doing?" His voice was low, intense, critical.

"Alba's neck was broken. And I think Mike's was too. And Van Oss was obviously—"

"Lenore, leave it."

"The three murders are linked," I said.

A pulse beat in his jaw. "Listen to me. Leave it."

Outraged, I stared, the pieces clicking into place. "You already know they're connected. You see it too."

The sounds of construction, cars, passersby were dull and sharp at the same time.

"And if you keep this up, you're going to be the next body found with a broken neck. Leave. It." He turned and strode down the street.

Nauseated, I stood frozen on the sidewalk, unsure if I'd just received a warning or a threat.

CHAPTER 23

Pensive, I walked down Main Street. I needed to start crossing suspects off my list. I needed alibis.

As if in answer to my wish, Steve Woodley popped out of the yarn store across the street. A tiny woman with white hair and wearing an old-fashioned floral print dress leaned on his arm.

I waited for a ghost carriage to pass, its wheels rattling, then I jogged across the road. "Mr. Woodley! Steve!"

He halted, looked up, and smiled. "Lenore. How are you? You remember my aunt Ethel?" In his free hand, he carried a cloth bag filled with pale blue yarn. In spite of the morning warmth, he wore a pressed, blue suit.

"Of course," I said. "Hello Mrs. Woodley." The woman had to be close to a hundred, but she stood straight, and her wrinkled skin had a soft, pink glow.

Her black eyes twinkled maliciously. "Ah, one of the magical Bonheim sisters. I hear you've had quite a time of it lately."

My muscles twitched. "Magical?"

"All triplets are magical." Steve laughed. "Isn't that what you always say, Ethel?"

"I'm part Indian, you know," she said.

Steve rolled his eyes. "It's Native American, you know that."

"I'll call myself what I want." She stepped closer to me, and I smelled peppermint and lavender. "You've been finding bodies. It's happening again, just like with your other sisters. It's no accident, you know." She lowered her voice. "She always knows."

I didn't know where to look. Was she another Alba? Mad enough to see the truth behind the fairy spell?

Steve patted her gnarled hand. "Perhaps we should get you home."

"But I want to hear about the murders." She drew closer to me. "So exciting. Did you see Alba fall? Terrible woman. I'm only surprised no one threw her out a window sooner."

"Poor Alba wasn't murdered," Steve said, "you know that. She killed herself."

"Did the police tell you anything?" I asked him. "I saw you there afterwards."

"My aunt sent me outside to see what was going on." He rolled his eyes, careful to turn his head so she wouldn't see.

"How else was I going to find out?" she snapped.

"So you were with your aunt that night?" I asked and looked to his ancient aunt. "I didn't realize you lived near Alba."

"On the same street," she said.

"I was the one who called Doctor Toeller," he said. "Ethel was feeling poorly."

"Nonsense," she said. "I was fit as a fiddle. You were the one feeling poorly, all twitchy and irritable."

"I was worried about you," he said. "You're the only relative I have left. I'd like to keep you around."

"All that poking and prodding," she said. "And what did the doctor tell you afterward? I'm fine."

He gave me a put-upon look. "My aunt will live forever."

"Doctor's exams are never much fun," I said to her, sympathizing.

"He wouldn't know," she said. "He was watching TV while I was subjected to all manner of indignities."

"You asked me to leave the room," he reminded her.

"Steve," I said, "were you near the Historical Hotel on Friday night?"

His silvery brows rose. "Friday night?"

"Between nine and eleven."

"No, I was visiting my aunt."

"We watched my program together." She pouted. "We watch it every Friday night. But I fell asleep and missed it."

"It's all right," he said. "I recorded it."

"Recorded?" She sniffed. "That doesn't seem right. Now you tell your sisters not to muck about in things they don't understand. We have a good thing here in Doyle. I won't stand for them ruining it."

Steve colored. "Perhaps I should get you home. Good day, Lenore."

Wondering, I watched them amble down the plank sidewalk. Was I going crazy? Had Steve's aunt…?

No. I had to stop listening to crazy people and interrogate someone whose mind was fully functioning. Dreading what I was about to do, I pulled my cell phone from my purse and called Peter.

"Lenore?" he asked. "What do you want now? Because I'm not going back to that bookstore. When I said I quit, I meant it."

"I know," I said. "But something's going on, and it has to do with your uncle. I'd like to talk to you and Gretel again."

He didn't respond.

"Please," I said.

There was a long pause.

I thought I heard murmuring in the background.

"We're at Alchemy," he said, "finishing breakfast."

"I'll be right there," I said and hung up.

Turning around, I strode down the street and crossed the road. Past the low stone bridge, the shops thinned out, giving way on one side to homes and barns.

Peter and Gretel sat at a table on the restaurant's sidewalk patio. I opened the metal gate and walked inside.

Gretel's mouth pinched, her expression sullen. They were both in casual wear – tank tops and slouchy shorts that showed off their tans. The remains of their breakfasts lay on white plates before them. Crumbs were scattered across the black tablecloth. Tall champagne glasses, half-filled with mimosas sat on the table.

"You again," Gretel said. Her loose tank hung from her slim shoulders and skimmed her breasts.

"I think Mike was murdered for something he had or he knew," I said. "That bookdealer, Van Oss, was involved in it, and so he was killed too."

Gretel's mouth fell open. "That's... that's ridiculous."

"And I don't believe it was a coincidence that Mike's neighbor, Alba, is dead either." I pulled out a metal chair. Its legs scraped against the rough pavement. Tucking my tunic dress beneath me, I sat. "Living next door to him, she may have seen something."

"Wait." Peter shook his shaggy blond head. "Mike died in his bookstore. Van Oss died in his hotel. Alba may have lived next door to Mike, but Mike and Van Oss didn't die anywhere near her. She couldn't have seen anything."

"Alba was at the hotel right before Van Oss died," I said. "She may have inadvertently helped his killer. She made a scene, diverting everyone from the stairs leading up to the rooms. Everyone was looking at Alba. Maybe she was looking at the killer."

"Why?" Gretel stabbed a piece of poached egg and popped it in her mouth. "Why kill Mike or this Van Whatever?"

I steeled myself. "Mike may have owned a book worth over a million dollars."

Gretel's tongue darted out, moistening her lips. "A million?" Contemplative, she sipped her mimosa.

"Did Van Oss approach you?" I asked.

Peter nodded. "He said he'd lent Mike a book of American folktales to appraise before he died and asked us to watch for it. He said there'd be a reward."

My brow furrowed. "Folktales?" Those again? I thought he'd lied about the book as an excuse to hang around and get his hands on the William Blake. But why send Peter and Gretel on a wild goose chase for a book of folktales? He could have just asked for the Blake. They wouldn't have known its potential value. Hell, I wouldn't have known its value if someone hadn't told me.

"He said it wasn't intrinsically valuable," Peter said. "A college professor on the east coast needed it for his research."

"Did he tell you the professor's name?"

Peter's boyish face twisted. "Are you kidding? He must have figured we'd try to sell the professor the book ourselves."

And they would have.

"So we wouldn't have killed him," Gretel said, triumphant. "There would be no way for us to get paid."

"Does that mean you found the book?" I asked.

They glanced at each other.

An SUV crawled past.

"No," Peter said. "We were looking for it when you ran into us at Mike's."

"Did you notice anything odd at Alba's place that day?" I asked.

"Why would we?" Gretel asked sharply. "We didn't have anything to do with her death."

"But you were nearby after she fell," I said. "And you must have walked past the house earlier."

A waitress in a short, black apron approached. "Can I get you anything?"

I shook my head. "No thanks."

"I'll have another mimosa." Gretel tossed back the remains of her glass and handed it to the waitress.

"Certainly," the waitress said. "And for you, sir?"

Impatient, I squirmed in my seat.

"I'm fine," Peter said, studying me.

The waitress disappeared into the restaurant.

"Alba was in her garden when we left the house," he said. "She shouted at us, called us names. We ignored her and walked on."

"Why did you return?" I asked Gretel.

Her gaze darted sideways, across the narrow patio. "Went for a walk, like I told you."

Liar. "And did you see or hear anything?"

"I heard Alba shouting," she said. "So I turned around and walked up a different street. I didn't want her to cuss me out again. Later, I heard sirens. It sounded like they were near Mike's place, so I walked back."

"What about you?" I asked Peter.

He shifted in the black, metal chair. "What about me?" Peter crossed his arms over his t-shirt.

"Where were you when Gretel was out for a walk?"

"Home," he said shortly. "Alone, cooking dinner. We had a stir fry."

"And Friday night?"

He blinked, and his blue eyes widened. "Friday night?"

"Between nine and eleven p.m."

They looked a question at each other.

"We were home," Peter said. "The both of us. Watching TV, I guess."

"You guess?" I asked.

His mouth pursed. "It's not something we calendar."

"We were at home together," Gretel said. "Why? Is that when that other guy died?"

I nodded.

"So we have an alibi," she said. "Happy?"

"Do you have any idea why someone would have wanted to kill them?"

One corner of her mouth quirked upward. "Aside from a million-dollar book? No."

"Well, thanks." I rose from my chair.

Peter looked up at me, his head cocked. "You think Van Oss was lying to us about the value of that folktale book?"

"I think he was lying about something." I left, deep in thought, and narrowly avoided walking through the ghost of a miner.

I'd been on the wrong track. The Blake book might be valuable, but the folktale book was worth something to someone too. I needed to find it.

My phone rang, and I exhumed it from my purse.

"Hi, Lenore." Karin sounded as if she were speaking from underwater, and I had to strain to understand her. "Any news?"

"Lots, but I'm having trouble making sense of it." I pressed a hand to my other ear to block out the street noise.

"I know it's early, but I'm starving. How do you feel about brunch?"

I wasn't hungry, but I did want to see my sisters. "Sure."

"Great. Jayce said as long as there are mimosas involved, she's in."

"Um..." I glanced over my shoulder at the restaurant. On the front patio, the waitress brought Gretel a mimosa. "Please tell me she hasn't picked Alchemy."

"I was thinking of a place in Angels Camp. Lux. I just feel we need to get out of Doyle to discuss things."

My shoulders relaxed. "Good idea."

She blew out her breath. "Great. I'll pick you up. Where are you?"

"I'm on Main Street, headed toward Ground."

"Perfect. See you there." She hung up.

I met Jayce, a dusting of sawdust in her brown hair, in front of her coffee shop. Karin pulled up in her red, Ford Fusion.

I climbed in, and we descended the mountain highway. The pine woods turned to aspen and scrubby oak on red earth cliffs. Jayce kept up a running lament on the perils of permitting and contractors, until we passed the sign for Arcadia Township. She sagged in the front passenger seat. "Are we paranoid, thinking we can't speak freely in Doyle?"

"I don't know," I said. "Steve Woodley's aunt said something strange to me today."

"What?"

"She said she knows everything, hinted we were witches, and said we should leave well enough alone. She reminded me of Alba."

"I've met his aunt." Karin glanced in the rear-view mirror at me. "She wanted me to write her a new will. In the end, I couldn't. I told Steve it didn't seem like she was in sound mind. Fortunately, they'd put together a medical power of attorney for her years ago, so he can take care of her."

"She was sure rambling today," I said. "I wasn't sure what to make of it."

"You're thinking maybe there's some truth in her crazy," Jayce said. "That she was talking about the doctor?"

"I guess I did," I said.

"It's all about sight, isn't it?" Karin slowed behind a lumber truck. "We can see what's happening around us because we're magic. People like Alba and Ethel see things differently too. Now I wonder if some of the things Alba said before were about the unseelie. Maybe that's why she was killed."

"But the doctor's never killed anyone that we know of," I said.

"She killed our mother." Karin's voice choked. "She was probably the midwife at all the births in our family, going back over a century."

"She won't be yours." My jaw set. But my faux-determination couldn't keep the stalking wolf of fear at bay.

"No." A vein pulsed in Karin's jaw. "Nick and I have decided to have the baby in San Francisco."

Over her shoulder, Jayce shot me a worried look.

San Francisco wasn't far enough.

CHAPTER 24

Angels Camp was a mining town, like Doyle. But it had Mark Twain going for it, and his Celebrated Jumping Frog of Calaveras County. We passed giant, green frog statues and antique shops, making our way up the main road to a tiny restaurant with a garden in the rear. Moss grew beneath its paving stones, and water trickled from a Spanish-style fountain on the patio.

We brunched in the lazy summer warmth. Nearby, bees feasted on fat wisteria blossoms trailing from the white-painted trellis.

Karin watched us drink mimosas, but her professed envy seemed a front for her obvious happiness. With a sharp stab I understood she was willing to die for this tiny life inside her. I understood it, but a small part of me felt betrayed.

"Have you turned up anything else while researching Doyle history?" I asked her.

She pushed garden potatoes around her plate with her fork. "Unfortunately, we haven't learned much."

Jayce sipped her mimosa. "What did you learn?"

"Doyle's reputation for healing waters grew so large in the early twentieth century that the town almost became a spa."

"What happened?" I asked.

"It started with Prohibition," Karin said. "The Bell and Thistle had been incorporated at that point into Arcadia Township. It couldn't make beer anymore – at least not legally – and the owner began to make the pub over into a health spa."

"You're kidding." Jayce leaned back in her chair, shifting the cushions.

"He'd lined up investors and everything," Karin said. "Then some prominent Doyle citizens got together and managed to shift the boundaries. You already know this, but that's when they made a little island of Doyle around the Bell and Thistle. I guess the Doyle police weren't as strict as those in Arcadia, and the pub continued on as a restaurant." She put the last word in air quotes.

"You mean a speakeasy," I said.

"Exactly." Karin swished her auburn hair behind her shoulders.

"Was the doctor one of these prominent citizens?" I asked.

"There's no record of Doctor Toeller being involved," Karin said. "But Nick and I are certain she's changed her name over the years. She would have had to, don't you think? At any rate, at the same time, there were a series of murders near the wellhouse. It got a reputation for being haunted. The town closed it to the public, and stopped up the tap. With the two most accessible sources of healing waters shuttered, the movement to make Doyle into a resort died."

"Wait," I said, leaning forward. "Movement? I thought it was just the owner of the Bell and Thistle who wanted to do it?"

Karin shook her head. "No, there was a committee and everything."

"Maybe it's not about boundaries." I bounced my foot, my legs restless. If I was right, this was very bad.

"What do you mean?" Jayce asked.

"Maybe Toeller didn't help shift the boundaries to keep the Bell and Thistle in Doyle for her magical purposes," I said, my insides shriveling. "Maybe she shifted it to keep it and Doyle from becoming overrun as a resort." If this was true, it wouldn't matter where Karin had her baby.

"You think she didn't want to share the water?" Karin asked. "It might track. There are stories around the world of fairy springs. When they're tampered with, bad things happen to those involved."

"Did bad things happen?" Jayce asked. "To the people pushing for the health spa, I mean?"

"The president of the committee was one of the murder victims at the wellhouse," she said.

My foot stilled. "It's strange. I've never seen ghosts at the wellhouse. You'd think if more than one person was murdered there – how many were killed?"

"Three," Karin said. "The killer was never found."

"How did we not know this?" Jayce asked. "You'd think that would be scandalous enough to make it into a modern tourism brochure."

"But the wellhouse was never developed as a tourist site," Karin said. "At least, not during our lifetime. It's–" Her face distorted.

"Are you all right?" I asked.

"Fine," she said. "I just feel–" She went rigid and fell sideways, crashing to the paving stones in a pile of glass and crockery.

"Karin!" I cried out.

Jayce and I leapt from our chairs and knelt beside her. People at nearby tables murmured, watching, their expressions uncertain.

Face ashen, Jayce lightly slapped Karin's face. "Karin!" She looked at me. "She's breathing."

I fumbled in my purse and grabbed my cell phone. Beneath my tunic, beneath my skin, my heart thundered, painful. I called nine-one-one.

A slender, blond waitress hurried to us. "What's happened? Is she all right?"

"Nine-one-one, what is your emergency?"

"My sister's unconscious," I said. "Please send an ambulance to..." I glanced at the waitress.

She gave me the address, and I repeated it to the dispatcher. "She's pregnant," I said, my voice tight and sharp. "We have a family history of preclampsia."

"Has your sister been diagnosed with it?" she asked.

"I don't... I'm not sure." Whenever I'd asked Karin about the pregnancy, she'd told me everything was fine. And I hadn't pressed, because I'd wanted to hear everything was okay.

The dispatcher was saying something.

"What?" I asked.

"An ambulance is on the way," she said. "Help will be there in ten minutes."

"Thank you," I choked out and hung up. "Ten minutes," I said to Jayce.

Her face tightened. Ten minutes might be too late.

"Lenore," she said in a low voice, "can you...?"

In answer, I took Karin's limp hand and closed my eyes. The other customers probably thought I was praying. In a way I was, asking the Divine to be with me, calling my animal spirits to guide me to wherever she'd gone.

Fleeting images passed before my closed eyes. A little girl with auburn hair in a blue dress. The sun behind redwood branches, swaying in a breeze. A rabbit wriggling into a hole in the earth.

Karin, where are you?

And then Karin and I were standing in the center of the labyrinth in her yard, the scent of lavender blossoms heady in the balmy summer air. One of the low bushes that made the labyrinth tickled the backs of my knees.

She grasped my hand. "Thank God you're here. What happened? How did I get here?"

"You fainted in the restaurant." I'd found her. She was still alive. Shaking my head, I briefly closed my eyes.

She blanched. "But how... Am I dead?"

"No. You only passed out. You're alive." For now. I rocked in place. I had to keep her safe, keep her well.

A crow settled on the sloped roof of her shingled bungalow and cocked its head.

Uneasy, I turned from it and focused on the labyrinth. "Why did you come here?"

Her brow furrowed. "I don't... I didn't plan it. One minute I was with you in the restaurant, and the next I was here and too afraid..."

"Too afraid to what?" I asked.

"To leave." She glanced down. The center of the labyrinth was a patch of tanbark no more than three feet across. "Labyrinths are portals, you know."

I didn't.

She gulped. "There are rituals surrounding labyrinths. When you enter, you're supposed to say thank you to the lady of the labyrinth, she who can never be unveiled."

Karin was rambling, fear wide in her eyes. I let her talk.

"When you leave a labyrinth," she continued, "you're supposed to back out the last three steps. Is that what I should do? I get the sense that if I stay here, I won't wake up, will I?"

Wings flapped. The crow croaked, harsh and loud.

I glanced at Karin's house. The turkey vulture had joined the crow. The smaller bird hopped, flapping its wings, as if attempting to drive it off.

"I should go." She turned toward the open path.

A sick certainty grasped my throat. "No," I said quickly. "It isn't safe."

"Why?"

"You feel safe here," I said. "So do I. This is your place, your power spot. It's been a power spot for us all. Remember when Jayce was attacked by those crows last winter? She was safe in here. They couldn't get at her." The vision of Karin and the labyrinth turned watery, and I grasped her hand more tightly. "Stay here until I come and get you."

My sister telescoped away from me. A mist formed between us.

"Karin? Karin!" And then I was stumbling backward. My hip struck a round table. Glass shattered. Paramedics surrounded Karin, and a police officer was pulling me away.

"Lenore?" Jayce asked, her green eyes dark with worry.

I shook my head, unable to speak. I didn't know what would happen to Karin now, or if I'd helped or hurt. I hadn't had time to plan. This wasn't the way a shamanic journey was supposed to happen!

"I'm okay," I told the policeman, and he released me.

We watched the paramedics lay our sister on a stretcher, followed them as they wheeled her through the restaurant. The other patrons stared, silent.

"Where are you taking her?" Jayce asked a paramedic.

"Doyle," he said.

"No!" I shouted. Toeller was at Doyle.

"It's the best and closest hospital," the paramedic said. "We're going."

"But—"

Jayce grasped my arm. "She'll be okay," she said fiercely. "We'll meet them there. We'll protect her."

"How?" We had no power there, no right to override the doctors. We couldn't protect her from Toeller.

CHAPTER 25

We paced the blue-carpeted waiting room. An African-American family huddled around a cluster of pale yellow couches and chairs, waiting for news of a loved one.

An old man sat slumped in a wheelchair beside the reception desk. The nurse behind it rose and rolled him through the swinging doors into the emergency room's inner sanctum.

Bloodied ghosts, some clasping their broken limbs, wandered, searching for help. I couldn't meet their gaze. Tonight was for Karin.

Nick strode through the automatic glass doors, his dark hair mussed. Tension lined his face, and his business suit was rumpled. "Lenore, Jayce! How is she?"

Jayce hugged him. "We don't–"

A doctor in blue scrubs walked through the double doors. Spotting us, he nodded and smiled briefly.

"There's the doctor," Jayce said. Toeller had been out of the hospital when they'd brought Karin in, and we prayed she stayed out.

"Ms. Bonheim, Ms. Bonheim," the doctor said to us. "Your sister is resting."

"She's okay?" I motioned to Nick. "Sorry, this is her fiancé, Nick Heathcoat."

The two men shook hands.

The doctor turned to me. "Your sister had an eclamptic seizure."

"But she didn't have any hypertension," Nick said. "We've been watching for it, since preeclampsia runs in her family."

"It's unusual, but some women do have eclampsia without exhibiting hypertension," the doctor said.

"Will she be all right?" Nick clawed his hand through his black hair.

"We're treating her with medication and rest, but the only real way to treat her is to deliver the baby."

I felt the blood drain from my face. We'd counted on having three more months to solve our problem, but an early delivery changed everything. How much time did we have left?

"But she's only six months along," Nick said.

"We'll see how the medication works," the doctor said. "Then we can make a decision."

"Can I see her?" Nick asked.

"We're moving her to a new room now. Give it an hour, and then ask at the desk. They'll tell you where she is."

Nick wrung his hand. "Thank you."

The doctor nodded and vanished through the swinging doors.

"How did it happen?" Nick asked, hoarse. "What happened?"

Jayce shot me a worried look. "We were having brunch—"

"Where?" he asked.

"In Angels Camp," I said.

He took a step back, his face paling. "You weren't in Doyle? But we thought..." He turned away. They'd thought what we'd hoped, that she'd be safe outside Doyle.

"Maybe it's the mountains," he muttered. "Maybe she wasn't far enough."

"I could use some coffee," Jayce said. "Nick, would you come with me?"

"Sure," he said absently.

"Can we get you anything, Lenore?" she asked.

I shook my head, unable to speak through the icy fear flowing between us.

"We'll be back soon," Jayce said.

I watched them leave, then I rose. I walked through the sliding glass doors and outside, into the parking lot. The sun, almost straight above me, warmed my shoulders and glinted off the snow-capped mountains.

Winding through the parked cars, I walked to the end of the lot, where the concrete ended and the forest began. Karin had once found a woman in these woods – an escapee from the unseelie's world. The old woman had died before we'd gotten the chance to ask her how she'd broken free. We'd taken her escape as a sign that the fairy's power was waning. I hoped to hell we were right.

A breeze shifted the tops of the redwoods. Their branches whispered against each other.

I stepped off the macadam and onto the bracken-covered earth. In the shade of the redwoods, the temperature dropped.

Fists clenched, I made my way down the slope, careful on the damp earth and leaves.

I brushed past ferns and coffee berry bushes until I reached a fallen log. Five redwoods loomed around it, forming a sheltered clearing. I listened and heard only the sounds of the woods. A bird twittered. Branches rustled. Far off, water trickled like running footsteps. I bent my head and thought I heard a far-off echo of sobbing.

This would do.

Karin was in danger. I'd gone to Lower World before to find the spiritual cause of infections and pull them from their host. This was no different. Doctor Toeller's curse was an infection in Karin that didn't belong.

I sat on the log. Closing my eyes, I went inward, to my breath, to the beat of blood in my veins.

Sinking deeper, I found my heartbeat. I followed the sound, my own internal drum. I imagined myself walking to the roots of the largest redwood. I dropped alongside the roots, into the earth and an underground cavern.

Crystals in the walls lit the uneven earth and the three passages sloping downward before me.

A man stood in the left-branching passage.

I froze.

Scars crisscrossed his face. His plain, white t-shirt, stretched too tight across his broad chest. The man's jeans sagged around his hips. Light from the crystals glinted eerily off his golden hair. The look he turned on me wrung my heart with memories of loss and missed chances. "Are you willing?" he growled.

"What are you?" I whispered.

Silent, he turned, vanishing down the left-hand passage.

I hesitated. The spirits always met me in Lower, Middle, or Upper Worlds. I'd never encountered anything or anyone in this passage between worlds before. "Willing to do what?" I called after him.

"Lenore." The word was a whispering echo.

Leaden, my legs stumbled forward, pulling me down the left passage. "Who are you?"

But the man had vanished.

His footsteps padded steadily down the corridor.

I stopped resisting and hurried forward. "Wait!"

I followed the sound of his stealthy footsteps down winding passages, going ever and ever deeper.

The air grew stale, warm. "Are you the Rose Rabbit?" My words bounced off the rough stone walls.

I rounded the corner.

The man stood beside an outcropping of stone, so black it appeared burnt. "Tell me who you are," I said. "Are you the Rose Rabbit?"

He ducked down and slithered through a gap in the rocks.

Getting on my hands and knees, I followed, grazing my elbows on the jagged stone.

His bare feet vanished through a gap in the tight tunnel.

The heartbeat that had guided me now thundered in my ears. Blind, I felt my way. The rocks were too close. I'd be stuck here, trapped. But the man had gotten through, and he was twice my size.

Ahead, a faint, watery light turned the passage charcoal. I thought I caught a glimpse of white fur.

Panting, I clawed my way forward. There was always a barrier like this on my journeys – usually through water, occasionally through fire. I always had to pass through one of the four elements to reach Lower World. This passage through earth was no different, even if someone or something had appeared to guide me here.

The light brightened, glittering off the damp rocks. A brilliant, vertical arc of light – the exit – made me wince. I was nearly there.

Something grasped my foot.

I shrieked, banging my head on the rock ceiling.

And then I was being dragged backward. I clawed at the earth. The light dimmed. The man howled my name, a fearful echo.

My fingertips scraped stone. I squirmed, my heartbeat exploding in my chest.

The grip on my ankle tightened, cold and hard as iron chains.

And then I was flying, the cave telescoping, the glowing crystals a blur.

Gasping, I tumbled backwards off the log and landed in ferns. Above me the towering redwood branches framed a blue puzzle-piece of sky.

"Did you really think I wouldn't notice?" Doctor Toeller stood over me, one corner of her mouth slanted upward. Dazzling, a sunbeam haloed her silver-gold cap of hair. A breeze stirred the hem of her ice-blue duster. Light streamed from her alabaster skin. Once again, I glimpsed her true form – pale and feral and glowing with power.

Fear coursed through my body, freezing me in place, hardening my stomach.

She cocked her head. "What did you think you were doing?" The vision faded with her words, and she was the doctor again, her skin merely odd in its perfection. She turned and walked away.

I scrambled to my feet. "Why?" My voice cracked. "Why do you need us?"

She paused and looked over her shoulder at me. "I don't."

"Every seven years, someone disappears. Why? Why take the Bell and Thistle and all the people inside? Is it a sacrifice, like Alba said?"

Her lip curled. "Alba was a foolish old woman." She waved her hand negligently, and a cold wave shuddered through me. "Besides, you'll all die one way or another. What are a few years?"

"A few years?! They're our lives! They mean something!"

"But you're meant to die. It's what makes your world so charming, so interesting. It's fascinating." Her blue eyes glowed. "It's why I became a doctor. To study you, to see all your pain and mortality in their full glory."

"You don't belong here." My voice trembled. I couldn't breathe, my chest constricting.

"You are the ones who don't belong."

I pointed a quivering finger. "Doctor Toeller, I banish you from this plane!"

She burbled with laughter. "You? Mousy little Lenore? Banish me? You barely exist on this plane yourself. And you thought you would invade my home and... do what?"

The wind stilled in the branches. The birds fell silent.

"You thought you'd treat me like one of your Lower World spirits? Rip me from your patient and discard me in lower world? You can't possibly be that arrogant, so I can only assume you're stupider than I gave you credit for. This is my world now. I like what I've created here, and I'm not leaving."

"No." But the word was a whisper, so quiet even I could barely hear it.

The doctor vanished.

Strings cut, my knees buckled and hit the soft earth.

There was a loud crack, and I looked up just in time to get a face full of rain. The sky was sullen gray. Had the fairy caused the downpour for dramatic effect? Could she control the weather too? I'd been stupid – stupid and arrogant – to attack something that powerful.

Something bit into my palm, and I opened my hands. A rough quartz crystal, partially covered in loose earth, lay in one hand. I stared, my mind a dull blank.

She'd pulled me out of the passage. She'd frozen me in place. She'd moved about by magic, appearing in the passage between worlds and vanishing in this one. My power was in my shamanic ability, and she'd easily thwarted me. I choked, nauseated.

Water puddled around my knees. I couldn't beat her. I was done.

CHAPTER 26

Muscles quaking, I pocketed the crystal in my tunic dress and stumbled up the hill, slick from the sudden rain. By the time I reached the hospital parking lot, my hands were muddy, my white dress stained and sodden. I raced the last five-hundred yards to the hospital. Steeling myself against the hospital's melancholy aura, I barreled through the sliding doors and into Connor's broad chest.

"Lenore!" He grasped my bare shoulders, steadying me.

"Connor." I panted. "What are you doing here?"

"Looking for you." His voice was heavy.

My blood ran cold. "Has something happened? Is Karin—"

"She's resting. Where have you been? Your family's out of their minds worrying."

"I was just..." I trailed off. The Emergency Room had grown crowded since I'd left. "I went for a walk to clear my head." And the crystal hadn't been anywhere on that walk. It was as if I'd pulled it from the passage between worlds, but that was impossible. That passage didn't exist in ordinary reality. It was on the astral plane. I couldn't bring real objects from it.

"For five hours?"

"Five? No. I've only been gone..." I glanced at the wall clock and stammered to a halt. It was nearly six o'clock. I grasped the sleeve of his uniform jacket. "Where's Karin?"

"Upstairs. Room four-seventy-two."

If they'd moved her, then she must be stable.

"Lenore," he said gently. "You can't run off on your own every time things get rough. It only makes it worse."

I grimaced. "I had no choice." There was no sense hiding it from him. Better he knew now who I was. Better we end things before they began. "I was on a shamanic journey. I thought I might be able to find whatever was hurting Karin. I can't help her any other way."

"Why didn't you tell anyone where you were going?"

"There was no time," I said.

"And those times you explored Mike's alone, knowing there was a killer on the loose? I talked to Mr. Pivens. He told me you'd promised not to go into that house by yourself."

My gaze darted to the sliding glass doors. "That wasn't…" I floundered before his obvious disappointment. Had I messed up that badly?

"Look, I can't imagine what it must have been like growing up a triplet, the need to be alone. But this was bad timing. Your family loves and needs you."

But he didn't love me, and a stone weighted my heart. "I was trying to save her," I said in a low voice. "That's why I journeyed, and that's why I had to be alone."

"I get it. Shamans are healers, and a shamanic journey goes inward," he said. "You needed privacy and quiet. But Jayce was so out of her mind with worry she called me for help finding you."

I gaped, stunned. Jayce had called Connor? And he hadn't just read up on shamanism. He'd studied it. "I'm sorry," I muttered.

"Tell that to Jayce and Nick. They had enough on their plates without having to worry about you."

I flinched. "There wasn't anything else I could do."

"You could ask for help," he said.

"No one could have helped."

"You should have asked." He stood for a moment, silent, as if waiting for me to respond. When I didn't, he strode through the sliding doors.

I stood for a moment, wanting to follow him, wanting to argue, to convince him. But wretchedness immobilized me, unable to go after him and unable to bear the sight of his departing back.

I'd always been a lone wolf. It wasn't such a bad thing, was it? And how was I to know Toeller would interfere with my journey and keep me away so long?

My mouth set in annoyance. Besides, Connor shouldn't try to change me.

Turning on my heel, I strode toward the doors that led from the emergency waiting room and to the main part of the hospital.

Five hours. Jayce would be worried and furious. And Karin…

I pushed through the swinging doors and hurried along a corridor. Through its windows, the leaves of semi-tropical plants danced beneath the rain. A ghost who'd lost her baby, her gown stained red, turned and stared bitterly at me.

I wasn't avoiding people. I was doing what I had to. I speed-walked down the tiled hallway to the elevators, pressed the up button. So I spent a lot of time alone. I worked in a bookstore, my job was to read and know the books. That wasn't a team activity. Something had to be done alone, like helping Mike cross over.

My heartbeat slowed.

Mike.

When was the last time I'd even tried to call his spirit? Had I been avoiding him too?

I reached into my sodden pocket and gripped the crystal. No. It didn't matter. Once Mike's murder was solved, he'd be at peace and could cross over. I wasn't being a reckless loner. I wasn't avoiding people I loved. I was taking action.

The elevator doors slid open, and I stepped inside, pressed four. The doors began to shut. A feminine hand inserted itself between them, and they slid open. The FBI agent stepped into the elevator.

"We meet again, Ms. Bonheim." Her ebony hair was in a neat bun. She unbuttoned the jacket of her navy business suit and glanced at the button panel. "I see you got my floor."

I swallowed and said nothing.

"You look like a drowned rat who's just seen a ghost," Agent Manaj said, one corner of her mouth curling upward. "Though as a poet I don't suppose you approve of mixing metaphors."

"Mix away."

"So have you?" She turned to face the closed doors.

"Have I what?"

"Seen any ghosts lately?"

I tried to sneer, but shivering in my sopping, muddy dress, I didn't quite pull it off. "Why would I?"

"Because you and your sisters are witches."

My heart thumped, fast and uneven. "I didn't think the FBI believed in the supernatural."

"The FBI is filled with all kinds of people. What do you believe in?"

"My family."

The elevator shuddered to a halt. The agent stepped aside, and I hurried past her into the carpeted hallway.

She fell in beside me, taking one long stride to every two of mine.

I pushed through a swinging door into a tiled corridor. The walls were painted a soft sand.

"I get the feeling you don't want to talk to me," she said wryly.

"If I had anything to share that might help, I would."

"Are you sure of that?"

I didn't know how to respond, so I walked on. But I hesitated at an intersection to scan the small signs on the walls.

"Four-seventy-two is that way." Manaj pointed down a corridor.

Why did she know where my sister was? "Thanks. I'm not sure Karin is up for questioning."

Her brown eyes glinted. "I'm not here for your sister."

My mouth went dry. Was she here for me? "Then what are you here for?"

"FBI business."

"Good luck then." I turned and walked away.

"What are you so afraid of, Ms. Bonheim?" she called after me.

"Nothing," I said.

"Maybe you should be."

I kept walking.

Are you willing? A masculine voice echoed in my head, and my footsteps slowed.

I scanned the empty corridor.

Willing to do what?

A heavy, gray curtain had been pulled across Karin's door. Soft voices drifted from the other side.

I rapped on the door frame and drew aside the curtain.

Jayce and Nick stood beside a hospital bed. Karin lay pale beneath the covers, her eyes shut. Tubes fed into her arm.

"Lenore!" Jayce hurried around the bed and hugged me fiercely. "Where the hell have you been? You're soaking wet!" She pulled away from me, a new, damp stain across the front of her blue Henley thanks to me.

"Sorry," I muttered. "How is she?"

"She's sleeping," Jayce said.

"Thank God."

She dragged me from the room. "Where were you?" Fear, anger and relief mingled in her eyes. "Why didn't you call?"

"I went on a journey."

"For five hours?!"

A nurse walked past and shot us a quelling look.

"I tried to find the unseelie's world," I said in a low voice. "Toeller caught me."

My sister swore softly. "Why didn't you tell me? I could have watched over you! Protected you!"

"Shamanic journeys aren't your thing."

"And traveling to fairyland isn't yours." She scrubbed a hand across her forehead. "What the hell, Lenore! You just took off. We didn't know where you'd gone or why you'd left, and anything could have happened to Karin. It's the sort of stupid, reckless stunt I would pull. What's gotten into you?"

"I had to do something."

"And so you took off and left us without telling anyone where you were going?"

"I didn't think it was going to take five hours."

"You ran."

"What does that mean?" I folded my arms. My wet tunic dress had grown cold and sticky against my skin.

"Instead of staying with Nick and I, or even telling us what you were thinking, you ran to Lower World. This is so typical!"

Stricken, I stared at my sister. "What are you talking about?"

She blew out her breath. "Never mind. I didn't mean anything by it."

"I think you did."

"Look, I get that books and Lower World are your coping mechanisms. Just... Next time give us a heads up, okay?" She turned and walked into the hospital room.

I stood in the hallway and stared after her.

A nurse walked past, pushing a food cart. She stopped in front of Karin's open door and glanced at her clipboard, then continued on.

Lower World was my coping mechanism? Well, of course it was. That was the whole point of the shamanic journey – coping, healing, figuring things out. And books weren't a coping mechanism, they were fun, relaxing. But...

Don't do this, Lenore.

You could ask for help.

Books and lower world are your coping mechanisms...

Are you willing? Clear and strong, the masculine voice cut across my internal chatter.

I swayed, bracing my hand on the sand-colored wall. Was it true? Was I using the otherworld of books and shamanism to avoid this one? To avoid... what? Not the people I loved...?

...to avoid thinking about losing them. If I didn't get close, I had nothing to lose.

Are you willing?

"Willing to do what?" I whispered. "To lose?"

No one answered.

I closed my eyes. Was I willing to risk? Willing or not, my sisters were in danger. Our coming loss was real. And if I avoided this fear...

My eyes opened. If I avoided that fear of loss, I would avoid risks that might be worth taking. This wasn't about me not asking for help. It was about my choice to be alone. Was avoiding the risk of getting hurt worth it?

Risks like Connor. Connor, who'd always been there when I needed him. Connor, who understood what I was and didn't laugh or judge. Connor, who was strong and smart and brave and quick to smile. And I knew I shouldn't be thinking of him now, not with my sister in the hospital. There were other things I needed to face, like breaking the curse so Karin could live.

Are you willing? the voice demanded.

I straightened off the wall. To save my sister, I was willing to do anything.

CHAPTER 27

Karin woke up enough to tell us all to go home. Predictably, Nick refused.

But I was shivering in my damp clothing. Giving her a quick kiss on the cheek, I left the hospital and drove home. The rainclouds had broken apart, beams from the setting sun setting the snow-capped mountain peaks on fire.

At my house, I changed into white jeans and a loose, cream-colored knit top. I'd just had my butt kicked on my own territory – the path between worlds. But I was still standing, and what had Doctor Toeller done to me after all? She'd pulled me out of the passage, but aside from a few bruises on my ankle she hadn't hurt me.

I laid the crystal on the work island in our aunt's kitchen and unhooked a bundle of dried sage from the pot rack.

Rules. This crystal's existence in our plane was a violation of those rules. Had the fairy changed the passage somehow, or had I changed? I laid the sage atop the crystal and made a list.

A) She needs sacrifices to stay here – they're taken somewhere and kept alive, b/c some escaped. Fairyland?

B) Hurts through curses – family curse, bad luck curse, eating disease?

C) Helps her favorites – known to gift some people with good luck.

D) Traditional fairy powers – knock down old buildings, change paths in the woods...

E) Crystal removed from passage btwn worlds - how?

I tapped my pencil on the yellow-lined paper. Curses and reverse curses seemed the same sort of power. But the ability to change paths in the woods was something else. So was kidnapping people from this world and taking them into the next. Changing paths could be an illusion, or a spell that confuses people in the woods. Or it could be real, a way of warping the reality in this world. And knocking down walls...

I made a frustrated noise. There had to be some logic to her powers, something that tied them all together. Didn't there? And why did the people of Doyle age differently? Why did our skin look so weirdly perfect? Was that a simple fairy glamour? Or...

I drew in my breath. What if her world was somehow bleeding into ours? A sort of dimensional layer? That would explain the changing paths in the woods that Karin and Nick had experienced. It might even explain the wall collapses – a sudden dimensional shift that weakened walls and foundations.

Could it explain us?

I paced. It might. People who'd been taken to fairy world were said to age differently. If that world was bleeding into this one, it could affect the people who stayed within the boundaries of the bleed. But tourists seemed to come and go with no ill effect. Even Nick seemed normal, and he was spending more and more time in Doyle. Maybe people needed to spend a certain amount of time in Doyle for it to change them.

I sighed. I'd talk it over with Jayce and Karin first. But for now, I had another painful duty to fulfill.

Mike.

Slipping the crystal into my purse, I drove to his Victorian. I hadn't stopped trying to locate his spirit because I'd been busy. I'd been avoiding it because seeing him was too painful.

The porch light automatically flicked on as I walked up the steps. I unlocked the heavy, dark-wood door and walked inside, fumbled for the switch. The chandelier illuminated the high ceilings, the grand staircase winding to the second floor.

The air was thick, expectant. Shaking myself, I flipped the light switch at the top of the steps. I walked down the hallway's worn, burgundy carpet, examining the antique photos of Doyle. Doc Toeller didn't appear in any of them.

I reached for a brass doorknob, cool against my fingertips, and dropped my hand to my side. I'd no right to be upstairs. My inheritance was downstairs, in the secret room. By sneaking up here, was I any better than Peter and Gretel? But they'd come here out of greed. I was here for love.

The purse slid from my shoulder, and I let it thunk to the floor.

"Mike? I'm worried about you. Are you here?"

At the far end of the hall, a brocade curtain stirred. A cool breeze whispered along the back of my neck.

"Mike? It's me, Lenore… You're probably wondering why I'm in your house."

No answer.

I blundered on. "The police are still trying to figure out what happened to you, how you died. But I think you were killed over a book. That man, Heath Van Oss, was looking for it, and he was murdered. I hid some valuable books of yours in a safe deposit box, but I'm not sure if they're the books the killer is looking for."

A door clicked open opposite me, and my breath caught. "Mike?"

Lightly, I pressed my hand against the door, opening it wider. A queen-sized bed covered in a simple, beige blanket with hospital corners. A brass clothing rack with a neatly pressed pair of khaki trousers folded over it and a leather belt. An antique bureau with elaborate scrollwork. A tarnished mirror hung on the wall.

Mike's bedroom.

This was the room Gretel had emerged from the other night, when I'd surprised her and Peter. Its closet door stood open, and a shoebox lay on the oriental carpet. I walked to the cardboard box, knelt, and opened the lid.

Men's leather shoes, polished to a high gloss. My chest constricted.

I stood. A movement caught the corner of my eye, and I turned.

The brown bed skirt rustled, a gentle wave rippling toward the head of the bed.

I walked toward it. "Mike?"

Beside the bed was an end table, stacked with books, and a desk lamp.

Smiling, I picked up the top book, The Hardy Boys – The Tower Treasure, still in its full-color, paper cover. It looked like mint condition, and I guessed the book was from the 1930s. My brow furrowed. No, not the thirties – the cover's colors were too soft. Was this a first edition from 1927? I opened the book and inhaled sharply.

This wasn't The Hardy Boys.

Gently, I removed the paper cover, exposing a leather-bound book.

The Folk and Fairy Tales of America, by Ichabod Langley.

"Holy shit." This was the book Van Oss had said he'd been tracking. I glanced up. "Sorry, Mike." He'd sworn like a sailor when in the mood, but it felt wrong to curse in his presence. I thumbed to the title page. First printing, eighteen fifty-five. The publisher was Ticknor and Fields.

I gnawed the inside of my cheek. I knew that publisher. They'd gone out of business around 1890, and they'd typically printed books at the author's expense. But they were well respected – they'd published Twain and Emerson and Hawthorne.

Maybe I had picked up a few things about old books from Mike.

He'd been hiding the book in plain sight, by his bedside. I sank onto the bed and skimmed the chapters. The book had been organized by region. I flipped to the section on the west, and my heart beat double time. The Legend of the Doyle Fairy.

I'd found Doyle.

I began reading and winced. No wonder this book hadn't got much traction. The Brothers Grimm had kept their stories simple, but the prose in Ichabod's tome was impossibly dense. The author had loved his own writing style more than the stories he'd collected. I plodded through the text. Mike had hidden this book. It was important, and it—

I swayed on the bed. It was all there. Everything.

How could I have been so stupid? The key to defeating the fairy was here, but it wasn't unique. I moaned. Stupid, stupid, stupid. I should have done more research. I should have known.

Returning the Hardy Boys cover to the book, I walked into the hallway and slipped it into my purse. Was this book the cause of the murders rather than the Blake? My God, had the doctor killed the men? She'd been on the scene right after I'd found Mike. And she'd been nearby when Alba had died – Alba, who'd seemed to know more about the doctor than was good for her.

I raced down the winding stairs. The doctor had never killed before – not like this. Or had she? Fingers fumbling, I locked the front door and hurried to my Volvo.

Inside the car, doors locked, I dug my cell phone from my purse and called Jayce.

"Karin's still okay," she said without preamble.

"Where are you?"

"I'm at the hospital. I know Karin told us to leave, but I don't trust that doctor, and–"

"Don't go anywhere. Don't leave her alone. I'm coming to you. Is Nick there?"

"Yes, but–"

"I found a book in Mike's house." One-handed, I clicked my seatbelt into place. "The missing book on folktales Van Oss was looking for. The doctor's in it."

"What?!"

"Well, the fairy. It's her name. The key to beating her is her name!"

"Doctor Toeller?"

"No. That can't be her real name, can it?" I asked, giddy. "But... I'll be there in twenty minutes."

"I'll meet you in the parking lot."

"No. Stay with Karin. Or make sure Nick does. I'll see you in twenty." I hung up and started the Volvo, pulled away from the curve.

I drove through Doyle and onto the highway. The pavement was shiny from the earlier rain, and I drove slowly.

An SUV sped behind me, tailgating, its headlights blinding. It passed, too close, too quick on the winding highway.

I adjusted my mirror and braked, giving it more space. Pines flashed past, monochrome in my headlights.

I pounded my palm on the steering wheel. It was so obvious! Everything about our fairy problem had been in the classical literature – the falling walls, the moving trails, the missing persons. How had we missed this?

Another SUV roared up behind me, flooding my car with sulfur-colored light. A double line made a twisted ribbon in the center of the road.

The SUV couldn't pass me here, though it obviously wanted to. But I wasn't about to speed up for it, not on this slick road.

I clenched my jaw. There was a pullout about a mile ahead. "You'll just have to be patient."

The SUV dropped back, and I breathed a small sigh of relief.

Amber light flooded my Volvo's interior. I glanced in my rearview mirror.

The SUV hurtled toward me, no doubt angling to pass.

I tapped my brakes and edged closer to the shoulder. If the idiot was determined to pass, I'd make it easier—

The car slammed into my bumper.

I rocked forward. The rear of the Volvo fishtailed, tires screeching.

The SUV struck me again.

The Volvo pinwheeled, the pines a dizzying, unyielding, unavoidable obstacle. My father had died in a car wreck on the way to visit my mother. My ending would be like his.

The Volvo skidded down a short embankment, and I was spinning again, vertically. My head slammed into something hard, and—

CHAPTER 28

I awoke upside down. Something hard pressed into my shoulder and hips. Uncomprehending, I stared, my only illumination the greenish glow of the dashboard. The airbag hung limp from the center of my steering wheel.

My head and neck felt like they had been beaten between the two jawbones I'd found, and a sharp ache pierced the front of my skull. The back of my arms brushed the soft, unyielding roof of the Volvo.

Unthinking, I reached for the seatbelt release, and I tumbled downward. I landed in an awkward heap, mostly on my shoulders and upper back. In an ungainly somersault, I twisted and sprawled along the Volvo's roof.

Broken glass scraped my hands, and I gasped. The car wasn't just upside down, it was at a sickening, fun house angle. The roof had compressed, breaking the windows, impossibly narrowing any path to escape.

I slithered to the door and grasped the handle, pushed.

It didn't budge.

Maybe I could crawl through a broken window and escape this coffin. The space had been made narrow when the top of the car had crumpled downward, but–

Footsteps sounded outside, the sound of someone sliding, trotting down a slope.

I drew breath to scream for help, then fear arced through my bones, and I clamped my mouth shut. There was something stealthy in those footsteps, crunching across the pine needles.

Someone had intentionally run me off the road. I'd no idea how long I'd been unconscious, but the Volvo's metal ticked and groaned. I imagined I could hear its wheels still spinning above me.

I froze, my heart rabbiting. If the police discovered me in the Volvo, my neck broken, would they chalk it up to an accident?

Connor wouldn't. But he was a patrolman, not a detective, and–

The person tugged on the car handle, the latch clicking.

Gulping down breaths to keep quiet, I pulled my arms and legs inward, crouching like a bug. If only I really could disappear into the other world.

My eyes blinked open. The crystal. I'd brought the crystal back. Did that mean... Had I physically been there, in the passage between worlds? This would make the third time one of us had physically traveled by magic, but it was the first time I'd left this world. The passageway was neither here nor there, but it was somewhere else.

Cowering, helpless, I let my mind run wild. The bruises on my ankle... I rubbed it now. Toeller had grabbed me. I'd assumed she'd seized my physical self in this world, but what if she hadn't?

A flashlight beam shone through the narrow remains of the smashed, driver's side window. Stomach granite hard, I winced at the glare and edged away. Safety glass dug into my knees leaving a trail of fire. The light traveled to the what was left of the other windows, the footsteps moving around the car.

I scooted sideways, avoiding its beam.

Whoever was out there wasn't Toeller. She wouldn't be afraid to call out my name. We knew each other as adversaries.

A stinging bead of sweat dripped into my eye. Gretel or Peter? If either was a killer, I'd put money on Gretel, filled with resentment and a sense of entitlement. But was she capable of snapping the necks of two grown men?

The dashboard light flickered and went out.

Peter could. He'd been nearby when I'd found Mike. He could have easily killed Mike, then walked outside and waited for me to find his body.

But why kill Heath Van Oss? He was looking for a book, most likely on someone else's behalf. Someone who wanted...?

I turned my head, frantic. A bolt of pain shot up my neck. The book. Where was it? And then I saw the Hardy Boys cover, the book lying beside my left foot. Bare foot. I was barefoot. Shaking off that mystery, I grabbed the book of folktales and clutched it to my chest.

Was this what my attacker wanted?

Outside, the flashlight flicked off, bathing me in pitch.

I blinked, trying to regain my night vision, and held my breath.

The person outside tried the other doors. They remained shut fast. What if the person was trying to help me? What if he or she left, assuming the car was empty? What if my silence was destroying my only hope for rescue?

I almost cried out then, but some instinct stopped the noise in my throat. There was something... wrong, about those footsteps, about the rattling of door handles.

Don't think about that. Think about the murders. If the book in my arms was the cause of these murders, why? It wasn't that valuable. The only reason it could be worth killing over was because of the information inside it, information Mike had read...

My head gave another throb. He'd hidden it inside a Hardy Boys cover. He'd known it was valuable. And he'd been studying it.

While I was willing to believe Doc Toeller could make an entire bar full of people disappear, I didn't believe she was the killer. Breaking necks wasn't her style.

The person outside was moving again, the flashlight beam angling inside the windows. Had the top of the roof not crumpled, narrowing the windows, whoever was outside would have had an easier time seeing me. But the angle of the car, the smashed glass, was working in my favor. Lucky me.

I shook my head. Pain rocketed through my skull. Think!

Alba. Alba in her madness had seen through the doctor's facade. Alba had lived next door to Mike. She'd caused a diversion at the hotel the night Van Oss was killed. Had she seen too much that night? While the hotel staff was trying to quiet her, had she seen someone creep up the steps to Van Oss's hotel room? If Alba had seen something, she wouldn't have remained silent. But would anyone have understood what she was talking about, or even listened?

And once again, there had been Toeller, conveniently at the scene of Alba's death. But others had been there as well – Gretel, Steve Woodley. I'd been right there too.

I thought back to Alba's death now. The shouting, the silence, and then...

Outside, the footsteps paused.

I stilled, imagining the person listening, and I gripped the book to my chest more tightly.

Silence.

There'd been a long silence before Alba had gone through the window. The fight had ended before she'd taken that fatal dive. The killer must have broken her neck and then flung her out to make it appear she'd jumped.

And then the pieces fit together, locking into place. I knew who'd done it, and I knew why. And they were outside, and I was helpless.

Running footsteps. Whoever had been outside, was running away.

I was alone.

For the first time in my life, I didn't like it.

My eyes readjusted to the dim light. White smoke drifted lazily above me, from the cavity near the pedals, and my heart jumped. Oh, God, was the car on fire? Was that why the person had run? But I didn't smell smoke or gasoline, and I blinked. Was I imagining the strange mist?

Out, I had to get out. I twisted, searching for the largest window opening. The front windshield was crushed. The back window was intact – wide enough for me to get through but impossible to open. My best chance seemed the broken, rear passenger side window. I wriggled between the seats and tossed the book out the window. It landed with a dull thump.

The bottom (top?) of the window was jagged with glass, but it was safety glass. I'd survive any scratches.

I stuck my hands out the window, as if I were a diver readying to take the plunge. I could get through it. The opening was narrow, would be close, but I could–

Two hands, rough as pine bark, grasped my wrists, and I shrieked.

CHAPTER 29

I screamed, a dry, cracking sound, and the grip around my wrists released.

"Lenore!" Connor peered through the narrow window, and I almost cried with relief. His swarthy face creased with worry.

"Someone ran me off the road." My voice trembled. "Someone was here."

"It's all right. We'll get you out."

"I can get through the window." The car was a tomb, and suddenly I had to get out, out, out. Heedless of the broken glass, I wriggled forward.

"Lenore, wait—"

But I wouldn't, couldn't wait. Sparks of agony nipped my palms, glass scraped against my back and stomach. I slithered through the Volvo's broken window.

Connor grasped my arms and helped me stand. His muscular form towered over me.

I swayed, dizzy, and scanned the tilting earth. Where was the book? I hadn't thrown it far.

"Come and sit down," he said, curling one arm around me, steadying.

"No." I tried to pull away, but his arms were unyielding. "The book! It's here somewhere."

"A book?" He scanned the uneven slope with his flashlight. Pine needles carpeted the ground. A manzanita bush, branches crushed where my car had slid or rolled through them. A snapped, baby pine, and the book beside it.

I gasped with relief and hurried forward, but my legs felt disconnected, and I sank to the ground instead. "The book."

"I'll get it." In two, long strides he swooped and picked it up, then returned it to me. "An old Hardy Boys. Cool. Not sure they're worth all the fuss though."

I reached for it.

He hesitated. "Your hands are bleeding. You sure you want this now?"

Surprised, I studied my stinging palms. Right. Blood plus old book, equals not good.

"Come on. Let me help you." He looped one muscular arm around my waist and hauled me to my feet, walked me up the slope to his patrol car. He sat me in the front passenger seat, leaving the door open so my feet brushed the ground. Reaching across the seat, he set the book beside me, and I could smell the piney scent of his cologne.

He cradled my head in his hand. "Here, look at me." He gazed into my eyes, and even though he was only checking for blurred vision, my breath caught.

Connor stilled, then seemed to shake himself. He pulled away. "Wait here." He walked to the back of the squad car.

I turned my head to follow his progress. Nausea twisted my stomach. I leaned forward, grasping the handle of the open door, and willed myself not to vomit.

The patrol car's headlights turned the ground the color of whiskey. Shadows twisted unevenly along the earth, and my stomach wrenched again.

"You all right?" He stood over me and shook his head, his smile wry. "Dumb question." One-handed, he draped a beige blanket over my shoulders.

Kneeling in front of me, he popped open a first aid kit. "You might have a concussion," he said. "Your head looks pretty banged up. I'll let the paramedics make that call, but we can clean up your hands."

He dabbed at them with cotton soaked in antiseptic, and I winced. "What's so important about the book?" he asked.

A car's headlights swept the highway. The car slowed, passed.

The book. If I told him, he might confiscate it. And we needed that book. But I didn't want to hide things from him any longer. "I need to take it to my sisters. It's important," I said, acutely conscious he was still cradling my open hand.

"A Hardy Boys," he said, bemused. "Okay, I'm going with concussed. You said a car ran you off the road. Did you get a look at it?"

"No. It was an SUV or a truck, but it was behind me and too dark to see much more. All I saw were headlights. They were high. But someone was here, before you arrived, walking around. I think... I think it was the driver." And I thought I knew who it had been, but I had no proof, and so I said nothing.

It would be a deadly mistake.

He nodded. "We'll treat this as a crime scene. Just in case."

I touched his wrist, and my skin burned at the contact. "I'm sorry. You were right. About everything."

His mercurial eyes looked at me for a long moment. "For the rest of our lives," he said, "I'm going to keep reminding you of that apology, because I know I'm never getting another." He grinned broadly, and I laughed.

He didn't hate me. Maybe there was even a chance for something more?

"Now tell me about this book," he said. "Is it valuable, like the others you found?"

"Not monetarily," I hedged.

"But you say it's important. Why?"

And here it was, the make or break moment when he'd either think I was a lunatic or join the team. I hesitated. "Have you ever noticed anything... strange about Doyle?"

He paused, the bloody cotton hovering above my open palm. There was a beat. Two. "I'd say a disappearing pub is strange."

"But that's not the only thing, is it?" I said, intent, hoping he'd understand.

He got back to work on my palm. "The Bell and Thistle isn't the first disappearance." Connor didn't meet my gaze. "Someone vanishes every seven years. For a while I was convinced Doyle had a serial killer." He laughed, a short, mirthless bark. "Before I became a cop, I figured I'd catch him. But serial killers don't make pubs vanish into thin air. And I don't believe in UFOs."

"It's not a UFO," I said, my hand warm in his.

He looked up at me and said nothing.

A wind stirred the pines. They bent, soughing.

"And then there's the bell," he said.

"What do you think it is?"

"People say it's the old bell from the Bell and Thistle."

"But what do you think?"

"I've hunted up and down, and I can never find that damn ringing bell."

I sighed. He'd never admit it.

"They say you and your sisters are witches," he said.

My face fell. "Witches didn't make the pub disappear."

"No. I'd never believe you would. Or your sisters." He released my hand and tore a fresh piece of cotton from the wad, soaked it in alcohol. "My grandmother was a curandera, a traditional healer."

"I didn't know that." His grandmother was a witch? There was so much about him I still didn't know. How I wanted to find out, to study him like one of Mike's old books.

"It wasn't something we publicized," he said dryly. "She practically raised me, told me stories about... other things. Older things. They scared the hell out of me when I was a kid."

"Did she tell you about Doyle?" Silken hope unfurled inside me.

He met my gaze. "She told me to leave." Gently, he lifted my other hand and dabbed at it with the cotton.

My face tightened from the alcohol's sting.

"She and my mother had raging fights over it. My mom had a good job here. She liked Doyle. And she wasn't superstitious."

"Superstitious about what?" I asked. Was it possible he believed?

"Old things. Things in the forest. And then my grandmother died, and my mother and I moved on. Or stayed, depending on how you look at it." And with his change in tone, the moment was over, his revelations done.

A siren sounded, faint.

"It's not in the forest anymore," I said. "What's doing this is in Doyle, affecting us, making our world more like its own. And it's taking sacrifices to maintain its power."

He met my gaze. "Sacrifices. Every seven years."

He believed, and relief bubbled through my veins. "I don't know why it took the Bell and Thistle, but I think its grip is slipping. Two of its prisoners returned last year, though they didn't last long in this world."

He nodded. "The old woman and the school teacher last summer."

"Maybe that's why she took so many this time–"

"She?" he asked.

"She, it, does it matter? That book..." I nodded to the book on the seat beside me, setting off a fresh wave of sickening pain. I closed my eyes against it. "If you look inside, it's not a children's mystery. It's an old book of folk tales, and I think it has the answers."

"Folk tales? Is that the book Van Oss was searching for?" He reached across me and opened the book, squinting in the dim light.

"The book Van Oss was hired to find," I said. My jaw clenched. He couldn't take it as evidence. He couldn't. "Connor–"

Another car approached, slowed, stopped.

Connor slid the book beneath my seat, his hand brushing against the legs of my jeans – white no longer – and my heart skipped a beat.

A car door opened. "Deputy? Is everything all right?" Steve Woodley asked. The councilman's figure silhouetted against the blaze of his headlights.

"Yes, sir," Connor said. "There's been an accident."

"Good heavens." He shielded his eyes with one hand. "Is that Lenore Bonheim?"

"Yes," I called out. "I'm fine."

"No, you're not," Connor said.

A paramedic's van drifted to a halt behind Woodley's SUV. Its blue emergency lights turned the forest and cars and men ghastly colors. The siren cut to silence, and two men in blue uniforms jumped from the cab. I breathed a sigh, recognizing Jayce's boyfriend as one of them – Brayden Duarte.

Brayden stopped, stared, cursed. "Lenore?" His muscular form raced to the squad car. He gripped a black, doctor's bag.

"I'm fine," I said.

Connor stepped aside, and Brayden knelt in front of me. He brushed a lock of his dark hair off his face. "You'd better be," the paramedic said, "or Jayce is going to kill me." He pulled a penlight from his breast pocket and shined it in my eyes. "Okay, can you follow the light for me?"

Connor moved away and spoke with Steve Woodley.

Anxious, I strained my ears, but I couldn't catch their conversation.

The second paramedic came to stand beside us.

Gently, Brayden felt my neck, my head. "Possible concussion. I want to take you to the hospital."

"No!"

He stared. "No? What part of Jayce is going to kill me if you're not okay didn't you understand?"

"I don't..." I stuttered to a halt, confused.

Connor walked to us and braced his hand on the squad car's roof.

Doc Toeller might be at the hospital. I'd been on my way there anyway, to see my sisters, but the book... I couldn't bring it into an Emergency Room. What if Toeller examined me and saw it?

"Don't worry," Connor said with quiet emphasis. "I'll take care of everything."

The paramedics edged away.

Grasping the top of the car door, I wavered to my feet.

Connor took my arm, his breath warm against my cheek.

I shivered, his nearness overwhelming. "But the..." The book, the book, we had to protect the book, had to get it to my sisters, keep it secret.

"I'll follow you to the hospital. Understand?" He unpeeled a lock of hair from my face and brushed it over my ear. "Trust me. I'll take care of it."

My heart thundered, fear and hope tangling. He understood. We were together in this now. I raised my bandaged palm to his cheek, and his breath caught.

Heedless of the men around us, we kissed. The men, the flashing lights, the forest vanished. In that moment, it was just us.

With a soft breath, he stepped away. "I'll follow you," he said. "You'll be okay."

It was a promise. I nodded, still feeling his mouth burning against mine.

CHAPTER 30

I slipped inside Karin's hospital room. My sisters looked up at me – Jayce from a lounge chair and Karin from her angled bed. They took in my bandages, the dirt and blood smearing my white jeans and loose, cream-colored top.

Jayce rose. Karin sat up, the metal bedframe creaking.

I glanced at the wall clock. It was nearly midnight, and suddenly I wanted to laugh, remembering our childhood, late-night whispered huddles.

"What happened?" Karin asked, aghast.

"Someone tried to run me off the road." I glanced again at the clock. Connor still had the book. At least, I hoped he had it and hadn't turned it in to the sheriff's department. Where was he? He'd told me he'd come to the hospital, and I'd seen him briefly in the emergency room, but then he'd gotten a call on his radio, and–

"Are you all right?" Jayce asked.

"I found the book," I said. "The Folk and Fairy Tales of America. Doyle's in it. So is our fairy."

Jayce's lips parted. "And?"

"There's a poem–"

Someone rapped on the door frame and scraped the curtain aside.

I turned.

Connor strode into the room, his deputy's jacket zipped to his collar. His mouth curved in a slow smile. "You're here."

"Connor!" I wrapped my arms around him. Something hard and angular pressed into my chest.

Pulling away, he unzipped his jacket. "I thought you might want to keep this secret." He withdrew the book.

I gasped. "You brought it. Thank you."

The radio on his shoulder crackled. Grimacing, he clicked its button and muttered into the small plastic device. There was a garbed response, and his face creased with annoyance. "I've got to go." Lightly, he rubbed my upper arm. "Will you be all right?"

"I will now." Seeing him again made everything all right. "Thanks for keeping this for me." He'd taken a leap of faith by bringing it to me rather than to his boss, the sheriff.

"I want to hear all about it when my shift's over." Kissing me on the cheek, he hurried out the door.

My sisters grinned at me.

"So," Jayce said, "you and Connor? When did that happen?"

An alarm went off down the hall. Footsteps pounded down the corridor, nurses racing to deal with the crisis.

"Priorities," I said, my skin warming. "This book has a story about our fairy. I think—"

"Connor brought it to you." Karin's forehead wrinkled. "How much does he know?"

"Almost everything," I said.

The ticking of the clock grew louder, and I rubbed my ear.

Karin shook her head, her hospital gown gaping over one bare shoulder. "It's dangerous for him."

"And for Nick, and for Brayden," I said. "But they had to know."

Karin's mouth tightened, but she nodded. "All right. What's in the book?"

I walked to her bedside and opened the book. It fell open to the first page on Doyle. Mike must have studied this chapter often. "It's another poem," I said. And I read:

"The pow'r of the fairy queen,
Lay in life at her feet,
Her name inscribed in stone,
Beneath her royal throne."

I looked up. The alarm echoed down the corridor, but the sound seemed farther away, muffled. The wall clock's ticks seemed to slow.

"That's it?" Jayce rubbed her bare arms, shivering in her tight, blue shorts.

But Karin's expression was thoughtful.

"It's her name," I said.

Karin rubbed her cheek. "That could work. The unseelie's real name can't be Toeller."

"What?" Jayce's gaze ping-ponged between the two of us. "What are you talking about?"

"In old magic," I said, "knowing something's true name gives you power over them." And there wasn't much older magic than the unseelie's.

"In the Bible," Karin said, "God asks Adam to name all the animals, and this gives man dominion over them. We name something, we identify it, we know its true essence, and that gives us power over it. If we knew the unseelie's true name, we might have a chance against it. I'd need to consult the family grimoire, but I'm fairly certain there's a binding spell in it that would work."

"Bind her?" Jayce asked.

"In her world," I said, "where she belongs. We can set things right."

"I'd rather you didn't do that." Steve Woodley stepped through the curtain and closed the door behind him. He held a gun.

CHAPTER 31

I edged backward, my thighs bumping into Karin's hospital bed.

The blood drained from Jayce's face. She half-rose from her lounge chair, but stopped at a look from the councilman. "Steve, what—?"

"I'll take that book." He smiled in a fatherly fashion.

"We're in a hospital." Paling, Karin laid her hands over the swell of her stomach. "One shot and everyone will come running."

"I think not," he said. "Everyone's busy at the other end of the floor, and the doctor will make sure they stay that way. Besides, I don't think you really want me to sacrifice one of your sisters."

"Take it." I tossed the book to his feet.

He didn't move to pick it up. "Have you read it?"

"No," I lied.

He scratched his silver goatee. "Why don't I believe you?"

I reached behind me. Karin slipped her hand into one of mine. Jayce grasped the other across the bed. A whisper of energy flowed up my arms. The overhead lights flickered, humming.

"Why?" Jayce asked. "Why do you want it? Why are you doing this?"

"I doubt you'd understand," he said, aiming the gun at her. "You're too young. You think everything's ahead of you."

"I know nothing is," Jayce said.

"He wants things to stay the same." I bit back a whimper. "He likes Doyle as it is, preserved under glass. He and Mike argued about it."

"Mike had no vision," Woodley said.

"No," I said, angry. "He understood the costs."

"Do you have any idea how old I am?" he asked. "Eighty-seven. I don't look a day over sixty, and I expect to live well into my hundreds — and I mean live well. It's a gift, don't you see?"

"It's a curse for others," Karin said. Her magic flowed, tingling, up my arm, through my heart, down my other arm into my other sister. Jayce's energy twined through it, moving in a circuit that prickled the top of my scalp, lifted the hair on my arms.

"A curse for your family, perhaps," he said.

"And for people like my assistant manager, Darla," Jayce said, "cursed with bad luck."

"What about all those people in the Bell and Thistle?" I asked, my chest aching with fear.

"Rather stupid to build a bar on top of a fairy spring." His gun didn't waver. He wasn't going to take the book and go. "Ignorance is its own reward."

My gaze expanded, softened, drifted. My breathing slowed. My heart beat loudly in my ears, and I listened.

"Ironic that Doyle has your great, great, great, whatever grandfather to thank for bringing her here. Your family started it all." His face hardened. "And I won't let you end it."

"You were the one who hired Van Oss to get the book," I said, stalling. I'd physically gone to the place between worlds before. With my sisters joined to me, we could go there together and escape this lunatic. If we could pull it off. This was big magic, magic we'd never intentionally attempted. "You knew Mike would never hand it over, so you hired Van Oss to steal it back. How did you find out about it?"

"I was looking for information on old Doyle legends and encountered Van Oss. He told me about the book he'd sold to Mike. I motivated him to get it for me."

"Why didn't you just let him do his job? Why kill him? Why kill Mike?" My words rose over the sound of my heartbeat, so loud now I half expected Woodley to hear it.

"Mike wouldn't let it go," he said. "It was more than just the book. I realized that even if I got it back, he'd keep trying to end the enchantment. And he had the brains to figure out how. All those occult books – where do you think his obsession started? He's known something was different about Doyle since he was a boy."

"And so you killed Mike." My grip on my sisters tightened. "You broke his neck and made it look like an accident, then left the bookstore before anyone saw you,"

In the corner, beside the dresser, a shadow stirred.

"I couldn't pass up the opportunity," he said.

"And Alba provided you another opportunity to get rid of Van Oss," I said. "She distracted everyone in the hotel while you snuck upstairs," I said. "Did Van Oss ask for more money? Try to double-cross you?"

"More money. I didn't need him, and he knew too much."

"But you did need an alibi for the murder," I said, "so you used your aunt. Her alibi isn't so solid. She's easily confused, but she knows her TV schedule. And Alba saw you at the hotel, didn't she?"

The room was shifting, changing. The walls slipped away, revealing translucent tall, white trees. The laminate floor softened to beaten gold beneath our feet.

"I'd hoped to be able to leave her be," he said. "No one ever listened to poor, demented Alba. But that damned FBI agent was sniffing around. She's different. She understands things. And I thought she might get something out of Alba."

The wall clock ticked, slowed.

A male figure, tall and blond, his face disfigured by scars, emerged from the shadows. He reached his hand out toward me. "Lenore."

"So you broke her neck." My voice trembled. "You carried Alba upstairs and threw her out the window." The words were a gasp, the circuit of energy dizzying. I could no longer tell where my flesh ended and my sisters' began. The ceiling vanished. A full moon rode high above the aspens and turned the sky a velvety blue. Undimmed by the moon, the Milky Way streaked the sky.

The clock stopped.

From a distance, a bell tolled.

His gun wavered. "Where are we?" the councilman barked, as if suddenly noticing our new surroundings. "What have you done?"

I turned. The aspen's yellow leaves rustled, and the hospital room, my sisters were gone.

CHAPTER 32

Aspens shivered in a warm breeze. Their white trunks gleamed in the moonlight, yellow leaves fluttering to the ground. The scarred man strode toward us and through the trees.

Woodley's gun wobbled. "Stop this nonsense. Send us back."

A twig cracked beneath the scarred man's feet.

Woodley turned, too late.

The man punched him in the jaw.

Woodley tumbled to the uneven ground and skidded to a halt against a papery tree trunk. He lay, unmoving.

The scarred man rubbed his knuckles and smiled.

I snorted, a short, disbelieving laugh. "Thanks." Where the hell was I? How did he get here? And how did Woodley come along for the ride? I shook my head, trying to rattle some sense into it. Anxiety unspooled in my chest. "Where are my sisters?" Steve was here, so at least they were safe from him. But where were they?

"They are safe, for now."

"But where—?"

"They are not here. I do not know where you have sent them. But the danger is here, so they are safe."

"You're the Rose Rabbit, aren't you?"

Slowly, he turned to me. "Once." He bent and picked up the gun, studying it. "Interesting weapon." He jammed it in the waistband of his jeans. "You have come for my lady's name. We must go." He strode down the slope.

"Do you know Toeller's real name?" I hurried after him. "The unseelie's name, I mean?"

"No."

"I think it's carved into the base of her throne."

"Is it?" he asked. "I have not seen it."

"Then... How did you know which direction we should go in?"

"I know we must leave this place. Danger approaches."

I didn't like the sound of that. If I was really here, and this wasn't just a vision, I could be hurt. I swallowed. "We can't leave him." I gestured up the slope to Woodley.

He paused. "Leave whom?"

"Steve Woodley. Not if there's danger."

"He is a murderer, and in the queen's pocket."

"He's vulnerable."

"The danger is not for him." He turned and continued on.

Steve was a killer. I shouldn't have cared what happened to him. But I followed the Rose Rabbit guiltily.

We crested a rise, and he paused. A black-and-white landscape sprawled before us, a mercury ribbon of river slicing it in two. Splintered trees lay scattered along the barren ground. Their roots were exposed, torn from the earth as if a flood had swept the valley.

"We must all play our role," he muttered.

"What are you?" I asked. "I've seen you in Doyle, in my dreams, but you're not a ghost. You're not a spirit animal."

One corner of his mouth slid upward. "You already know me."

"But aside from a man of few words, what are you?" He had to be an unseelie, like his queen, but I desperately needed him to deny it.

"A soldier." His mouth pressed into a white line.

"My Queen crouches beside the spring." I quoted. "Her hands fist. The babble of water drowns her muttering, ripples off her lank hair, raises the flesh on my scalp. She turns, her expression a diamond grotesque on a burning castle wall."

He halted. His broad back straightened.

"I saw that in a dream," I said. "My poems – they came from you, didn't they?" I'd thought they'd been figments of my subconscious, but like Blake's visions, my poems really had come from another place.

The muscles in his shoulders went taut as bridge cables.

"And you gave my poems to Mike," I said. "Why?"

"It was the only way I could converse with him."

"But why Mike?"

"Because he understood. I tried to reach you, but you wouldn't listen."

"The ghosts that kept coming through when I was trying to call Mike. You sent them."

"Of course."

"But what did Mike understand? How did you meet him in the first place?"

"Another tale. Come." He strode down the hill toward the river.

"How is it possible?" I trotted after him.

"You ask me?" He whirled on me, his eyes burning with fury. "How is it possible that my White Lady reaches into my dreams and waits for me on the other side? You are meant."

Karin raced up the steps to the attic, fumbled in the antique secretary for the grimoire.

Dizzy, I stopped short beside a cracked boulder, blackened as if burnt.

"What is wrong?" he asked sharply.

"My sisters..."

"Are playing their roles to finish our tale."

"What roles?" Uselessly, I flapped my hands. "What tale?"

He shrugged, his muscles rippling beneath the tight t-shirt. "Whether it is comedy or tragedy, we cannot know until it is done."

Jayce peered into a rough gap in the earth, purple thistles tearing at her bare legs.

"What is happening?" I whispered. If I stilled myself, I could feel my sisters' hands gripping mine, the energy of their magic pumping through my veins. But I couldn't still myself for long, my muscles clenching and unclenching in agitation.

"What is meant." The Rose Rabbit pointed past the river. "The throne is there."

An uneven structure of turrets and crenelated walls stood on the opposite side of the water. "A castle," I murmured.

"The castle." He extended his hand to me. "Come."

I reached for him, then dropped my hand. If I took his, would I lose my connection to my sisters?

"As you wish," he said. "Come." He strode down the hill.

Leather-bound tome clutched to her chest, Karin clambered through the attic's trap door.

I stumbled over ditches, hopped dried streams, tramped through tangles of tall, desiccated grasses. The land was blasted, the trees dead, the plants wilted. No small animals scrabbled in the dried brush. No birds or bats wheeled overhead. The world was silent except for the rush of the river, growing louder as we approached.

I made more abortive attempts to get my guide to explain who he was, what this place was, how I'd come here. His replies were cryptic, annoying.

I gave up, and we traveled without speaking.

He moved surefooted over the rough terrain.

My feet skidded on loose earth. My hands clutched at branches that snapped off when I clutched them for balance.

Finally, he found a thick, gnarled branch, about four feet long, and handed it to me. "Use this." He continued on down the hill.

Head bowed, the FBI agent walked past Jayce, thistles scraping her trousers. Jayce stilled. But the agent didn't notice her. Jayce was a ghost, a spirit, insubstantial, and terror rose in my sister's throat.

A pulse of hot, fearful energy whipped through me, and I gripped my makeshift walking stick. It was rough and dusty, but it kept me from falling. I willed Jayce to feel my presence.

The Rose Rabbit and I reached the river. Tumbles of dried brush, white and curving, clumped along its banks.

Panting, I stumbled through the damp soil. I knelt beside the water and reached–

"No!" He swatted my hand away and yanked me to my feet. "It is poisoned."

"But–"

"See." He pointed toward some brush.

"That's a..." I stared. Not sticks. Bones. An animal's ribcage, bone cage, a cow's I guessed by the size.

"The crossing is not far."

We walked on and on. A fallen tree took us across the river. A winding path that only my guide could see led us through the broken landscape. A sulfuric smell rose around us, and I wrinkled my nose. And still we walked.

Karin hesitated outside the labyrinth of lavender bushes. Their scent rose around her. A breeze stirred their blossoms.

We walked. My tongue grew thick in my mouth. My walking stick grew heavy, and I dragged it behind me, dropped it. My eyelids drooped.

We walked. I wilted.

The Rose Rabbit's step lengthened his back straightening. "There," he said. "The castle."

A crenelated silhouette loomed over the twisted landscape. The moon sank behind its fractured walls. The castle was crumbling like everything else in this dying land.

An echo of music, laughter. And then the sound was gone.

Pins and needles danced across my scalp.

I halted. "There's someone inside the castle."

"They will not bother us." He kept walking.

I stumbled after him. "The people who've been taken – the hikers, the people from the Bell and Thistle – are they here?"

"Here. Not here."

"We have to help them." I clutched at his muscular arm.

He stopped and stared down at me. His eyes glittered. "You do not know them. They are strangers."

"They're prisoners."

One blond eyebrow lifted. "And?"

"They're innocent."

Jayce steadied her breathing. No, she wasn't dead. If she was dead, there were plenty of better places to haunt. Lenore had sent her to the site of the missing pub for a reason.

The Rose Rabbit said nothing for a long moment. "Yes." He turned and walked down a cobblestone path.

I followed. "Then we can send them home?"

"Perhaps."

Perhaps. I'd take perhaps. But I was so thirsty, and my legs trembled with fatigue.

An open drawbridge lay across a dried moat. We walked inside the stone fortress walls and into a garden of dead brambles. Four paths converged at the garden's center. Inside it stood an empty, marble fountain crusted with muck. In its bowl, a stone woman poured nothing from an empty vase. Four crumbling halls rose around us, forming a square.

He pointed toward the hall beneath the setting moon. "This way."

A ripple of laughter and music stirred the air and faded to nothing. I stopped short, swaying toward it.

The snippet of music had been unspeakably beautiful, my soul written in its chords. "Did you hear that?" I whispered.

"Lady of the labyrinth," Karin whispered, "to she who can never be unveiled, I ask safe passage." The lavender rippled in a wave of invitation or warning.

"Do not be lured by the music," he said sharply. "You have little time. Come."

He turned and strode down the garden path, through the high, arched entry to the stone hall.

An instrument twanged.

I glanced toward the sound.

"This way," he urged.

And I followed, because he'd gotten me to the castle, and a throne should be in a castle. That proved he was helping, didn't it? But doubt niggled inside me. Why was I so quick to follow, to believe?

Because I have no other choice, Jayce thought, and knelt beside the gash in the earth. Water echoed faintly beneath, and she tilted her head.

Tattered banners wafted like spider webs in the vaulted ceiling. Real spider webs decorated the corners of stained glass windows and draped suits of armor. The stone hallway widened.

The Rose Rabbit grasped the handles of a double door.

"Are you real?" A young woman in shorts and a blue hiking t-shirt touched my arm, and I jumped. She seemed to have appeared from nowhere. Athletic and tanned, with high cheekbones and gray-blue eyes, she reminded me of... Karin's fiancé, Nick. A small raven tattoo adorned one side of her slim neck.

Karin stepped inside the low labyrinth, and her skin tingled as she passed through a wall of energy.

My skin tingled. "Emily?" I asked. "Emily Heathcoat?"

She blanched. "You know me? Who are you? Are you here to get us out?" She clutched my wrist. "You have to help us!"

"Get away from her!" The Rose Rabbit roared and made as if to swat her away.

She cringed.

"Stop it!" I shouted. "She needs help."

"Help her by getting the name," he said.

"No, don't go through those doors." Eyes wild, she grabbed my arm and tugged me away. "Don't go in there. It's dangerous. You can't go in. If you go in, you won't come out."

The man's jaw clenched. "She is ignorant and delaying us. Leave her."

"He's lying to you," she said. "He belongs to her. It's his fault the others are here. Don't go in there."

"What do you mean, it's his fault?" I turned to him. "What does she mean?"

"She knows nothing," he said, impatient.

"He didn't tell you, did he?" she asked. "He belongs to her, loves her. He's a traitor."

He stiffened.

"No one trusts him," she continued. "He brought twenty-two strangers. It isn't supposed to be that way. He's only supposed to take one!"

His expression hardened. "I had no choice."

Horrified, I stared at him. "You took the Bell and Thistle?"

"It was the only way to end this. Finish this and all of them, including those She took, will be free."

"He's lying, he's lying," Emily insisted.

"But why…?" I hesitated. Whatever his game was, I needed Toeller's true name. And I didn't think we had much more time. "I have to find the throne."

"No," Emily shrieked. "You can't go in there. For God's sake, listen to me."

I wrenched free and ran to the doors.

The Rose Rabbit flung them open, and I raced past. A long carpet the color of blood. High, narrow windows and beams of wavering moonlight. Flagstone floors and bone-like ceiling and a stone chair on a dias.

Emily sobbed outside the open, arched doors.

The Rose Rabbit came to stand beside me. "She thinks she speaks the truth," he said. "But she is only half right and much confused."

"Which half is right? You admit you kidnapped twenty-two people!"

"But only twenty-two. My Queen took many more before then."

Water? But the spring beneath the Bell and Thistle was supposed to be dry. Kneeling, Jayce raised her hands over the crevice and felt for the energy.

"So what part is 'half right?'" I repeated.

"I do love my queen, and I am a traitor. To her." He pointed to the throne. "Go. Take the name."

I glanced toward the open doors.

Emily shook her head and looked away.

I walked down the scarlet carpet to the throne. Climbed the three steps. Stared.

The stone was smooth.

Frantic, I ran my hands over the cold steps, the legs of the throne, beneath the seat. I tossed the cushions to the floor.

Nothing.

Karin walked the tanbark path. There was only one way into the labyrinth's center and one way out, but her steps were jerky and uncertain.

"It's not here." I recited the poem: "The pow'r of the fairy queen,

Lay in life at her feet,

Her name inscribed in stone,

Beneath her royal throne.

It should be here, unless..." Unless he'd tricked me, and this was the wrong throne.

He reached behind him, lifting his shirt, and drew a short blade.

I couldn't speak, couldn't move.

"In life," he said. "It is there. It requires life – human life – to be seen."

I went cold. He'd brought me here to die. "You needed me to get the name," I said, voice rising. "My life isn't like the others in this place, is it? You lied—"

He grasped my wrist, his hands as unyielding and cold as manacles. His jaw hardened.

A muffled groan escaped my throat. I'd failed us all.

The energy of the fairy was there, dark and cold and powerful, and Jayce connected to it. It seized her, choking.

In a swift motion, he drew the blade across my palm.

I yelped in pain.

He held my hand over the steps, My blood dripped onto the stone.

"Apologies," he said, "but we have little time and none for arguments."

The steps shimmered pink, and letters appeared.

He released me. Sheathing the knife, he smiled. "It is a beautiful name and worthy of a queen."

Karin reached the center of the labyrinth and opened the book to the binding spell.

I closed my eyes and felt my sisters' hands, hot with my blood. Waves of their energy passed through me.

Jayce felt her sisters' magic pour into her, but instead of wrenching free, she grasped the dark energy of the spring.

I could see the book in Karin's hands, hear her speak the words. She, Jayce and I chanted in unison.

"Hear now the words of three sisters," we said.

My scalp tingled.

"Of secrets we hid in the dark."

Candles in the chandelier above burst into flame.

"The oldest of powers we invoke," we said.

"Lenore, stop this," the unseelie said.

Power whispered across my spine.

"Our great work of magic we three provoke," we said.

The ground rumbled, splitting. Jayce staggered, but didn't fall into the widening fissure.

"Remain here and rule in my place," the queen whispered. "Both our worlds will be made right."

The throne room spun, and I stood among the dying aspens.

The doctor leaned against a tree, her arms folded, and smiled. Steve Woodley lay at her feet. "I'm glad you're here." Her ice-blue tunic shimmered in the moonlight, her cap of gold and silver thread glimmering wetly.

"I don't believe you." I wanted to run, to hide. But there was no hiding in her kingdom.

She straightened off the tree trunk. "My knight thinks if he drags me back here, everything will return to normal."

"And he's wrong?"

"He's probably right," the unseelie said. "The Rose Rabbit usually is. He's quite annoying that way. But there's a better solution for us both. You can take my place."

A dirt-covered hand burst from the crevice. Jayce reached for it, and her own hand passed through its flesh. Behind her, the FBI agent shouted.

"Why would I want to do that?" I asked.

"Let's face it," Toeller said, "you've never really fit into your world. I've never fit into mine. You'd be perfect here."

I glanced at the ruined landscape and shuddered.

"Oh, you could fix that," she said. "If you sat on my throne, this land would be yours to make as you wished. No more worries about what other people wanted or expected. No longer would you scrabble for work and money. You could read and write poetry to your heart's content. You could make this land your poem. Imagine."

And I did imagine. Verdant leaves whispered in the aspens. Birds soared above fields of rippling wildflowers. I smelled herbs and wild grasses, heard the rushing of many streams. The trees trembled, and green buds burst from their dried branches. Involuntarily, I stepped backwards, my heel twisting on a rock.

She laughed. "See how easy it is. All you need do is imagine, and you have plenty of imagination, Lenore."

A world of my own. A world that I fit into because it was mine.

"You've never been at home there," she said.

And she was right. The real world had never quite fit me. I'd spent my life escaping into books and the otherworld, half-living between in the world of spirits. "If it's so wonderful, why did you leave?"

"I wanted to experience something else. Why settle for staying in one world when I can explore another?"

What would it be like to live in this place, to make it my own? I licked my lips. Connor might even like to come. And my sisters... Karin and Nick wouldn't have to die. Maybe that was the solution, switching places and freeing us all.

"And would you leave me?" The Rose Rabbit emerged from the budding forest. The air around him shimmered, and he was no longer scarred and blond. He was Connor – tall and swarthy and in his deputy's uniform.

"It's a trick," the unseelie said. "You can't trust him."

"She's half-right," he said. "It is a trick, a reminder. Your knight waits on the other side."

"Is it true?" I asked him. "Could I fix this place?"

"Yes. But you do not belong here."

"I'm not sure where I belong," I said.

"Aren't you?" he asked in Connor's voice.

I touched my lips, remembering his kiss. Love in the messy real world was worth the risk – not just Connor's, but my sisters, and the love I'd felt for Mike. I felt them all now, their energy glittering around me. Yes, I was willing. I'd take the world as it was, for all its challenges and its rewards.

And I was back in the throne room, the words dancing before me.

"On this night and on this hour," our voices boomed together.

The Rose Rabbit stood beside me, and his face changed, shimmered, the scars fading.

"We call upon our ancient power," we said.

A light expanded on the throne, and the doctor – how had we ever mistaken her for a doctor? – sat upon the great stone seat. Her hands clenched its arms. Her hair grew long, flowing in waves down her back. Her teeth sharpened. Her eyes enlarged.

"Laudine, we bind you in your fairy bower," we shouted.

"No!" the unseelie screamed.

"You are bound, you are bound, you are bound." Our words rose in a roaring wind. The banners brightened, snapping. The candles blew out but the light grew, golden sunlight pouring through the high windows.

And then we were in the hospital room, holding hands, my back to the bed, Jayce behind me, and Karin beneath the covers.

Unconscious, Steve Woodley lay on the floor, and the gun lay beside his hand.

I moved to grab it.

He gasped, raising himself up. His cheeks and eyes grew hollow. His silver hair yellowed. Deep furrows appeared on his face and hands. He wheezed and collapsed.

CHAPTER 33

Steve Woodley gave a rambling, raving confession to Connor in the emergency room.

The sheriff opted not to take the multiple murderer's statement herself. She was too busy with the returnees from the Bell and Thistle. The building never returned, but the people inside had emerged from the ground like gnomes, blinking in the moonlight. Others crawled from the earth as well – Nick's sister and other hikers who'd disappeared over the years.

Like the other missing persons, Nick's sister, Emily, had no memory of her "abduction." But she'd developed a dread fear of closed places, anemia, and what the doctors were calling PTSD. After so many years missing, her return to the real world was rocky. But she had Nick and her parents, and we were hopeful the nightmares and phobias would fade.

Spinning theories, reporters descended on the town. A cult. Hallucinatory gases. The speculation on the Internet was wilder – UFOs were high on the list. But none of the returned could remember where they'd been, and those who did remember could only recall odd fragments.

Forty-eight hours after the returned climbed from their underground prison, a missing persons report was filed for Doctor Evelyn Toeller. The police seemed to believe Woodley was responsible for her disappearance as well.

I let them.

Three weeks later, Connor took me to dinner at a restaurant high in the mountains. Afterward, we walked a path by an alpine lake. The Sierra darkness was complete, the moon not yet risen, our only light from the stars. They reflected off the black lake, making their own miniature universe.

He clasped my hand. "How's your sister?"

"Karin's blood pressure is normal and everything seems okay. But the doctors are still watching her. They don't trust her recovery." But I did. The unseelie's power was broken. The evidence was all over Doyle. A sudden outbreak of acne had struck the local high school. A small red bump had even appeared on my forehead, and Jayce's hair had gone frizzy. Darla had won two thousand dollars in the lottery. And Steve's aunt, aged well over a hundred, had died gently in her sleep.

Karin wept at her funeral. She felt guilty. We all did. The town didn't look quite so perfect anymore. Bricks tumbled from their walls. Paint peeled and flaked off.

But we were all free.

Connor led me down a short set of steps to a narrow beach that gleamed faintly in the starlight. A log lay fallen on the sand, and we sat on it.

A fish jumped, plopping into the water.

Connor pulled me close, and I leaned my head on his shoulder. We sat there for a long while, not speaking, the Milky Way a glittering path above us.

The moon rose, a flash of gold against the mountain ridge. Inexorably, it rose higher until it hung, pendulous, in the black velvet night and washed away the nearby stars.

He drew a deep breath, his chest expanding and falling against me. "Tell me now what really happened."

And I did. Everything.

He didn't laugh or stiffen with skepticism or argue the rationalist's point of view. He simply listened and nodded. When I'd finished, he pulled me close again.

"So why did the fairy flood your bookstore with customers that day? What was she trying to keep you from?"

"I don't know," I said, uneasy. I didn't like not knowing, but Toeller was gone, so it probably didn't matter.

Probably.

"How did Woodley figure it out?" he asked. "How did he know what was going on with the doctor?"

"He'd been around a long time, long enough to see people weren't aging normally. Mike figured it out. I suspect other people knew as well – people like your grandmother. But how do you tell others there's a fairy in town without sounding crazy? And what do you do about it even if you have figured out Doyle was wrapped in fairy magic?"

He rested his chin on the top of my head. "Woodley thought he had the answer – if you can't beat 'em, join 'em. And you're right. Everyone thinks he's crazy. His defense attorney is bringing in a shrink to prove it."

"Mike wasn't crazy." He'd understood what was happening long before we had.

"He was a good man," Connor said.

A lump formed in my throat. God, I missed him.

"So life will return to normal." He brushed a kiss across my jawbone.

"I don't think you can say that. Doyle's never been normal, so for us, everything from here on out is new territory."

"And now you're rich."

The first edition by William Blake had proven to be authentic. We'd found several others in his private collection that were also quite valuable. I wasn't sure what I was going to do with the money yet, but I had a vague idea that Doyle would need some help. And I had a bookstore to run. "Is that why you're dating me? For my riches?"

He laughed into my hair. "I just want discounts on the books."

We kissed, and I knew, though nothing would ever be the same, everything would be all right.

And that is how three sisters came to live happily, if not ever after.

SHAMANIC DREAM SACHET

Shamans travel while waking, and they travel in dreams. Make this simple, intention-inflused sachet to make it easier to sleep and dream.

You'll need:

A lightweight, muslin bag (4-6 inches tall);

Dried lavender;

Dried rose buds;

1 tsp dried mugwort;

Lavender essential oil (10-12 drops).

In a bowl, gently mix the essential oil, lavender and rose buds, while concentrating on your magical intention. It could be restful sleep, or hearing your inner voice in your sleep, or safe dream journeying, for example. Pour the herb mixture into the muslin bag. Keep it near your pillow at night, where you can smell it. When the mixture no longer has any scent, you can refresh it with more essential oil and intention.

Welcome the Day Ritual

Shamanic witches like Lenore are in touch with nature's rhythms and grateful for the opportunity to spend time on this planet. Start your day right by looking outdoors and saying "Good morning," to the sun. (Just don't look at the sun directly, or you'll hurt your eyes). Take a moment to feel gratitude for the coming day. Before you go to bed, say "Good night," to the moon and take some time to reflect on the good things you experienced during the day.

BOOKS BY KIRSTEN WEISS

The Witches of Doyle Series
Bound | Ground | Down | Witch | Fey |

Doyle Witch Supplements
Spirit on Fire | Shaman's Bane | Lone Wolf | Tales of the Rose Rabbit

Doyle Cozy Mysteries
At Wits' End | Planet of the Grapes

The Perfectly Proper Paranormal Museum Cozy Mysteries
The Perfectly Proper Paranormal Museum | Pressed to Death | Deja
Moo

The Riga Hayworth Paranormal Mystery Novels
The Metaphysical Detective | The Alchemical Detective | The Shamanic
Detective | The Infernal Detective | The Elemental Detective | The
Hoodoo Detective | The Hermetic Detective

The Mannequin Offensive

Pie Town Cozy Mysteries
The Quiche and the Dead | Bleeding Tarts

Sensibility Grey Steampunk Suspense
Steam and Sensibility | Of Mice and Mechanicals | A Midsummer Night's
Mechanical

ABOUT THE AUTHOR

Kirsten Weiss authors genre-bending stories of mystery, suspense, and enchantment.

She worked overseas for over fourteen years, in the fringes of the former USSR and deep in the Afghan war zone. Her experiences abroad not only gave her glimpses into the darker side of human nature, but also sparked an interest in the effects of mysticism and mythology, and how both are woven into our daily lives.

Now based in San Mateo, CA, she writes paranormal mysteries, blending her experiences and imagination to create a vivid world of magic and mayhem.

Kirsten has never met a dessert she didn't like, and her guilty pleasures are watching Ghost Whisperer reruns and drinking good wine.

You can connect with Kirsten through the social media sites below, and if the mood strikes you, send her an e-mail at kweiss2001@kirstenweiss.com.

Follow her on Twitter: @KirstenWeiss

Check out her story world boards on Pinterest: www.pinterest.com/kirstenweiss/

Sign up for her newsletter for cool free stuff and book updates at: kirstenweiss.com

DOWN

A DOYLE WITCH COZY MYSTERY

KIRSTEN WEISS

Made in the USA
Coppell, TX
04 February 2021

49566228R00118